W•CLARK
PUBLISHING
A STATEMENT IN LITERATURE

KARMA 2:

For The Love of Money

D0071750

This is a work of fiction. Names, characters, places, and incidents either are the product of the author's imagination or are used fictitiously, and any resemblance to actual persons, living or dead, business establishments, events, or locales is entirely coincidental.

Wahida Clark Presents Publishing, LLC
60 Evergreen Place
Suite 904
East Orange, New Jersey 07018
973-678-9982
www.wclarkpublishing.com

Copyright 2010 © by Tash Hawthorne
All rights reserved. This book, or parts thereof, may not be reproduced in any form without permission.

Karma 2: For the Love of Money
ISBN 13-digit 978-0-9828414-0-2
ISBN 10-digit 0-9828414-0-X
Library of Congress Catalog Number   2010931322
  1. Urban, Contemporary, Women, African-
      American, Cuban-American – Fiction

Cover design and layout by Oddball Dsgn
Book design by NuanceArt
Contributing Editors: Jazzy Pen, R. Hamilton and M.D. Phillips

Printed in United States

WAHIDA CLARK PRESENTS

KARMA 2
For the Love of Money

TASH HAWTHORNE

Dedication

He who has a why to live for can bear almost anyhow.

- Friedrich Nietzsche

This book is dedicated to the greatest warrior I know, my brother, Durron Buchanan. You are the most courageous, selfless, compassionate, humble person I know. Our unbreakable bond exists because of the unconditional, unyielding love our mothers had for each other. We have shared laughter, we have shared tears, we have shared love and we have shared loss. But most importantly, we have shared this life. From you I have learned be a better daughter. You have taught me to believe in hope. And you have taught me to keep my faith in God and be grateful to Him in our darkest hours. We are bound by blood, and with that said, I will continue to walk beside you until the very end. I'm so proud of the man, the father, the example you have become; I know Uncle Durwin and Aunt Brenda are too. I love you always and forever.

ACKNOWLEDGMENTS

"Some say we are responsible for those we love. Others know we are responsible for those who love us."

- Nikki Giovanni

I am deeply indebted to God for his grace, mercy, comfort, and forgiveness throughout the years. Thank YOU for never taking your hand off me. And my family---mother (Leslie), husband (Chris), grandmothers (Lorraine and Martha), aunt (Lorelei), mother-in-law (Carmela), father-in-law (Ormand, Sr.), grandmother-in-law (Lottie), brothers-in-law (Ormand, Jr. and Jonathan), godmothers (Claudette and Theresa), great-aunts (Gloria and Claire), all of their children and grandchildren, the overabundance of maternal and paternal aunts, uncles, and cousins that I have, and extended Williams/O'Neal family, whose love, support, wisdom, encouragement, and belief has sustained me through it all.

My sincerest gratitude goes to my cousins (Karma, Maiiya, Shaun, Chad, and Lamar) and dearest friend (Vontica) for their bravery and unselfishness in being my muses for the Karma series, the ORIGINAL Valley family who are forever bounded by shared blood, sweat, tears and fears: The Allens, The Anthonys, The Baileys, The Battles, The Brodies, The Bronsons, The Browns, The Buchanans, The Burwells, The Caraways, The Davis', The Fernandes', The Fords, The Gardners, The Gibson-Whites, The Golsons, The Gomez's, The Gwaltneys, The Holmes', The Hunts, The Irvins, The Joneses, The Joyners, The Lassenberrys, The Longs, The McCrees, The McGriffs, The Parks', The Pearsons, The Peters', The Poaches', The Porches', The Roberts', The Simpkins', The Taylors, The Thurstons, The Tynes', The Willis', The Withers', and The Woolfords (Thank you all for exemplifying the true meaning(s) of LOYALTY and HISTORY), the greatest black female educators of our time who instilled in me the importance of our history, self-worth, humility, and the conception, belief, and will to achieve our dreams: Mrs. Effi Barry (RIP) Mrs. Joanne Brooks (RIP), Mrs. Katherine Carter, Mrs. Logan Chappell, Mrs. Candace E. Holmes, Mrs. Lillian Nails, Mrs. Carol Pinner (RIP), Mrs. Kimberly Watkins, Dr. Karen Turner-Ward, and Mrs. Shirley Hunt-Williams.

I wish continued success and happiness for my Forest Street, Heywood Avenue, Orange Middle, Orange High, and Hampton University friends. You all know who you are (especially those who trekked through the snow storm last December to attend the Karma: With A Vengeance release party; my very FIRST celebration). We've lost many (in death and in translation) along the way, but it is up to us to continue to listen, live, let go, and love.

I outstretch my appreciation to Ms. Wahida Clark and the entire WCP family (Tanya, Wahida Marie, Hasana, Yah-Yah, Rozy, Ebony, Al-Nisa, Cash, and Missy) for their belief, support, warmth, criticism, guidance, patience, and trust in me. It has been a pleasure and a blessing knowing you all. The road has been long and tiresome, but we made it to this place...this moment of accomplishment TOGETHER. I love you all!!!

A special thank you to Mary Ellen, Ms. Mauline, and Ms. Harriet for your positivity, counseling, and prayers over the years. I carry you with me always!

And lastly, I'd like to take this time to celebrate a number of our fallen leaves. May they continue to rest peacefully in the arms of our Lord: Raven Battle, Wanda Britt, Anna Ruby Brown, Willie "Junie" Brown, Buddy Boy, Brenda "Bren" Buchanan, Jean Fernandes, Mr. and Mrs. Hunt, Audrey Irvin, Ann Jackson, Carl and Michael Long, Nella "Auntie" Lovey, Emily "Emmy" Marsh, Hassan C. Miller, Jr., Melvinlene Milton, Jean "Cokey" Monroe, Allen and Shelly Simpkins, Maxine K. Singleton, Steven and Michael Thurston, Theresa "Teta" Thurston, Keyonna J. Willis, Jenny Wimberly, Denise and Peggene Withers.

Chapter 1

Karma gently massaged Mekhi's scalp with her fingertips as he suckled the milk from her swollen breast. The light creaking of the rocking chair mother and son were sharing, created a whispered sonata composed only for them. Mekhi cut his eyes lovingly at his mother while he swallowed the consistent flow of her rich sustenance. Karma looked down at her baby boy, her eyes connecting with his. She watched the tide slowly turn in his two blue oceans. There was no judgment there. He was simply a child, *her* child, who knew nothing of his mother's sins. She could wade peacefully in the cool waters of his unconditional love for her. If she drowned, so be it. She would let go and let the waves wrap their arms around her and rock her to sleep.

How she loved her baby boy so. He stopped taking to his formula recently, forcing her to start breast feeding him again. She stopped a month or so after he was born because it had been too painful for her, but Mekhi wasn't having it any other way. Karma winced in pain as the baby's jaw locked around her tender nipple again. She would never get used to this breast feeding thing, especially when her son had the "jaws of life."

Fortunately, the pain never lasted too long and she was able to enjoy the special bonding time with him.

Motherhood had surprisingly come natural to her. The *maternal instinct* so many women spoke of definitely kicked in after his birth. She knew what each and every one of his cries meant, what his facial expressions read, his eating habits, sleeping schedule---everything. There wasn't anything Karma wouldn't do for her son. When she looked at him, she saw the goodness of her better self. He not only brought her joy, but a sense of calmness, something she lacked for the majority of her life. Her temper was a thing of the past now. The little things no longer bothered her as much as they use to. She thought before she reacted now instead of reacting first and thinking about her actions later. Karma Alonso-Walker was officially *grown*. She wouldn't trade woman or motherhood for the world.

Mekhi slowly pulled away from her aching bosom, signifying his fullness.

"Finished, Pooh? she asked with a tenderness only a mother could convey. She picked him up and quickly pecked him on his plump cheek before placing him over her shoulder to burp him.

As Karma went back and forth from rubbing to patting the baby's solid back, she wondered what he would have looked like had he been her first love's child. Joaquin was heavy on her mind. It was his birthday today and she didn't know how she was going to get through the day without someone noticing her sense of loss. She was sure it was going to show on her face.

She sighed heavily at the thought. Everyone would notice the difference in her mood, everyone except Money. The relationship between the two had become strained overnight. After she and the baby came home from the hospital, Money suddenly became distant. He asked for more hours at work, which kept him away from her and the kids. He even stopped reaching for her at night.

Karma's recovery from her emergency C-section had almost been non-existent because of Money's negligence. Luckily, she had his mother, her cousin Indigo, and her aunt Maggie for support. Money's drastic change in behavior didn't make sense to her and she had run out of options for how she should deal with him. The couple had their share of arguments about it, usually with Money storming out of the house and Karma left shedding tears of fury. She'd given up on him two months ago. She'd given up on *them*. Now, more so than ever, she wished she'd kept her heart to herself. She wished Joaquin never died.

~~~~~~

Originally born and raised in Cuba until the age of three, Joaquin Armando Garcia hopped into a boat alongside his parents and grandparents in search of a better life in America. Unlike his grandparents, who survived the journey, his parents died at sea and were thrown overboard, leaving the elders and the toddler to set out to start anew in the foreign country.

Joaquin spent most of his early years in Miami, Florida working in his grandparents' bodega. As the years passed, the city began to overcrowd. His grandparents, overwhelmed by the mass of incoming immigrants (like themselves), decided to relocate to New Jersey where they finally settled in the Ironbound Section of Newark. They opened a chain of bodegas throughout the city with Joaquin managing two of them, andit was in one of those bodegas where a sixteen-year-old Joaquin met a fourteen-year-old Karma. He was well aware of who the young beauty was the first day she walked into his family's mini-market. She was the girl he'd seen and read about in the High School Sports section of The Star-Ledger every week; the track star. Desperately wanting to know more about her, Joaquin introduced himself and the rest, as they say, was history.

Joaquin was the most selfless person Karma had ever met. He was a sixteen-year-old man among twenty to thirty something-year-old boys in the city of sun-dried clay. She had been hesitant to speak to him because her perception of Cuban men had been shaped by that of her uncles. Karma saw how they treated her mother. They were overprotective to a fault, so she wanted no parts of the young Cuban man with the sun-kissed pecan-colored skin, sugar cane lips, and deep chestnut brown eyes that reminded her of the coffee beans that were grown and shipped from the place their kin called home. No, she didn't want any parts of him. Like the rumba, the beating of his kind heart pulled her into him and she redefined what a Cuban man truly was. He was a man tailor-made by God in His perfect image of goodness.

There was no one more compassionate than him. He genuinely cared about people and did for anyone who was in need. He dreamed of becoming a child psychologist, believing children were the world's hub of communication. And when they went unheard, so did God. He epitomized an upstanding citizen. He was a Big Brother in the city's Big Brother/Big Sister program, a camp counselor for special needs children during the summers, a college honor student; the list went on and on and on. Most importantly, he was a gentleman. Karma told him right off the bat she wasn't allowed to date until she turned sixteen and Joaquin respected that. He told her he'd wait sixteen-hundred years if he had to. All he wanted was a little bit of her time.

As the friendship and love between them grew, Karma and Joaquin found it befitting to introduce the other to his/her family. While Joaquin's grandparents welcomed Karma with open arms, her father, more so than her mother, found it difficult to accept the young man. Lorenzo immediately reiterated what Karma had already told him in regards to dating, then shamelessly asked what his intentions were for her. Karma, embarrassed to the point of tears, silently pleaded with her mother to intervene before he said anything else. As if on cue, Soleil excused her husband for being so forward. Lorenzo, full of mixed emotions, left the house without another word.

Stunned by his sudden departure, Soleil moved quickly to save what was left of the meeting as well as her daughter's crushed feelings. She offered Joaquin a glass of milk and brownies while explaining her husband's unacceptable behavior.

"She's his only child, his little girl," she said. "Now, by no means did he have the right to attack you the way he did, Joaquin. I'm not excusing him for that. But please understand that he's been dreading this day for quite some time."

"I understand.And I want you to know that I would never challenge any of your rules. I respect your wishes," Joaquin replied. "I can wait."

"I'm very happy to hear that. Because I already know that you two are in love. And although love is a beautiful thing, it can be dangerous. Love will make you do crazy things. So it's up to you to stay sane until May first," she jested, rubbing his broad back.

"I will," Joaquin smiled.

"Good. I'll work on her father. He'll come around eventually. That I promise you," she assured him.

And Soleil had been able to keep that very promise. Lorenzo ultimately submitted to the inevitability of a relationship forming between the two teenagers. Joaquin even came to him and asked him for his permission to court Karma the day she turned sixteen. Lorenzo couldn't knock the proper way the boy had been raised. Not only did Joaquin earn Lorenzo's respect, but that of Karma's uncles Victor and Miguel as well. He helped out at the restaurant when he could, played dominoes with them, and accompanied them to a number of Yankees games.

Now, of course, Joaquin had his flaws. He'd inherited the very same overprotective nature Karma's uncles possessed and was very much a slob. He had a short-term memory and more admirers than he could count. But one thing about him , he never strayed.

If one were to ever ask him what his greatest achievement was, Joaquin never hesitated to admit that his greatest achievement, his greatest joy, was being Karma's man. He was sincerely proud of his position in her life. He was even prouder the night she came to him with tears falling from her eyes and told him what her father had done. Lorenzo had broken her mother's heart and his solemn vows to her.

Joaquin loved Karma even more then because in that moment, she didn't look at him as just another triflin' man who would do the same thing to her one day. She looked at him as better. He made it his mission from that night on to help her understand the importance of forgiveness and embracing the God within her. Forgiving her father hadn't been easy, but with Joaquin's assistance, it had been done.

******

Sitting there in the nursery, rubbing Mekhi's back now, Karma thought about how loving Joaquin had been as natural as breathing. When she looked back on the nine years they were together, Karma couldn't help but appreciate the time that was spent with him. If only he hadn't gone into the service. He told her he had no other choice. After his grandparents passed away, he was left with their debt. He sold their chain of bodegas in an effort to pay it off, but he fell short by the thousands. The Marines promised to pay off everything in exchange for his life. Of course they didn't actually say that, but that was the obvious unspoken truth of the matter. Joaquin told her the four-year tenure would go by quickly and not to worry herself over him. Karma, in response, cried and cursed him for making such a decision. But deep down inside she knew there was no other way for him to surmount his financial obstruction. He left for Afghanistan in the fall of 1998. She prayed for him. He asked for her hand in marriage in the spring of 2001. She said yes. He reenlisted in the summer of 2002. She cried. He died in a road-side bomb attack in the winter of 2005. She swore to herself she'd never love again.

Karma wiped away a tear as she repositioned her sleeping son in her arms. Her worries with Joaquin were nothing compared to the issues she had with Money. She'd made a terrible mistake by giving Money her heart. He didn't know how to take care of it. One can't love a loveless man. *So why couldn't she stop loving him?*

******

Money awakened to the sound of humming near his ear. He wiped his heavy eyes and glanced over to the left side of him and noticed the usual warm spot beside him was cold and vacant. He felt for the love of his life, but she wasn't there to be touched. Money rolled back over toward the soprano voice that was resonating within the space between the bed and the nightstand, and picked up the small white monitor it was coming from. He turned the volume down a little and noticed the time on the digital clock radio as he placed the monitor back on the nightstand. The time read: 2:45. Money would be so glad when Mekhi grasped the concept of time. His son stayed up all night long and slept all day, until he wanted something to eat, of course. Once his hunger was satisfied, he went right back to sleep. It was what Karma called a " full-tummy coma."

Money listened to Karma hush Mekhi as he fussed. He knew she'd put the baby monitor on his side purposely to wake him when the baby cried to be changed or fed so she could sleep. She needed as much rest as she could possibly get while he was home, but nevertheless, Karma was always the one to hear the baby first and tend to him by herself. Money didn't mean for her to have to do everything on her own, but his job as an officer was starting to wear on him. Before her and Mekhi, it was just him and Mimi. Feeding two mouths went to feeding four overnight. That meant going to work every day and working overtime just to bring home a decent check. The *overtime* he claimed he was working every other night was anything but. It was actually an excuse he told Karma to keep her from knowing he was spending time in the streets of Orange, Newark, East Orange, and Irvington searching for Jimmy. He was out speaking to every pimp, prostitute, dealer, messenger, and wino who would listen. But he came up empty-handed every single time.

Money had made it his mission to devote the little time he had in his troubled life to find his father. The Alonso-Cruz family, with the exception of Karma's uncle Miguel, had long given up on their search. Even Karma had given up hope. Well, at least that's what Money thought.

There were questions that needed to be answered like, *how did he become the monster that he'd grown to be? Or, did he even know about him? How could he beat, rape, and turn out the woman who brought his son into the world? How could he do the same to Karma's mother? And why did he kill her?* Money needed to know what caused that man to go astray and turn the lives of so many upside down. No matter his father's answers or lack thereof, the story he'd written about himself wouldn't be able to be changed or erased. It was etched in one of the stones rejected by God's building.

Since his taking of *extra shifts*, Money and Karma had an argument over finances and his long hours. They were never the *You don't make enough. We don't have this or that.* fights. They were the, *We're already financially stable. Why do you choose to put more on yourself than you have to?* disputes. Even though he hated entertaining Karma with his lies, Money knew there was no other way to approach and execute his quest. He had to keep Karma at a distance until he found Jimmy. Then he would tell her the truth.

It was no secret that he'd forced her into her current ill-condition. The daily stress of holding the couple's relationship together by herself had taken a toll on her health, her spirit. It wasn't just the bags under her eyes, or the narcoleptic spells she'd fall into whenever she sat down somewhere, or the mood swings, or the lack of intimacy between them. It was the look of emptiness in her eyes when she looked at him. He was doing more harm than good to her. And he was fine with that because she had Indigo, Maggie, and his mother for support.

Money thought about how involved his mother had been with Karma and the baby since his birth. She'd taken the young mother under her wing, loving her like the daughter she never had.. Three months seemed to have flown by so quickly. In those three months, Money had said all of *"Hey," "Yes," "No," "I don't know,"* and *"Bye"* to his mother when she came to the house or when he dropped Mekhi off at hers. The relationship between mother and son had become strained as a result of Money discovering his father's identity.

The day of his only son's birth was supposed to be a day of gaiety. He was to cry tears of joy, but instead Money found himself crying tears of rage. He didn't know how to tell Karma about it then and had yet to tell her. *"What's goin' on between you and your mother?"* or *"When are you gonna tell me what happened between you and your mother?"* had become regular questions in her daily conversations with him. His response was always *"Nothing happened."* Now, Karma was no fool and Money knew it. He knew she was well aware that he was lying to her every time she asked, but she never pressed the issue. The way she'd been feeling toward him for the past three months was far from compassionate.

Money repositioned his manhood in his boxers as he rose from the bed and made his way to the baby's nursery down the hall. Since Mimi was staying with his mother for the evening, he was able to bypass her room. As he walked toward the dimly lit sanctuary, Money thought back to the night he found Karma cradling her mother's lifeless body on the floor of that same room. He didn't know exactly how she felt about its transformation then or even now. Karma seemed grateful at the time he surprised her with it. He noticed how hesitant she was before stepping into the room on a daily basis. She always walked around the infamous spot she and her mother shared that dreadful night when she went to pick up Mekhi, put him down, take something into the room, or get something out of it. Karma never *ever* walked across that spot. Money hadn't asked her if moving the baby's things to another room would make her more comfortable, but he figured she would tell him in time.

As he stood in the doorway of his son's bedroom and watched the love of his life place their hushed prince into his crib, Money's mind drifted yet again. It took him back to the moment he first laid eyes on Karma. He'd never seen anything more beautiful in his life and he knew he had to have her. He couldn't believe, even now, how beautiful she was from behind. The fitted, white wife beater and boy-cut shorts she was wearing gripped her body like static to a strand of hair. She'd bounced back almost immediately after having Mekhi. The only evidence of his birth she had to show was the stretch marks and caesarean section scar on her stomach. Her stomach had since become a little pouch due to the surgery, but Money didn't care. The pudge suited her midsection area nicely. His woman still had the body of a track star.

He watched as the muscles in her arms flexed as she placed the baby's blanket over him. It made him wonder if she missed that part of her life...the running. She'd told him running was her life before her mother was stricken with cancer years ago, but she had stepped away from the sport altogether. Her reasons behind her retirement were still unknown to him. Why she never went back to the sport after her mother went into remission was another question he didn't know the answer to. He wondered how far she would have gone had she not quit. Karma always made him wonder.

"Do you miss it?" he asked her as he walked up behind her and pressed his body against hers.

Karma jumped a little at the sound of his voice and froze under his touch. She couldn't bring herself to relax in his embrace as he wrapped his strong arms around her waist. It had been so long since the two made any kind of intimate contact. Karma breathed deep as she pondered over Money's question.

She wasn't sure what he'd meant by it. He couldn't have been talking about his manhood because it wasn't erect at the moment. She had no clue where he was going with his question and feared the worst.

"Do I miss what?" she asked, turning her face toward his, and then directing her focus back to the baby.

"Running," Money replied sincerely.

Karma turned away from the crib and faced him. She folded her arms at her chest as the father of her son stepped back and stood before her with curious eyes.

"What makes you ask a question like that?" she asked in confusion.

"I know it was a big part of your life at one time and I was just wondering if you missed it," he said with a shrug.

Karma tilted her head back a little and squinted her honey brown eyes in an attempt to read him. For the year and some months they'd been together, never once had Money brought up that part of her life. Karma thought he must have come across the tapes her mother kept of her throughout her former career. They were Soleil's own personal video diaries of her from the time she put her first pair of track shoes on to the time she hung up her last pair. That was the only valid reason she could think of as the cause for his sudden outburst of interest.

"You come across my old tapes or somethin'?" she asked with a slight attitude.

"No, I don't even know where those tapes are. You hid 'em, remember?" he replied.

"Uh-huh," Karma said skeptically.

"I didn't. I just...I would really like to know," Money admitted.

Karma sighed and shook her head.

"Money, I don't see how me missin' track or not is important. It's three somethin' in the mornin' and once again I was up, *by myself*, tendin' to our son," she huffed.

"I know. Look, I'm sorry about that. I don't mean for you to...," his voice trailed off.

Karma, with her arms still folded at her chest, watched her man struggle to apologize for his lack of participation in caring for their son. He fidgeted and mumbled things under his breath. Even though her patience was wearing thin, Karma waited. She waited patiently for the apology she ever so deserved.

Money nervously rubbed the back of his neck, trying to find the words to muster an admission of guilt, but he couldn't find them.

"I've been fuckin' up. I know. I don't know what else to say. Can you just, uh, answer my question? I'd really like to know if you miss it or not," he managed to say while trying to soften Karma's hard glare with puppy dog eyes.

"No," Karma spat as she turned back around to watch her son sleep.

"No, you don't miss it or no you're not going to answer the question?" Money asked in sincere confusion.

"Take the 'no' any which way you like, Money. I really don't care," she replied smugly.

"Damn, Karma. I'm not trying to argue with you, baby. I just want an answer to my question. I mean, am I asking too much of you? I don't think I am. Why can't you just answer a simple question?" Money sighed.

"The same reason why you can't answer mine in regards to you and your mother," Karma fired back over her shoulder.

Money ran his massive hand over his mouth while looking up toward the ceiling. Had he known he was going to set her off, he would have stayed in the bed and blinked at the ceiling until he got tired and drifted back to sleep.

"I already told you. There's nothing going on between me and my mother," he lied.

"If you say so, Money," Karma smirked in disbelief as she turned around to face him. "If you wanna keep lyin' to me and yourself, for that matter, then that's on you. I just thought we were better than that," Karma admitted. She looked him dead in the eyes and waited for him to respond. When he didn't and looked away instead, Karma shook her head and grunted. "Unbelievable. I'm goin' to bed. My breasts are killin' me," she said as she walked around the infamous spot and lightly brushed past him out the door.

Just be patient with me, baby, Money thought to himself. He didn't know how to tell her Jimmy was his father. He was scared he was going to lose her if he did. Karma would have to continue to roll with the punches until all was said and done.

Money walked over to the crib and melted at the sight of the replicated man-child below him. He made a promise to his son that night that he would put an end to his mother's suffering soon. He had to. *But would it be possible?*

Money gently ran his masculine hand through his son's curly locks. He couldn't believe, even in that very moment, the

precious little life beneath his touch belonged to him. Blessed.
Money bent down and kissed his hushed prince before exiting
the room and making his way back down the hall. He knew
Karma thought their discussion was over, but it wasn't. She
wasn't going to get off that easy.

Money quietly pushed the bedroom door open, stepped into
the room, and then closed it behind him. He watched his queen
lay motionless as he approached the bed. Her eyes remained
closed, her face strained with misery. She'd situated herself in a
fetal position with her back facing his side of the bed. Money
was not surprised by the sight. It had become all too familiar.
Karma had been sleeping in that position for the past three
months. She stopped reaching for him at night. He stopped
calling for her. Their bodies no longer intertwined, and he
understood. But it didn't change the fact that he missed her.
Every piece of him missed her and deep down inside he knew
she missed him just the same, but she was far too hurt to ever
admit it.

Money climbed into the bed, pulling the covers over his
strong, bare legs and pressed himself against Karma. Her body
was so warm and solid. Before he knew it, his manhood had
grown into a full erection. It was so hard it hurt. He needed to
be inside of her. An apology wouldn't fall from his lips, but he
knew it would fall into her once their hips touched. He needed
her to look into his eyes so she could read how sorry he was.

Money inched his nose close to her neck and took in the
sweetness of her skin. It was a mixture of her natural almond
scent and Baby Magic. He couldn't help but gently push his arm
through the space between her bent arm and waist to hold her

tight. She belonged to him and she needed to know he still needed her. He kissed her softly on the earlobe.

"Are you asleep, baby?" he asked, peeking over her shoulder.

Karma remained silent and still. She felt the growth of Money's member snake up her back. She just couldn't bring herself to respond. It had been so long since they last made love, she was sure that if she gave into him, the pain would be too much for her to bear...physically and emotionally. The minute he slipped his arm around her, a tear fell from her eye. Another followed, then another one after that.

"Yes," she replied in a shaky voice.

Money cringed. He had no idea she was crying. Her body was so still. He knew he was the cause of her pain. And for some reason, he believed he could ease it by filling her up with the extension of himself. He leaned over her and watched the tears stream down from her left eye, run over the bridge of her nose, then slide onto her praying hands. He hated to see her cry, but she was even more beautiful when she did. Money took Karma's face into his left hand and slowly pulled it in his direction. Karma closed her eyes.

"Look at me, baby," he said in a stern whisper.

Karma shook her head in response.

"Please?" Money asked in an even tone.

"I c-can't," Karma replied in a hiccup. The tears wouldn't stop falling. She needed him to let her go so she could find solace elsewhere in the house. But he wasn't going to. She felt his eyes on her. The more he looked at her, the harder she cried.

"M-M-Money, ple-please," she begged. "Leave m-me alone."

"No. I'll never leave you alone. Never. I love you. Look at me," Money countered. "Look at me, baby."

As much as she didn't want to, Karma slowly opened her eyes and stared back into those of her love. They were filled with so much sorrow and regret. Money took his thumbs and gently rubbed her tears away.

"Tell me where it hurts, so I can fix it," Money whispered.

"Money," Karma grimaced with pain.

"Tell me. Tell me where it hurts," he replied, licking his full lips.

Karma sniffled as Money's hand traveled from her face to her swollen breasts. Her eyes closed momentarily as she squirmed under his touch. Her breasts hurt so much. She wished he could take the pain in them away, along with all that was in her heart. The pain was so great, Karma wasn't sure which of the two hurt more.

"Tell me," Money repeated as he got on top of her, slipping his body between her legs and carefully tearing the tank top off of her.

"All over," Karma sighed heavily as Money gently took one breast into his mouth.

"How's that feel?" he asked while massaging the other breast with his free hand.

"Good," Karma replied in an almost inaudible tone. Money was being so careful with her. She felt like a porcelain doll under his touch. He took his time outlining her auburn colored areolas with his tongue all the while making sure he was very careful not to lick or suck them too hard. The last thing he wanted to do was cause them to leak. Money cringed with pleasure as the area of skin shriveled beneath his lips. He made sure his strong mouth encapsulated her sore, hardened nipples fully, leaving little air for them to breathe.

Money was trying to breathe life back into Karma's worn body. He was appreciating her as the giver of life...WOMAN. The two things that nourished their son's little body on a daily basis needed nourishment of their own. Without her milk, Mekhi wouldn't grow to be a strong child. Without her heart, he wouldn't develop into a good man, a better man than his father and grandfathers. Without her mind, he wouldn't be able to teach others. Money was a man on a mission.

As he continued to tend to Karma's swollen breasts, the thought of running his fingertips along her stomach crossed his mind. Money knew she'd become self-conscious about the scar left behind from the caesarean section, but he thought the moment they were sharing was perfect. It would give him the opportunity to show her how and why to appreciate it like he did. It was the mark of motherhood, the ultimate mark of survival. Money decided to follow through with his thought. Seeing that Karma was well under his hypnotic spell, he brought his head back up and locked eyes with her.

"I want to touch you *there*," he whispered while caressing her face. "Can I?"

Taken aback by Money's humble request, Karma blinked back the fresh tears that were brimming in her eyes. She knew where he wanted to feel, but she wasn't sure if she was ready for it. Her body had gone through so many changes during her pregnancy. She enjoyed the way she looked during that time. Of course she had her moments of feeling like a beluga whale, but all things considered, she had carried the extra weight well.

When the time came for her to bear her son, she was ready to use all of her might to push him out, but God had other plans. The two had gone to war. He'd fought to take her life during labor and she'd fought to keep it. Luckily, Karma had a team of doctors on her side. They believed her life was in *their* hands, and they helped her bring her son into the world, healthy and whole. Karma would be forever grateful to them for saving her life, but the ugly scar that was left behind would never let her forget. No, He wouldn't let her forget that she overstepped her boundaries and took a life. He couldn't let her forget that He, indeed, forgave her, but He was still God and not her. What she did by taking Jimmy's life was an act only He was justified to make, not her or anyone else.

Karma couldn't let Money touch her in that place. She had been spared for reasons he would never understand. God let her live because it was so much harder to do. Dying was too easy. Murder was her cross to bear. The only problem with that notion was she still didn't feel guilty about killing the man. She didn't think she ever would. It had been very difficult at the beginning to look Money in the eye and not tell him about her mortal sin. But as time went on and his behavior began to change, any unsettled thoughts she once had went right out the window.

He couldn't touch her *there*. He couldn't touch her anywhere, but she wasn't putting up a good enough fight to resist him. Her tears were silencing her and before she knew it, she was giving him the answers he wanted to his questions. Karma couldn't avoid his gaze. His eyes were so intense and sad. Even though her mind was troubled and her soul was weary, her body was yearning for him. Before she could stop herself, she raised her hands and cupped his face and neck with them. She outlined his meticulously trimmed goatee with her golden eyes before hesitantly permitting him to touch her in that place she wished didn't exist.

Money bit down on his bottom lip as he allowed his right hand to travel down from her bosom, to brushing past her rib cage, trailing to her navel, then finally settling *there*. He watched Karma's eyes flutter as he began to rub it. Her discomfort was obvious. She began to have second thoughts about the whole situation and tried to push his hand away, but Money shook his head in disagreement and politely placed it back on his neck.

"No more," Karma murmured with pleading eyes.

Money ignored her plea. He couldn't promise her no more lies about what happened between him and his mother. He couldn't promise her no more lies about why he consumed himself with work. He couldn't promise her no more lies about why he wasn't doing his part as the father of her child. He couldn't even promise her that he would never touch her *there* again. But what Money could promise her was euphoria by the end of the night. With that thought in mind, he ran his hand back up her bronzed body to her chiseled face, leaned in and kissed her ever so gently. Karma fought the urge to part his lips with her tongue, but lost the battle. She slipped her tongue in between his succulent lips and tied it with his. That response alone gave Money the go-ahead to continue his expedition.

As the lovers' tongues continued to dance, Money began to peel Karma's shorts off. Her heart began to race as she watched him remove his boxers. Her mind raced back to the first time they made love on the living room floor downstairs under the Christmas tree over a year ago. She'd abstained from sex for two years and lying with Money that night felt like she'd lost her virginity all over again. The same feelings emerged the night she gave herself to him after fully recovering from the C-section.

Money was well endowed, not only in length but in girth as well. It was common for him to hit her cervix when their bodies met. Thankfully, he was never too rough with her, which gave her some comfort during their lovemaking. He knew what he was working with and did his best not to hurt her. ButKarma wasn't too keen about what she was in store for tonight. The man hadn't gotten any in two months. The experience was either going to be a slow and controlled one or fast and furious.

After throwing his boxers onto the floor, Money knelt between Karma's legs, ready to reclaim what was rightfully his. He took her thick legs into his hands, throwing them over the crux of his muscled arms. He was hungry for her and she saw it in his eyes. Like he'd done so many times before, he lined himself up with the entrance of her wet channel and gradually edged himself in. A slow low moan escaped from his lips as Karma's sugared walls enveloped him completely. He remained for a minute, basking in the pleasure of being inside of her again. Money ran his hands up Karma's thighs, leading them to her ample behind where he palmed and squeezed it. The feeling of her cushioned skin in his hands was almost too much for him to handle. So he took all the love within him and began to thrust in and out of her. His hands moved from her behind to her wide hips.

Karma, unable to speak or keep her eyes open, reached above her head and held onto her pillow and mattress brim. Her body grinded against his slow, deep thrusts. Her tight, wet tunnel pulled and pushed back on his outstretched muscle. She could handle this lovin' tonight. She'd missed it so bad, she found herself dripping wet some mornings as a result of dreaming about him the night before. But Karma wasn't sure if it would be another two months before she'd give into him again. He didn't deserve her goodies. They both knew that. But there she was on her back, moaning and hissing to each and every one of his strokes. She was going to be pissed with herself in the morning.

Karma continued to steadily ride Money from below. Through hooded eyes, she watched as the crinkles between the space of his furrowed eyebrows dug themselves deeper into his skin. Money's hands slid from her hips to her legs again. He took them into his grasp, throwing them over his shoulders. As he leaned forward and made a trail of kisses from her ankles to her knees, he slowly began to lower himself on top of her. He continued to move forward until Karma's legs were finally behind her head. The sight before him and the spot he'd suddenly reached inside of her instantly triggered something inside of him. Before Money knew it, he'd stopped balancing his weight on top of Karma and let himself give way. He'd found a spot that welcomed the head of his member with open arms every time he knocked on its door. His measured, steady pace and deep thrusts unexpectedly changed to fast, violent strokes.

Money blacked out. He was so far gone he didn't hear Karma asking him to stop. He didn't hear her telling him how much he was hurting her. He didn't hear her requests turn into begging, her moans turn into stifled screams. She couldn't breathe. He didn't hear her. Her freshly fallen tears were choking back her cries.

Karma struggled to push Money off of her, but her efforts were of no use. He just continued to pound into her. A sharp pain began to creep along the layers of scarred, stitched tissue within her stomach. Any moment now, she was going to pass out. She scratched at Money's shoulders and chest in an attempt to snap him out of the maniacal trance he was in, but failed yet again.

Gone. Karma could feel herself fading away. The pain was too great for her to bear and it seemed like Money was never going to stop. *How did it come to this?* An image of Jimmy sodomizing her mother flashed before her eyes. Karma struggled for air. An image of her mother's blood running down her legs flashed before her. She gasped for oxygen again. An image of Jimmy laughing during his evil act blinded her. She faded to black, thinking about Joaquin. He would have never done anything like this.

Chapter 2

Karma awakened later that morning sprawled out in the middle of the bed with the sheet thrown partially over her nude body. She blinked a couple of times, trying to adjust her eyes to the brightly sunlit room. Her eyes were so dry and sleep encrusted, they burned. She needed to regain full consciousness. The previous night's events seemed to have become a distant memory. She was unsure why the sheets were drenched with sweat. She couldn't understand why her body ached. The stench of stale blood and sex filled the air, but she couldn't figure out for the life of her where it was coming from.

Karma raised her hands to rub her face and noticed it was stained with dried tears. She could hear Evelyn moving about downstairs, which meant Money had already left for work. With that conclusion, Karma threw the worn sheet off of her and slowly rolled onto her side. She noticed there was a sticky substance clinging onto the insides of her thighs. Knowing exactly what it was, she shook her head in disbelief. She rose from the bed on unsteady legs with the intention of going to the bathroom, but had to sit right back down because the pain she experienced from the night before returned. Unfortunately, sitting down was just as painful as standing. Her vulva was swollen.

"Oh, my God," Karma uttered to herself as she leaned to one side with her hand between her legs. She looked back over her shoulder to see if her nose had been telling the truth about the smell of blood in the air. When her eyes fell upon an area in the bed that was soaked in red, her suspicion was confirmed.

"Oh, my God," she repeated in a hushed tone. Images of the previous night's events came back to her full force. The incident had been so traumatic that her brain repressed any recollection of it. Had it not been for the pain and bloody sheets, she surely would have gone on with her life like nothing ever happened. *How was she going to face Money after this?* She didn't know how to feel. A part of her felt like maybe she deserved it because she'd kept it from him for so long out of spite. The other part of her just felt violated. Sitting on the edge of the bed, holding herself, Karma should have hated Money for what he did to her. She should have wanted revenge. She should have been ready to call Stuff to kill him. Instead, she just sat there dazed and confused.

Karma could hear Evelyn walking up the stairs with the baby in tow. She had to snap out of her haze. The last thing she needed was Money's mother trying to read her. She would never tell the woman who loved her like her own mother had, her son raped her. Mother and son weren't on good terms as it was. If she knew her only child's spirit had taken on that of his father's, it would surely kill her.

Karma gathered as much strength as she could from within, rose from the bed again, and shuffled across the room to retrieve her favorite plush robe off the bed's matching chaise. She put it on, tying the belt securely in the front before making her way back to the bed and stripping it. She tossed the sheets to the side and picked up the comforter off the floor, placing it back on the bed.

"Knock, knock," Evelyn said softly as she peeked through the slightly opened door.

Catching the woman's warm eyes, Karma mustered a weak smile and gestured for her to come into the room. Evelyn walked in, clutching Mekhi close to her chest as he sucked on his index and middle finger Karma's baby boy, dressed in a pastel blue onesie, was the color of maple syrup with big, jet black curls that reminded her so much of her mother's raven locks.

"Good morning, baby," Evelyn voiced as she kissed Karma on the cheek and handed the baby over to her.

"Morning, Mother Evelyn," she replied with averted eyes.

Evelyn, quite conscientious of the young woman's normal behavior, studied her long and hard. Something was wrong. Karma's steps were uneven and she was cradling Mekhi like his life had just been threatened.

"Karma, baby, are you all right?"

Karma, finally finding the courage to look back into the woman's eyes, cringed at the thought of her mother-in-law-to-be seeing right through her. She sighed deeply as she shook her head up and down.

"Yes, I am. I just, uh, I just had a bad dream last night," she lied.

"Oh, no. Well, if you don't mind me asking, what was it about?" she asked sincerely.

"My mother," Karma replied wearily. She felt horrible about using her mother as an excuse for the way she was looking, acting, and moving, but it was the first thing that came to mind. Unbeknownst to Evelyn, there really was truth to her lie. Karma did have nightmares about her mother. She just hadn't had any as of late.

"But don't worry about it, Mother Evelyn. I'm all right," she continued, waving her hand in dismissal of the question.

"I don't think you are, hun," Evelyn countered as she moved toward Karma, reaching for her face. "Let me look at you," she insisted. She held her head back slightly, determined to see the truth in the young mother's eyes.

"Now, I don't want you to take what I'm about to say the wrong way. Okay, baby?" Evelyn asked sincerely.

Karma nodded in response.

"I, too, lost my mother at an early age. Not like the way you lost yours, but I was left alone early on like you. I did all that I could do to handle it the best way I knew how. But my way wasn't good enough. I needed to talk to someone," Evelyn hinted.

"Mother Evelyn, are you tryin' to tell me I need to go see a shrink or somethin'?" Karma inquired. The conviction in her voice was almost hard. She hadn't meant for it to come out the way it did, but she was insulted. Here this woman was trying to tell her she needed to go see a doctor to tell her what she already knew—her mother's death was haunting her and so was Jimmy's restless spirit. Karma was well aware of what was irking her. How dare her man's mother come to her and suggest such a thing when she couldn't even get three words out of him when their paths crossed.

"They're costly, I know. But maybe it'll be good for you," Evelyn responded earnestly.

"Well, thank you for bein' concerned, but I'm all right. Really," Karma lied again through a weak smile.

Defeated, Evelyn simply patted her flushed face and smiled.

"All right, well, if you say you're fine, then you're fine."

Karma shook her head up and down in agreement.

"I am."

"Well, all right," she said while taking Mekhi back into her arms. "Oh, yes," she continued, remembering something important. "I came up to tell you that your uncle, Victor, I believe it was, told me to tell you that you don't need to come back today. Enjoy the baby a little while longer."

"He did? But my maternity leave ends today," Karma replied in confusion.

"Well, it looks like he had a change of heart. And I agree with him, honey. In fact, you should use this time to catch up on some of the sleep you've been missing. I'm here with the baby and Mimi's at school. Take a day to pamper yourself, Karma. You deserve it," Evelyn sang.

"I don't know, Mother Evelyn," Karma began.

"Oh, you just hush your mouth," Evelyn responded playfully. "You need to take care of *you* sometimes. Those who truly love you will understand. Hmm?" Evelyn raised her eyebrows for emphasis and smiled warmly. "Say, *'You need to put yourself first sometimes, Mommy,'*" she playfully instructed Mekhi in a child-like voice. " *'Now, get some rest so you can play with me later,'* " she continued in the same voice. Mekhi gurgled and squealed merrily, his legs kicking under him in response to his grandmother's indirect demand. Evelyn nodded in Karma's direction once again before exiting the room with the baby.

Rest was the last thing Karma needed. What she needed was an emergency appointment with her gynecologist because she just knew Money killed her chances of having anymore children.

******

Money embraced his uncle, Dermont, with a firm hug. His uncle had called to tell him they needed to meet. Money had no clue what his uncle wanted to talk to him about, but he was certain the conference was not going to be a pleasant one. The relationship between him and his mother was worsening as the days progressed. Money had a feeling his mother had reached out to her big brother and expressed her feelings about the matter to him. But the dysfunction between him and Evelyn was the last thing on Money's mind. The previous night's incident was where his thoughts remained. He didn't know what happened. It was like his mind and body had taken on lives of their own. He'd lost all control of himself. He'd slipped so deep into Karma waters, he tried to drown himself. He tried to rid himself of his father's wrongdoings and drain the tainted blood, semen, and temper shared between them from his body.

When he woke up that morning, he looked over at Karma and noticed how still she was. Usually when he made any type of movement in the bed, she stirred. She didn't in that instance. Alarmed, Money watched for her chest to rise and fall. When he saw that it barely lifted, he began to panic. He started to lightly slap her face and call her name, but she didn't respond. So he lightly slapped her face again and called out to her; still no response. Terrified by the outcome of his cruel act, he began to shake her. Fortunately, Karma subconsciously turned her face away from him and regained regulation of her breathing. Relieved that she was somewhat okay, he probed her body with his heavy eyes, taking in every inch of it. He saw the streaks of dried tears on her face. He saw the dried semen and blood inside her thighs. He saw the stained sheet beneath them. *What had he done?* There was no way he was ever going to be able to fix the damage he'd done. It was one thing to try to apologize to her for not being there for her and the kids, but it was a completely different story to try to ask her for forgiveness for stripping her of her dignity.

It didn't take long for Money to flee the house. He threw on his sweats and boots, tossed his uniform and backpack over his shoulder and left. He had to get away from her as quickly as possible. He didn't want to be there when she woke up. He couldn't bear to think how she would have looked at him had he stayed. Him being gone for hours on end had become routine. Today was no different, but he would stay away just a little longer.

For as far back as he could remember, Money only saw his uncle whenever he got into trouble. It didn't matter if it had been in school or at home with his mother. His uncle was the primary disciplinarian of the Parks family. Money understood his mother could only do but so much in raising him to be a man. Boys needed their fathers or a father-like figure in their lives. Being very much aware of that, Evelyn made sure her brother was a permanent and visible fixture in his life. And Dermont "Hawk" Parks took his position very seriously.

"I got here as soon as I could, Unc'. Had a run-in with some knuckleheads on the way over. But look, I can't stay long, 'cause I'm on call," he informed him.

"I understand, son," Hawk responded with his gap-toothed smile and strong pat on his only nephew's back. "I'm not going to keep you too long." He gestured for Money to have a seat in one of the chairs set before his desk as he sat down in his leather swivel chair. Money obliged, removing his nightstick and gun from his belt before sitting down.

Hawk reclined in his chair and folded his hands under his chin as he studied his nephew from across the desk. He wanted to dig into his behind the moment he stepped in the door. Evelyn had called him the previous night, sobbing. He could hear her struggling to lift something from her shoulders, but couldn't bring herself to hand the burden over to him. Once she finally calmed down, she was able to bring him up to date with the event that occurred between her and Money three months prior. Since Hawk had been in and out of the country for the last three months, spending the majority of his time with his devoted wife, Sarah, and trying to shut down he and Jimmy's drug distribution franchise, he was totally unaware of what happened between his sister and nephew. Like the loyal older brother that he was, Hawk told Evelyn to dry her tears and put her worries behind her. He was going to take care of Money. With reassurance from her brother, Evelyn found temporary relief in his bonded word and left matters in his hands.

Now, here Hawk was watching his nephew's every move.

"So how are you, man?" Hawk quizzed warmly.

"Oh, I can't complain, Unc'," Money replied. "Life is good, you know?" He lied. "Got a beautiful fiancé and two healthy, beautiful kids at home. This job's kickin' my ass, but at least I have one, you know? Everyone can't say that. Got a roof over my head, clothes on my back and food in my stomach. So, as far as I'm concerned, it's all good in the hood."

Hawk nodded his head and smiled.

"That's good. Very good, son. Speaking of that fiancé and those two little blessings of yours, how are they?"

Money shrugged his shoulder and smiled.

"Aww, Unc', Karma couldn't be a better mother to Mekhi *and* Mimi. Mimi loves her to death, man. She's calling her Mommy Karma now and Karma's eating it up. She loves every minute of it. And as far as little man goes, he's getting bigger by the hour."

"Oh, yeah?" Hawk asked in light surprise.

"Yeah, man," Money responded proudly. "I couldn't have asked for a better family."

Hawk was so happy to hear Money say that. It was the perfect opening for him to begin his cross-examination about the drama between mother and son.

"I have to come by. I haven't seen Karma since she gave birth," Hawk admitted regretfully.

"I know, Unc'. You really have to. She asks about you all the time. I think she'd be really happy to see you."

"I definitely will. I know she's a good mother," Hawk hinted as he tilted his head back.

"She's better than good, Unc'," Money agreed without hesitation. "She's...she's amazing." A look of wonderment blanketed Money's face as thoughts of Karma with their son and his daughter shaded his mind. "When I see her with Mekhi and Mimi, Uncle D, man...it's...I don't even know how to explain it."

"You don't have to, son," Hawk nodded slowly as he thought about his own mother. "Mothers are the greatest gifts to the world. Many may argue that children are the greatest gifts. But, I disagree. God's greatest gift to our existence was woman. Without her, mankind wouldn't exist. What is it that we refer to nature as? *Mother*. Africa is the *motherland* of our people, the original birthplace of civilization. The world would be a much sadder place than it is now had we not been birthed by women, son...our mothers. Like God, they are all-knowing," he shook his head in confirmation.

Money squirmed in his seat from his uncle's last remark. He knew he was wrong for going off on his mother the way he did at the hospital. He also knew he was just as wrong for distancing himself from her. His mother was his best friend. But best friends didn't keep secrets from each other.

"I guess so, Uncle D. I wouldn't know. I'm not a mother," he replied uneasily.

"Well, the last time I checked, you had one, right?" Hawk asked disgustedly.

"Yes, sir," Money answered against his will.

"So why is it that my sister called me last night, telling me that you haven't spoken to her in the last three months?"

Money noticed the venom in his uncle's voice. He never liked challenging him, even as a child and teenager. His uncle's beatings were something terrible. He had the hands of a prize fighter. And they were the same hands that taught him how to fight.

Money didn't know whether his uncle was going to try him today or not, but he was prepared to stand his ground. His mother was wrong. As far as he was concerned, there was no need to discuss it any further.

"Uncle D, why are you even asking me about this, man? I'm sure she told you everything that happened between us," Money countered.

"I know exactly what she told me. Now, I want to hear what you have to say about it," Hawk replied calmly.

"I don't have shit to say about it. My mother lied to me. The end,"Money retorted.

"I hate to break this to you, Money, but that's what mothers do to protect their own," Hawk said in disbelief. "You think she wanted to lie to you about your father for the past thirty-one years? Would you have rather her painted a picture of him as some God-fearing, hard working, respectable family man, knowing damn well he wasn't worth two shits?"

"I didn't say all that,"Money replied.

"Then what the hell are you saying, son? Better yet, what is it that you're *not* saying that you *want* to say?" Hawk inquired. His nephew was just a little boy in a man's body. Even though

Hawk didn't appreciate the treatment Money was giving his sister, he knew Money was rightfully upset.

Money sighed heavily as he shook his head from side to side. A dull, aching pang was starting to form around his temples. The drama between him and his mother was the last thing he wanted to talk to his uncle about. Every time he thought about what she'd done, it infuriated him. He would become blinded with rage. And to hinder Karma and the children from feeling his wrath, he would stay away from the house until his fury subsided. "She should have told me is all I'm saying, Uncle D," Money replied adamantly. "I mean, what the fuck? I went straight *to* her after Karma's mother was killed. *Straight* to her. I told her what happened from the time the nigga crashed Mrs. Walker's party to the time we found out his ass disappeared after killing her. I ran the muthafucka's name *and* stats down to her, Unc'," Money emphasized by punching his fist into his hand. "I asked her if his name rang a bell since she'd been in Newark all her life and he was tied to the biggest drug dealer of Essex County. And she sat there, looked me dead in my face, and said no. The woman sat there and listened to me tell her I stood less than two feet away from the man who killed my woman's mother. The same muthafucka she knew was my father! And I'm wrong for not having shit to say to her after all of that? Whateva, Unc'. I don't even care anymore," Money said, slouching down in his seat, enraged at the whole situation. "I should have called you and asked you about him," he mumbled under his breath. "Maybe then I would have gotten the truth," Money sulked.

"But you didn't," Hawk replied curtly. "This September will mark the two-year anniversary of Mrs. Walker's death. Never once did you come to me and ask me about Jimmy. For two years I knew nothing about the conversation you had with your mother."

"She didn't come to you afterwards and tell you I approached her about him?" Money asked in disbelief.

"No, she didn't. And I'm sure she had her reasons. But what's done is done and we have to move forward. Now, I know you're upset and you're entitled to be just that. But you're wrong for treating your mother the way you have," Hawk responded seriously. "I truly believe she was doing what she thought was right. Had Karma's mother not been killed by your father, you still wouldn't know who he is, to all of our benefit. And I mean that to say, you wouldn't have had to get a firsthand account of what kind of sick, low-down cock suckin' bastard he truly was. And your mother and I wouldn't have to clean up this mess that's been left behind," Hawk said. "You need to be thankful you still have my sister in your life, son. Because she *was* Karma's mother once upon a time," he admitted as he leaned forward, placing one of his bended arms on the desk. "She too was abused and had she never left him, you *both* would be dead today. Your mother saved your damn life, boy. You need to take Karma's mother's death as a life learned lesson. Not everyone has a big brother like me for a nigga to answer to. And from what I understand, Karma's mother has two of them," Hawk said distastefully as he sat back in his chair. "Maybe she should have told you. Maybe. I don't know. It's not a place in her life she likes to relive. And neither do I.

But if you really want to know about your father, you ask *her* about their time together."

"All right, Uncle D, I, uh, I gotta get back on the road. I've been here longer than I intended to be," Money stated as he rose from his chair and placed his baton and gun back into his holster.

"I sure hope I'm the only one you've said that to, nephew," Hawk stated, eyeing Money closely.

"What the hell is that supposed to mean, Unc'?" Money asked in frustration. "I mean, what's with the fuckin' riddle, man?"

Hawk laughed as he watched his sister's son unravel before him. He knew things weren't right between him and Karma at home. Evelyn had filled him in on the couple's troubles.

"I think it's best you calm down, Money. I'm taking your disdain for your mother's actions into serious consideration right now. That's the *only* thing that's keeping me from jumping up out of this chair and knocking your black ass out for cursing me," Hawk said, cracking his knuckles before folding his hands and placing them back underneath his chin.

"I mean no disrespect, Uncle D, but one man laughing at another doesn't sit well with me. It never has, especially when the nigga that's laughing knows the other one is at his worst," Money replied insulted. "It's not right."

"Niggas laugh at you every day, Money. Just like they talk about you every day. You just don't hear and see them. Now, I don't know if that's by choice or what, but niggas are gonna laugh and talk about you when you're here and when you're dead and gone. My great-grandmother hipped me to that, son.

Niggas laugh at you out of spite. Niggas laugh at you out of their own misery," Hawk schooled him calmly. "But the reason why *I* was laughing at you was simply out of pity. I was laughing at you because I know your mama isn't the only woman you're having problems with right now. I was laughing at you because you're falling apart and haven't allowed your woman to do her job *as your woman*. Karma should be your backbone when you can't stand. She should be your eyes when you can't see. She should be your ears when you can't hear. Your woman should be the shoulder you need to lean and cry on when the world is against you. And you're not letting her, Money," Hawk admitted sincerely. "If something doesn't change soon, *you* are going to be that nigga who's left laughing at himself out of his own misery."

"My mother just told you everything, huh?" Money asked with a disgusted smirk. "Goddamn."

"My sister told me what she knew," Hawk replied.

"Oh, yeah? And what was that?" Money asked with an attitude.

"That Karma's doing everything by herself," Hawk snapped. "Now, your mama said she could be wrong because she doesn't know *exactly* what's going on between you and Karma. But, from what she's seen, you're not taking care of home, son."

"My mother doesn't know what she's talking about," Money hissed.

"You calling my sister a liar?" Hawk asked as he rose slowly from his chair.

"Man, what'chu gettin' up for?" Money asked as he watched his uncle rise from his seat. "I wasn't calling Mama a liar, Uncle D. I'm just saying she doesn't know first-hand. She's just going by what she's seen and hasn't seen. Her perception of me and Karma's situation is distorted and shit."

"If you didn't understand this when I said it to you the first time, let me repeat it. A mother knows," Hawk responded. "Women have something that we as men lack, son, and that's intuition."

Money looked away and shook his head in defeat.

"Look at me, Money," Hawk demanded quietly as he approached his uniformed nephew. He placed his masculine hands on Money's broad shoulders and shook him a little. Money allowed his eyes to meet his uncle's as his nostrils flared. He knew his mother meant well by telling her brother her worries about his deteriorating relationship with Karma. He knew she didn't mean any harm by going to him to settle the dispute between them. Money just didn't want to hear he was wrong. It was already bad enough he was reminded of his wrongdoings every day in his home. Hearing his uncle express he and his mother's concerns only made him feel worse. He didn't know how he was going to mend either relationship.

"Surrender your heart to your mother and woman," Hawk continued as he looked directly into Money's deep brown eyes. "They mean well. Let them take their positions in your life. If what happened between you and Evelyn has affected your relationship with Karma, then, you need to fix it, nephew."

"I don't know how to do that," Money confessed, fighting back tears. "I fucked up, Unc'...bad. I don't know how to make things right with either one of them."

Hawk lifted his hands and placed them on each side of Money's thick neck. He held on to it tightly as he smiled endearingly.

"First, you ask your mother for her forgiveness. Then, if you really want to know what she went through with Jimmy, you simply ask her so that you can find the peace you so desperately need. But before you do, I warn you to take her feelings into consideration. Then, after you have made amends with her, you go home, take that beautiful fiancé of yours into your arms and tell her how much you love her. Then you go on and tell her the reason why you've let her down these past couple of months. Lay her down and make those sweet nothings you've whispered into her ear so many a night, into sweet *somethings*," Hawk concluded with a pat to Money's neck. "Go home and make things right, son. Do it while you still have a candle burning in their hearts for you."

Money stood in silence as he thought about the impossibility of ever relighting Karma's candle again. He'd blown it out last night, watering it down with his uninhibited self-indulgence. *Who was he kidding?* There wasn't enough wax in the world to recreate her candle.

Chapter 3

Karma lay on her stomach, watching Indigo change baby Desiree's diaper as her legs dangled in the air behind her. She was able to see her doctor before she arrived at the condo. Expecting to hear she wouldn't be able to have any more children as a result of Money's manhandling, she heard the contrary. Her uterus had not been affected by the rape, but her vaginal canal was inflamed and bruised as a result of the chafing. She'd also acquired a urinary tract infection due to his mercilessness. Her doctor prescribed some medication for the UTI and Percocet for her pain. While she waited for her prescriptions to be filled at the pharmacy, she made sure she purchased the morning-after pill as well. The last thing she wanted was another baby by Money, especially a rape baby.

Karma kissed the baby's plump jaw as she marveled over her beauty. She couldn't get over her only cousin becoming a mother just one month after she gave birth to her own child. Indigo was still as naturally beautiful as ever. Since the birth of her little girl, she'd cut her hair into layers, letting it rest just an inch or so below her shoulders. With the exception of Karma, Stuff, and Miguel, the rest of the Alonso-Cruz clan totally disapproved of Indigo's new do and made sure she was aware of it. Her mother cried and prayed to the saints to restore the strength she believed Indigo possessed in her hair. Her father stopped speaking to her for a week because he felt her decision was disrespectful to Stuff as his wife. Karma, knowing how dramatic her aunt and uncle would be, simply pulled her beloved cousin to the side and comforted her with hugs and kisses.

Indigo still had much of the baby fat left over from her pregnancy; mostly in her chest, thighs, and backside, but the extra weight complemented her five-foot seven-and-a-half inch stature well. Since Indigo had been a dancer for most of her life, Karma was afraid her cousin wasn't going to be able to gain much weight during her pregnancy. Fortunately, all uncertainties were cast aside when the pounds began to creep up on her like a cat ready to pounce on its prey. Karma hoped Indigo was enjoying what was left over from the pregnancy just as much as she knew Stuff was.

To Karma, it seemed like just yesterday Indigo and Stuff moved into her old condo. But, in truth, that transition happened nine months ago. Since then, Indigo and Stuff finally settled down as man and wife, bringing Stuff's life in the drug game to a complete halt. He'd saved enough money to support them for the next ten to twenty years, but Indigo insisted that he look into going to college to become something greater than a retired drug dealer. Stuff was a math whiz. And she believed her man could go farther than he ever imagined in life if he'd just apply his natural mathematical abilities elsewhere. There was a baby to think about now and whether Stuff knew it or not, drug money, like any other kind of money, was disposable.

Stuff took his wife's suggestion and enrolled in a couple of courses at Essex County College to see what interested him the most. It was no surprise to Indigo that banking/finance caught Stuff's attention. He was now taking night classes to earn his Associate's degree in Banking/Finance and working at a Chubb's Bank in Parsippany as the firm's manager. It's something else how one has the ability to manipulate the truth about his former occupation on a resume' without getting caught. Now, Stuff wasn't proud of his actions, but if getting a nine to five was what he needed to do to make Indigo happy, he was going to do it and he did.

Karma couldn't have been more proud of Stuff. Even though walking on the straight and narrow had been a challenge for him in the beginning, he followed the footsteps that had been imprinted by God in his path nonetheless. Stuff was the ideal husband and father. She would watch him interact with Desiree when she dropped by and wished Money had the same enthusiasm and interest with Mekhi. Most men prayed for sons so they could continue the family name. But Money didn't seem to want Mekhi, her, or even little Mimi. It didn't matter now because the relationship was severed beyond repair.

Karma took Desiree's chubby little hand into hers and kissed it as Indigo finished snapping her onesie shut. Desi was such a good baby. She was a spitting image of her mother with the exception of her complexion, hair color, and mouth. She was a redbone like her daddy and had inherited his full, pink lips. Her hair, unlike her parents', was red. The family couldn't fathom where she inherited red hair. Karma figured the future generations of Alonso-Cruz's were all bound to be marked by the girls' late grandmother Ava Alonso-Cruz. Whatever the case, she just hoped Desiree would be spared of the woman's hatred like her mother had. The baby girl was going to be a little heartbreaker indeed. And it hurt Karma to the core to know her mother would never have the chance to see little Desi or Mekhi.

"*Mirar*, I love Desi and all, but I can't wait to go back to work," Indigo said as she rolled the soiled diaper up and threw it away in a sanitized waste basket on the other side of the room. "I know I just have a month left until my leave is over, but it's taking forever," she went on to say as she walked back over to the bed. "Do you know that sometimes she and I just stare at each other like, *Okay, now what? 'Cause I'm bored*," Indigo stated seriously.

Karma grinned weakly at the seriousness in her cousin's confession as she continued to kiss Desiree's hand. She could understand why Indigo was feeling such a way. She was never one to stay in one place for a long time. Indigo was always on the go and if you weren't able to keep up with her, then that was a fault of your own.

"I tell you, *mamita*, there's but so much you can do with a baby in a day. And call me crazy if you want , but I think she likes her father more than she likes me," Indigo admitted.

Karma's eyebrows furrowed as she looked at her seemingly troubled cousin in disbelief. She figured the new mother was experiencing a little bit of post-partum depression. It was the only thing that made sense to her because she refused to believe the baby wasn't absolutely in love with her mother like everyone else was.

"It's true," Indigo exclaimed as she removed the baby wipes and other child care things from the bed. "When that man comes in the door and opens his mouth to speak, this little girl will wake up out of her sleep just to see her daddy." Indigo shook her head, laughing while walking back and forth to set things back into their rightful places. "Mommy said I used to do the same thing to her with Papi, but I think she's lying. I don't remember acting like that toward her."

Karma shot Indigo a *You know damn well you did* look.

"All right, maybe I did," Indigo shrugged, sucking her teeth. "But that woman is worrisome and just as wicked as she wants to be. I can't help it if I'm a daddy's girl," she smiled. "I think, in a lot of ways, she wished we had the relationship you and Auntie Sol had, but--"

"Money raped me last night," Karma blurted out.

Indigo stopped in her tracks and closed her gaping mouth shut. She slowly walked over to the bed and sat down beside the baby. Desi wildly flailed her fat arms at her mother as a gesture to be picked up. And without hesitation, Indigo did so.

"What did you say?" Indigo stressed as she tried to wrap her mind around her cousin's sudden outburst. "Karma, what did you just say?"

"Money...he raped me last night," she admitted sadly. "I don't know what happened. We were makin' love and the next thing I know...he wouldn't stop, Indigo. He wouldn't get off of me. I tried to fight him off, but he just kept goin'. It was like he didn't even hear me." Karma held her head in her hand. She closed her eyes, awaiting the migraine she knew was coming on. When she reopened her eyes and looked back up at Indigo, her heart immediately sank. Indigo sat shivering with rage, tears falling from her eyes. The terror behind them reminded her of her own the night she found her mother dead.

"I'm going to kill him," Indigo confessed through sniffles. "I'm going to tell Stuff and--"

"You're not gonna tell Stuff anything," Karma replied earnestly. "You're not gonna say one word to him, understand? I don't want him to know. Not him, Uncle Vic, Uncle Miguel...no one, you hear me? I'll take care of Money. I have to do it my own way."

"Are you serious? He raped you, Karma. I can't just sit back and not say or do anything about it," Indigo cried. "I don't care what you say, I'm telling him anyway," she exclaimed, rising from the bed. Karma jumped up and grabbed her arm.

"What did I just say, Indigo? You think I'm playin' wit'chu? Don't say anything to him," Karma emphasized with wild, blazing eyes. "If you love me, you'll do what I asked."

"Don't even go there with me, Karma," Indigo countered as she traveled over to the crib to put Desiree down for her nap. "Don't try to pull that *"If you love me..."* crap because you already know the deal. My love for you is unquestionable. Don't stand there and try to make me feel guilty for wanting to tell Stuff. Money needs to be dealt with."

"You don't think I know that already?" Karma responded dejectedly.

"Well, what do you plan on doing about him then? You don't want me to say anything to anybody, so what is it that you're going to do?" Indigo asked disgustedly. Partner or not, she was ready to have Money put into an eternal slumber and there stood her cousin protecting the man. Indigo couldn't believe who Karma had become. She was her aunt, Soleil, all over again. Indigo understood how much Karma loved Money, but damn all that. He raped her and that couldn't fly.

Standing in that small space, Indigo wished she never introduced him to her in the first place. She was just as much to blame for the rape as he was. At least, that's how she felt.

"I don't know," Karma whispered as she sat back down on the bed.

"You *don't know*?" Indigo asked with an unusual hardness in her tone.

"No," Karma replied with her eyes averted to the floor. She didn't have to look up at her cousin to know she was looking at her the same way she looked at her mother the day she confessed her love for Jimmy. Karma couldn't bring herself to meet Indigo's eyes. If she did, her cousin would surely see how torn she was.

"Please stop lookin' at me like that," she uttered shamefully. Indigo continued to stare. She never saw her cousin so vulnerable before. Karma was supposed to be the strong one. And there she sat, looking like a lost child waiting for someone to tell her what to do next. Indigo knew this was only the beginning with the abuse from Money. It was unfortunate, but he had it honest. He was his father's son through and through. She just wasn't sure if Karma knew it.

Indigo walked back over to the bed and sat down beside her cousin. She looked around the room in search of something to say. Karma still hadn't lifted her eyes from the floor. The silence between them was too loud.

"Do you have *anything* figured out yet, K? I mean, have you seen a doctor yet?" she asked in a softer tone.

Karma's eyes trailed the floor. "Yes."

"Okay, okay. That's good. That's a start," she rubbed her moist hands on her thighs. "What did the doctor say?"

"She just said I'm a little bruised and swollen down there...nothing too serious. I have a UTI, but she gave me a prescription for that and something else for the pain."

Indigo closed her eyes and breathed deep. She didn't want to hear anymore.

"I think I'm gonna break off the engagement," Karma continued, her voice cracking.There's nothin' left between us

Another silence fell in the room. Indigo wrapped her arms around Karma's neck and rested her head against her shoulder. She finally found some comfort in knowing Karma was breaking up with the man or at least thinking about it. Thinking about it was better than not having the thought cross her mind at all.

"I won't say anything if you really don't want me to," Indigo proclaimed against her better judgment.

"You promise?" Karma asked, turning her face toward her cousin.

Indigo sighed. The last time she made a promise to Karma, two people ended up dead. Then again, when she tried to hold Karma back from taking control of an uncontrolled situation, her aunt ended up dead as well. She couldn't win.

"I promise," Indigo mumbled. She knew best not to give her cousin her word, but she knew even better not to cross her.

******

Money leaned against the archway to the kitchen of his former home, watching his mother pull out a huge pan of his favorite meal---lasagna. The aroma of the baked pasta filled his nose as he continued to watch his mother bop her head and sing along to Albertina Walker and Rev. James Cleveland's gospel tune *Please Be Patient With Me.* For as long as Money could remember, his mother always threw on a gospel record to get her through the most trying times in her life. But in all the years, he never thought he would be the cause of one of those times. He'd called her an hour before arriving at the house to tell her he was coming by to pick up Mimi, but unbeknownst to him, Karma had done so already. Evelyn hadn't heard Money enter the house due to the high volume of the music.

"Pleeease be patient with me. God is not through with me yet," she sang as her head snapped from side to side. "When God gets through with me...when God gets through with me, I shall come forth; I shall come forth as pure gooold. Lord, Lord, Lord, Lord, Lord," she ended the verse.

Money fiddled around with the keys on his keychain as he took in each and every pained inflection of his mother's call to the Lord. Three months was a long time to hold a grudge against the most important person in his life. He was sorry he hadn't spoken to his uncle or Karma about the rift between them sooner. Money understood his actions had been selfish; not only toward Evelyn, but to Karma and the kids as well. The moment his uncle explained his mother's reasons for hindering him from the truth about his father, Money forgave her. He had seen the man with his own two eyes and what he saw wasn't that of a man. He'd seen a foul-mouthed, illiterate drunken fool with no respect for himself, his woman, or his woman's daughter. He'd seen a murderer in the flesh. It infuriated him even more to know that the same man who killed his fiancé's mother had laid the same hands on his own mother. His uncle had been right. It could have been his mother instead of Karma's who was dead. And for that, he was thankful to Evelyn for doing what she'd done.

Some time ago, Money asked Karma what his approach should be the next time Mimi asked him about her mother. And instead of Karma telling him to lie to the little girl, she showed him a way to tell her who her mother was and how to continue to love and acknowledge her despite her personal indiscretions. Karma made the most complex situations so uncomplicated and he loved her for it.

Thinking about it now, he should have turned to her after the dispute between him and Evelyn, he was sure she would have spoken the same truths as his uncle. Whether she would have agreed with the way Evelyn went about doing things or not, Karma would have *made* him understand. *But would she have really taken Evelyn's side?* Her mother was dead. Nothing could change that. His father was the one who killed her. Nothing could change that either. Money just shook his head in dismay. He didn't have a clue about how he was going to break the news to Karma once he faced her.

"Yeah, yeah, yeah," Evelyn continued to sing still oblivious to Money's presence.

"You still have the voice of an angel," Money said with his head down and eyes remaining on his keys.

Evelyn jumped at the sound of her son's voice. She swung around with her right hand placed over her erratically beating heart.

"Money! Lord, have mercy. You scared me, son," she replied with a nervous smile. "How long have you been standing there?"

"No longer than five minutes," he responded as he slowly looked up at his visibly shaken mother. "I didn't mean to scare you."

"That's all right. That's all right," she smiled again. "I thought I'd cook you a little lasagna tonight since I haven't made it in awhile," she said as she turned back to the stove to retrieve a spatula. "I know how much you love it."

"Yeah, Mama. I do love it," Money agreed without hesitation. He walked over to the round, wooden dining table and sat down. "Where's Mimi?"

Evelyn paused for a moment before cutting into the platter of pasta with the spatula.
"Well, Karma came by and picked her up about an hour ago."Evelyn could feel Money's eyes on her back. She figured he had a look of disbelief on his face. It was one that said, *'Mama, you knew damn well I was coming by to get Mimi. You're not slick.'*

"She did?" Money asked with a smirk.

"Yes, she did," she sang as she dished their plates. "I just love that child. She's such a good mother to Mimi," Evelyn continued as she shook her head. She could feel the tears brimming in her eyes. The way Karma had accepted Mimi as her own always made her break down and cry. Mimi never took to any of her father's former girlfriends the way she had Karma. Evelyn was more than ecstatic about the relationship between the two.

"My baby just loves her to pieces." Evelyn proceeded to pile Money's plate with a nice amount of buttered spinach and a chunk of Italian bread before walking over and placing it before him on the table.

"Thanks, Ma," Money said, looking up at his mother and placing his manly hand firmly atop hers. "For everything you've done for me," he stated seriously.

A tear fell from Evelyn's eye as she looked into her only son's deep brown set.

There were traces of Jimmy in his eyes, nose, and mouth today. She never wanted to believe he looked like his father, but she couldn't deny it looking at him in that moment. The infamous temper the two men shared hadn't been seen since the day the youngest Hayes man was born. She knew it was there hibernating inside of him.

A mother's touch was the cure to any wound. With that unspoken truth in mind, Evelyn intertwined her fingers with Money's, balled their bound hands into a fist and pressed it against his heart. She placed her free hand gently on his face and said, "Everything I've ever done in my life has been for you." She rubbed the tear that streamed down her son's face and uttered with wide penetrating eyes, "I lied, but I'm not sorry for doing so. Know that I did it out of love...and *my* love has *no* boundaries when it comes to you."

Lost in each other's shared thoughts and feelings, an unspoken apology from a son was requested and accepted by his mother.

Chapter 4

Karma kept a painfully steady pace as she cleared and cleaned the tables around the coffee shop before closing it for the day. It was a quarter to twelve and she knew the lunch crowd would be swarming in soon to eat in the restaurant. She had yet to write the day's specials on the easel and didn't have a clue if her uncle's restocked colored chalk for the board.

Her mind was everywhere. Money hadn't come home the night before and she didn't know if it was because he couldn't face her or because he just didn't want to. She knew he hadn't been hurt in the line of duty because the precinct would have sent a car out to inform her. She just knew he couldn't have stayed at his mother's house because they weren't speaking. Karma didn't know what to think. For all she knew, he could have slept in his car outside the house last night without her knowing.

Karma walked behind the counter and placed the wash cloths and table rags in a bus pan in a cupboard below. She went through every single drawer and cabinet in search of a box of chalk. Nothing.

Karma slammed the last drawer she looked in shut, then walked back around the counter and proceeded to make her way into the dining hall. She was going to scold anyone in sight for not restocking the chalk when she noticed the lunch specials had already been written on the easel. She stood in front of the wooden structure shaking her head. *Had she been that out of it today?* The first thing she did when she came to work every morning was write the lunch specials on the board and today was no different.

Karma sighed as she looked around the vacant room. Money had a serious hold on her and she didn't like it. He was interfering with her job. If he had only called her cell or the house phone and left a message about his whereabouts, she would have tried not to care even though she obviously did.

The chiming of the bell that hung on the coffee shop's main door brought Karma out of her disgruntled trance. She turned around and stared into the eyes of the man who'd taken her womanhood. He stood before her with his hands hidden in the depths of his cream colored leather bomber jacket. He wasn't in uniform. *Did he take the day off*, she asked herself. His dark chocolate skin shimmered under the shop's dim track lighting. A matching off-white skully covered his low-cut hair.

She watched him lick his thick lips as he outlined her body with his deep brown, slanted eyes. Karma suddenly became self-conscious. She was wearing an apron over an oversized t-shirt, both with the restaurant's logo on them, fitted jeans, and a pair of Swamps. The only thing close to presentable on her was the new mohawk she was sporting and her flawless, naturally beautiful face. She'd put a hint of MAC lip glass on her lips, but that was it. The look in Money's eyes was remorseful but the lust that shared the same space spoke louder than his repentance. He was violating her all over again. Once again she remained, trying to fight him out of her.

Even if she wanted to deny it, Karma couldn't. Money was absolutely beautiful. He had to be the closest thing made in God's true image of perfection. In that same perfection, the man before her held the devil's flaws. With that thought in mind, a look of surprise turned into a scowl. Money watched the light in her honey brown eyes grow into a blazing fire. He knew he didn't have much of a fighting chance to extinguish the flames.

"Are you busy right now? I, uh, I wanted to talk to you about the other night. Why I didn't come home last night," he said while taking his hands out of his pockets and rubbing them together. "Can we go somewhere and talk?"

"I really don't think this is the right time or place to discuss what happened the other night," Karma replied with grave eyes. "I mean, there isn't much to say...at least not on my end. The damage is done." Karma turned her back and proceeded to walk down the corridor toward the restaurant.

"Karma," Money mustered through a raised whisper. "Karma," he called again.

Karma kept her eyes straight ahead. She untied the apron from around her waist and snatched it from around her neck. A handful of waiters and waitresses watched their boss hobble through the area from a distance. Money stayed close behind as he followed her through the maze of tables before reaching her office in the back of the building. He noticed the severe limp she had as she walked away from him, giving him more proof than he needed to confirm the crime he committed.

Karma threw the apron down in one of the office's corners before turning around to see Money closing the door behind them.

"Money, get out. Please, I don't want you here," she said, pacing back and forth with one hand on her head and the other on her hip.

"No, Karma. I need to say this," Money insisted.

Karma stopped pacing and looked over at him warily. She placed her hands on her hips and submitted to his stern declaration.

Money ran his hand over his goatee, thinking about what he wanted to say to her. It wasn't going to be easy, but he had to try to explain himself.

"I would never *ever* hurt you on purpose. You have to know that," he began."I've been trying to figure out why I did what I did the other night, but I can't find the reason behind it. There is no reason. There's no excuse," he sighed. "I don't know what came over me, but you have to believe I didn't mean it. I love you. I would give my life for you. I swear to God I would. And, and, last night, I was at my mother's house. I fell asleep over there by mistake," Money admitted while removing his skully.

Karma looked over at him in disbelief.

"I don't believe you."

"You don't believe what?" He asked sincerely.

"I don't believe you fell asleep at your mother's. You haven't said more than two words to the woman in the last three months. I'm supposed to stand here and believe that?" she asked.

"Well, yeah. It's the truth," Money countered. "I went over there last night to pick up Mimi, but she told me you had already come by and got her. She was making my favorite dish when I walked in, you know? And I can't turn down my mother's lasagna, Karm. You know that. Seeing her hook that up for me, I knew it was her way of making peace. So, I accepted her apology and we ended up talking for the rest of the night. I got so caught up in our conversation that I forgot to call you and fell asleep, baby. That's the God's honest truth," Money stated sternly.

Karma raised one of her perfectly arched eyebrows and smirked. She removed her hands from her hips and began to wipe them on her thighs.

"Are you finished?" she asked unmoved by his story.

"No, I'm not actually," Money spat back. He hated when Karma was pissed off. Everything that came out of his mouth went in one ear and right out the other. "Do you want to hear why I stopped talking to her in the first place or not?" he asked impatiently.

"No, I don't. And you wanna know why, Money? Because I don't have time to listen to anymore of your bullshit," she snapped. "You're bringin' somethin' to me *today* that should have been addressed three months ago. Instead of bein' my other half, *my man*, and confidin' in me when the shit first went down between you and her, you shut me the fuck out and let the shit fester. And now that you're *ready* and you all of a sudden found a moment that's most convenient for *you*, you want me to be all ears. Well, you know what, my love, it's not gonna happen. You can't get that because you don't deserve it. Just like you didn't deserve what you took from me the other night."

Karma's last remark cut Money deep. She was right and he knew it. He chewed on his bottom lip and sighed as he studied the mother of his son. Karma was fed up. She had every right to be. He had to switch gears. Meeting her hurt and rage with his own wasn't going to fix the situation. It would only make it worse.

"How you goin' to throw that shit back in my face, Karm? Like I didn't just apologize to you?" Money asked brokenheartedly.

"Because you didn't," Karma replied matter-of-factly. "Not meanin' for somethin' to happen is not the same as bein' sorry for it. You consider what happened the other night a mistake? 'Cause if you do, that just confirms that the whole thing could have been avoided. Mistakes are nothing more than unwise decisions. The other night was not a mistake. You don't make a mistake and rape somebody."

"You sayin' I did that shit on purpose?" Money fumed.

"Are you sayin' that it was a 'mistake'?" Karma seethed.

A loud silence fell between them.

Money cast his eyes toward the floor in search of something to say. The guilt was eating him alive. He'd expected Karma to fear him after their encounter. At least then he would have had a better chance of swaying her.

"Did you tell anyone?" he asked with his eyes still roaming the floor.

"You're still alive, aren't you?" Karma countered.

Money raised his eyes while scratching his chin. There was nothing more to say in regards to the rape. He truly was sorry for what happened. He thought his apology came across loud and clear, but it hadn't. It wasn't good enough for her. It probably wasn't good enough for any victim. He wished her mother was alive because she seemed to be the only one who could get through to Karma. Little did he know, Soleil hadn't been able to do much with her either.

"I stopped talking to my mother because I found out that Jimmy's my father. And because she never said a word to me about it, even after I told her what he'd done to your mother, I stopped talking to her," Money admitted, letting out a sigh of relief from the burden he'd been carrying. "That's why I've been so fucked up for the last three months. I didn't know how to come to you with that shit, Karm. Mekhi had just been born and it was supposed to be the best day of our lives...*my life*. And don't get me wrong, baby, it was. But when I found my mom's wallet lying on the floor in the waiting room, flipped through it to make sure all of its contents were still there, and came across a wedding pic of her and Jimmy...I shut down," Money confessed. "She caught me with the pic in my hand. I asked her about it, and that's when she told me. I know I've been telling you that I'm working overtime these last couple of months and I have been for the most part."

"What 'chu mean *for the most part*?" Karma asked with blazing eyes.

"I, uh, I use most of my time on the beat looking for Jimmy. I've been looking for him since I found out," Money confessed in a stern tone. "I'm out there in the streets longer than I have to be because I hate coming home and facing you. When I look at you, I see your mother. And after I blink, I see my father beating her to death," he said in a firm whisper. "Don't you see, baby? His blood runs through my veins. And I've passed that shit on to Mekhi."

Money's words hit Karma like a ton of bricks. There she stood, expecting to hear that he was out cheating on her with some other woman and all he was doing was running away from one problem and trying to solve another. For the first time in months, she felt guilty for killing Jimmy. The thought of Money wanting to find and confront the man, not only for her but for himself as well, never crossed her mind. He had so much disdain for Jimmy long before he knew his true identity that she didn't think he would ever want to face him.

"Right after I told you I was pregnant with our son, you told me you were a better man than your father could *ever* be. And I believed you," Karma spoke slowly through silent tears. "You let a coincidental thing consume you and then used it as a crutch for the last three months. You can't help who your father is, just like I can't help who my mother was. And as far as *your* mother is concerned, her admitting she knew Jimmy would not have changed the fact that my mother's dead. I have no beef with your mom. She's not the one who killed my mother. My beef is with Jimmy and it will always be with him." Karma sniffled as she placed one hand on her hip and let the other wipe her tears away. "There is no excuse for what you've put me through in these last couple of months...the other night. What you've done to your children. I almost died bringing our son into this world and you didn't do a goddamn thing to make things easier on me. Not when I was recovering in the hospital, the time in between, or now. I've accepted and treated your daughter as if she were my own and what have you given me in return? *Nada*." Karma took a few steps backwards and sat on the edge of her desk. "Long before we even knew who your father was, you told me you would be nothin' like him. But I don't see much of a difference. I told you what he did to my mother. How he raped her over and over and over again," she paused. "How do you expect me to stay with you after what you put me through, Money? You did the same thing your father did to my mother. Which brings me back to our son who you haven't done one damn thing for," Karma said taking a deep breath in. "You know what? It doesn't even matter. You've showed me that you serve no purpose in his life or in mine. So with that said, you can kick rocks," she said tersely.Money blinked excessively, clearly taken aback by Karma's curt response.

His eyebrows furrowed. He struggled to register what she'd just said to him. A half smile formed on the right side of his face as he looked back at her in disbelief.

"So what'chu sayin'?" he asked, fidgeting with his nose like a fiend in need of a hit. "You sayin' it's over between us? You puttin' me and my daughter out on the muthafuckin' street? Is that what'chu sayin'? Here I am pourin' my heart out to you, tellin' you how sorry I am, why I've been fuckin' up and you sittin' there tellin' me to kick fuckin' rocks?"

Karma watched the monster build up in the man she told herself she didn't love anymore. His nostrils were flaring and he had begun to sweat. He was one second away from turning into the raging lunatic she'd seen on New Year's Eve and outside of his mother's house over a year ago. She held her ground then and she was prepared to do so now. He had the nerve to swell up on her then, but she never backed down from him. And even though he hadn't laid a hand on her, she was more than ready to fight him if she had to. She knew the thought of hitting her had crossed his mind. But he'd fought the urge. And now that the truth was out about his tainted bloodline, Karma would match his with her own. She was Ava Alonso-Cruz's granddaughter, the city of Newark's greatest learned disciple. And their child had taken out New Jerusalem's most notorious drug lord. If she had to, she'd do the same to his son.

Fighting was the last thing she wanted to do with this man. She just didn't have the strength. She was tired and still in tremendous pain, but that was to be expected for *WOMAN*, right? As was the unavoidable confrontation that was about to erupt. *Remain calm*, Karma thought to herself.

"That's right. But don't get it twisted. I'm not puttin' you and your daughter out on the street. I'm puttin' *your* black ass out on the street. Mimi's got nothin' to do wit' this," Karma said, sliding off the desk while pointing back and forth between herself and Money. "She's more than welcome to stay wit' me or alternate between me and your mother's house if she likes. I'm not gonna keep her from seein' her little brother. But *you*, you got to get the hell up outta my house *tonight*."

"Aww, hell no! If I'm goin', my muthafuckin' daughter's goin' with me! You're not her mother! You don't have no muthafuckin' say in where she goes and stays," Money screamed.

"I don't have to be her mother. But the next time you ask her who her mother is, I bet you she won't say Lachelle," Karma replied snidely. "Yeah, dat's right. I said it. She may have given birth to her, but *I'm* the one who's breakin' *my* back to raise her to be a better woman *than her mother. Me*," she pointed to herself. "I'm *Mommy* all up and through dis bitch."

"Bitch, you ain't shit! I don't --"

The sting of a hard slap across Money's cheek cut him off in mid-sentence. He hadn't seen Karma run up on him. She'd been swift and made a perfect connection with her hand and his face. Money called her a bitch that same New Year's Eve night and received the same reaction. He should have seen the slap coming then, but he'd missed it like the one that was just served. Unlike the quarrel on that holiday evening, Karma didn't continue to pound on him. She merely stayed in his space and waited for him to make his next move. There was no more room for words between them.

Money wasn't stunned. He just didn't know what to say to her after being struck. The argument had gone awry. It was supposed to go down with him apologizing for his actions and her forgiving him for his indiscretions. But they'd gotten lost in translation. She'd come out of left field with wanting him out of her house. Breaking up with Karma had been the farthest thing from his mind. It obviously hadn't been from hers.

Money rubbed his stinging face as he looked down at Karma. Both of her hands were balled into tight fists. She was breathing heavily, causing her full chest to heave. Her face was beet red and her eyes were flooded with tears. He'd hurt her to the point of no return. It was deeper than having called her a bitch. He'd scorned her on the inside. He'd left her to fend for herself just like the police and her family had two years ago. The family had done it when they stepped away from her mother, leaving her in the hands of his father. And the police had done it by dismissing her mother's case altogether. Soleil went down in the books as just another foolish nigger spic bitch, another victim of domestic violence, another statistic. Cold case wide shut.

Money couldn't handle the sight of Karma crying, so he reached out and attempted to place his hand gently on her face, but she slapped it away.

"Don't touch me," she sneered. Money's words had hurt her deeper than the pain she endured during the rape. His heated words were always spoken out of lies, but the conviction behind them would make Karma believe they were true.

Unbeknownst to Money, today was a new day. Karma was going to regain control over her mind, over her spirit, and over her life. "You callin' me a bitch? I ain't shit? No, I beg to differ, sweetheart. *You* are the one dat ain't shit. You and dat punk ass *bitch* father of yours," Karma scoffed through tight lips.

Money watched the tears flow like a river down her flushed cheeks. She never took her glossed eyes off of him. Like she'd done to her mother in the past, Karma kept her eyes locked with Money's. He needed to see her pain and the reflection of himself in them because he was the cause of all of it.

"Your ring...is in...your duffle bag...with the rest of your things at the house." Karma mustered between sniffles. "All the clothes...that I couldn't pack...in your duffle...are in garbage bags."

"Karma, come on. Don't do this. We can fix this. What can I do to fix this, baby? I know my actions were selfish. My Uncle D and my mother opened my eyes to that. I didn't see it then, but I do now," Money pleaded with heavy eyes. "You and I not being together has never crossed my mind. It didn't two years ago after all the shit I put you through and not today. I can't just walk away from you that easily, Karma. I love you. You bore my son and that means more to me than life itself."

Karma shook her head in protest as she tried to control her breathing. The hard crying she was doing was making it difficult to speak. Money's begging sounded real good to her ears, but not good enough. In the months he'd left her to do everything by her lonesome, she learned more about herself than she ever did before. The magnitude of her spiritual, mental, and physical strength surpassed that of anyone she'd ever met. She'd found her independence in Money's absence. His control over her was no more. She'd embraced her role as a single, working mother like her mother had in the absence of her father. "When I get home tonight, I don't wanna see you or any of your stuff there. I don't wanna see you anywhere near my house. Because if I do, I promise you, Money, I will get a restraining order against your sorry black ass. And the next time you see your son will be under a court appointed, supervised visit," Karma confirmed gravely.

"I've hurt you that much that you'd threaten to keep me from seeing my son on a regular basis? You'd get the law involved? Have you forgotten that I am the law, baby girl?" Money asked with wide, wild eyes.

"Nigga, please. You better be grateful I'm even lettin' you see 'im after what you did to me. And have *you* forgotten that my uncle was the law before your ass was even a nut in your daddy's sack?" Karma countered. "You have no juice in this town, *Officer* Parks. I own every brick in this city," she smirked. "Shed blood and fallen tears speak volumes around here. I suggest you start playin' catch-up wit' those of us who've already proven ourselves and paid our dues."

"I wish I never fuckin'..." Money began before stopping himself.

"What?" Karma asked, already knowing the answer. "You wish you neva met me? You wish you neva fucked me and fell in love wit' my ass? Or is it that you wish it had been somebody else who had your son?" Karma looked for a response to her questions in Money's eyes. There wasn't one strong enough to read. His eyes were on the brink of shedding tears. And that in itself finally forced her to look away.

"Well, I guess that makes two of us then. But you know what? I don't regret havin' him. He's the *only* thing I don't regret out of dis," she said half-heartedly in reference to their relationship. Karma limped back to her desk and sat down on the edge of it again. *Where had they gone wrong?*

"When your mother died, she took the best of you right along with her," Money replied as he studied Karma's stoned face.

"I don't think so. Because every time I look at that precious little baby boy of ours, I see the best of me," she said, looking back at him. "He's my redemption. And I suggest the next time you look into those sky blue eyes of his, the very same ones I had, find the redemption *you* undoubtedly need in them." Karma crossed her ankles and tilted her head slightly, taking in every inch of her ex's frame for the last time. She loved Money and she would always love him. But sometimes in life, it was best to love from a distance.

"Now..." Karma said, rising from the desk and shuffling over to the door. "...if you would be so kind to do us both a favor and leave my place of business without making a scene, I can continue with my day and you can continue with yours." She opened the door and waited for Money to exit. Money remained where he was, looking down at her hurt beyond comprehension.

"So that's it, huh? We're through," he said in a cringe.

Karma simply nodded. She wanted to voice it, but couldn't bring herself to do so.

"Un-fuckin'-believable. You're a piece of work, you know that?" Money asked as he put his skully back on his head.

"That's what they say," Karma replied, maintaining her strong front.

"Fuck it then," Money responded with a wave of his hand. "I'll be by to pick up my son tomorrow."

"Oh, that won't be necessary. Your mother will have 'im every single day of the week for ten hours, sometimes more, with the exception of Saturdays and Sundays.

You can see 'im when he's with her," Karma countered coolly. She didn't want to give Money a reason to come by and show his face. He was the last thing she wanted to see. And since she was unsuccessful in helping him bond with their son, she was more than willing and ready to turn the job over to his mother.

Money bit the inside of his cheek. Karma had an answer for everything. She'd been hip to him trying to use Mekhi as an excuse to see her. He was out of ammunition.

"I'm out," he said, as he turned abruptly and walked out of the door.

Karma closed the door behind him and pressed her back against it. *Who was she kidding?* She would have to see the man for the next eighteen plus years of her life, whether she liked it or not. He'd used the discovery of Jimmy being his father as an excuse to not do his part as her partner and father to his kids. Karma didn't understand how he could let something like that stand in the way of taking care of his responsibilities. When her mother died, she still went on and carried out her daily tasks. Business was always taken care of.

Back to basics, Karma thought to herself. Money wasn't the first to grow up without a father and he surely wasn't going to be the last. Only time would tell if Money would step up to the plate and take care of Mekhi. But Karma wasn't holding her breath.

Chapter 5

The 40/40 club in Atlantic City was filled with bodies beyond its capacity. It was officially summer and everyone in attendance was ready to bring the hottest season of the year in right. Money stood amongst four of his fellow law enforcement buddies against a wall with a glass of Hurricane in his hand. He'd gotten back into the club scene a month or so after he and Karma broke up. And to his surprise, he hadn't lost his swagger. He had any and every woman at his disposal and he took advantage of it.

His forced bachelorhood was something he'd gotten used to quickly. It was no secret the women meant nothing to him. Money would tell them from the beginning that he didn't want anything serious. He had an insatiable appetite for sex and he needed it to be fed. His one stipulation---no kissing allowed. Kissing was an intimate thing done between two people who loved each other. Money had no love for hos. And even though some of them tried to win him over and fill the void Karma left in his heart, they never succeeded. Money's heart was still with Karma and always would be.

It had been five months since his break-up with her and each day that passed seemed more unbearable than the last.

They'd see each other in passing when she came by to pick up Mekhi or drop off Mimi at his mother's house. But that was it. The two didn't say a word to each other outside of those conditions. Money would try to spark up a little conversation between them, but Karma would barely respond. He'd try to give her a kiss on the cheek or take her hand in an attempt to get her to look into his eyes so he could see if the love was still there, but she'd pull away and avoid all eye contact with him.

Money didn't know how to fix Karma's broken heart. His mother told him to let time mend it. Evelyn truly believed Karma would come around once she was ready. She knew the girl still loved her son. She just needed to be by herself for a little while. Money understood what his mother had told him and decided to fall back until the time was right to pursue Karma again.

Since the break-up, he'd stopped working overtime and spent more time with his son, trying to make up for the time lost when he and Karma were together. Every time he looked into his little man's eyes he was sorry he ever neglected him. And he was even sorrier for ever hurting his mother. He made a promise to Mekhi every night that he'd make things right with Karma because he believed a *real* man never left a woman to stand alone. He was a man of his word and he needed to stay that way.

A dark-skinned beauty walking in Money's direction caught his attention. Her face was familiar to him, but he couldn't put a name with it. She was wearing an all white denim catsuit with a gold chain belt and stilettos to match. Her thick afro was full with straw set curls. Her African features were prominent in her nose, mouth, cheeks, and thick bones, but nevertheless breathtaking. Her solid frame was accentuated by wide hips and thick thighs. Her chest and waist were small, making Money wonder how such a small torso held everything below the belt up so well. Money watched the woman politely decline an offer to dance from a guy who was dressed in a tweed suit.

As she came closer and her face came into full view, Money realized he was looking at Mimi's mother, Lachelle. She wasn't the same emaciated, snot-nosed, chap-lipped fiend he'd kicked off his stoop so many months ago. Lachelle was healthy and she had that beautiful face and body he'd been allowed to sex and stress him five years ago. Feeling a pair of eyes on her, Lachelle snapped her head in the direction of the group of men standing up against the wall. Her eyes locked with Money's, causing her to stop in her tracks. The sight of her daughter's father watching her like a hawk suddenly made her want to run away and hide. She'd been clean for eight whole months and hadn't seen Mimi one time since her sobriety stint. Lachelle was too busy living it up in the clubs up and down the East Coast to reclaim her place in Mimi's life. The club scene was her second home. And it was in the club where she'd met Money five years earlier. Here they were once again under the same setting.

Lachelle averted her eyes first. Maybe he hadn't recognized her. She cursed under her breath as she tried to rush past him, but Money caught her by the wrist.

"Damn, La. I didn't even recognize you," he said, looking her up and down in disbelief. He knew she had intentions of bypassing him, but he refused to let her off that easy. Money wanted to know what she was doing at a club all the way down in South Jersey. *Was she clean? If so, how long had she been clean? Why was she sober enough to party but not sober enough to come by and see her daughter?* He had to approach the situation wisely. He didn't need his temper to get the best of him, especially in a public place.

"What you doin' down here in A.C.?"

Lachelle looked down at her grasped wrist, then back at Money. Money, catching Lachelle's drift, released it, and then placed his hand back in his pant pocket. He tilted his head back and waited for Lachelle to answer his question.

"I should be askin' you da same question," she replied, sizing up Money's towering, strapping figure.

"Don't play with me, La," Money countered seriously. "I don't have time for your games. Now, what the fuck are you doin' down here?"

"I'm partyin' like da rock star dat I am, baby," she said with her broad white smile.

"I see that. Now, correct me if I'm wrong, but doesn't that lifestyle consist of drugs and sex too?" Money asked in disgust.

"It does, but not in mine. Well, at least not da drugs part," she smiled mischievously. "Been clean and sober for eight months now. Eight months and countin'," she said proudly.

Money folded his arms across his broad chest as he continued to look down at the chocolate beauty with suspicious eyes.

"Oh, yeah?"

Lachelle placed her hands on her lower back and looked up at him defiantly.

Money looked good enough to eat. He was wearing a baby blue, short sleeved linen pant suit with a crisp, white wife-beater underneath his shirt. A matching pair of white Air Force Ones donned his feet. His body was stripped of any jewelry, with the exception of a silver watch on his left wrist. As she gave him a good once-over, Lachelle let her eyes stop at the bulge in his pants. The thought of Money's manhood anywhere near the mouth on her face or the one between her legs forced her to lick her lips.

"I'm glad to hear that," Money responded as he studied Lachelle's body language. There were no signs of the addict that used to house her body, not one trace of her. But he did see the freak who used to let him do whatever he wanted to her. He wasn't close to being drunk, but he was way past horny. The thought of taking Lachelle back to his hotel room and running up in her for the remainder of the night crossed Money's mind. But it was soon clouded by an image of Karma, then Mimi. He'd forgotten *that quickly,* Lachelle told him she'd been clean for the past eight months. And in those eight months, she never once picked up the phone to call him about Mimi. Money's mood quickly changed.

"So why haven't you called me since you've been clean? I know Mimi would love to see you, bein' that you're her mother and you're clean and all now," Money said haughtily. "You remember her, don't you? Your daughter? She's five now."

Lachelle stepped back and placed her left hand on her hip, shifting her weight to her left leg. She proceeded to point her finger in Money's face.

"Don't start dat shit wit' me in here, a'ight? I know how old my daughter is," Lachelle hissed. She closed her eyes momentarily, trying to keep herself from unraveling. She didn't want to black out on the man she once loved. It was no secret she hadn't been a mother to any of her nine children. She had her first child at the age of thirteen and hadn't stopped until she reached her twenty-fourth year of life. All of them had been boys and all of them she'd lost to the system, with the exception of Mimi who was her last born and only girl.

Lachelle was a recovering drug addict. She'd been an addict since birth. Her mother had been one of the many who had fallen victim to the crack epidemic in the '80s. Unlike her mother, Lachelle hadn't been given a choice. She was what she was. Take her or leave her.

"I'll see her when I'm ready," she said calmly.

"What's wrong wit'chu seein' her now...sober? She's already seen you high. It'll be good for her," Money protested with the shrug of his shoulders. "I mean, you makin' time to be all up in this club tonight to shake ya ass. I'm sure you got time to come by and see your daughter," Money declared angrily.

"What I do is my business, Money," Lachelle replied with an open hand in mid-air. "It always has been and it always will be. You don't tell me when da time is right to see my child or not. I make dat decision," she pointed at herself. " Dat's your problem. You always have to control shit. Tellin' people what they need to do instead of doin' what *you* need to do. And since we're on da subject, who's watchin' her while you down here posted up on a wall lookin' for some bitch to smash?"

"Don't even try to play me, La. You know Mimi's well taken care of. My mother's got her this weekend," Money waved his hand in dismissal of her stupid question.

Lachelle grunted and rolled her eyes.

"A'ight, well, I guess I can't say it was good seein' you again," she said with a smirk before stepping past him.

"Wait a minute, La," Money said, grabbing her by the wrist again. Lachelle sighed deeply as she pulled her hand away. Money was messing up her game for the night. She was there to show off her new outfit, reformed body, and use both to get free drinks from guys she knew wanted to take her home. Lachelle had to get rid of Money.

"This isn't how the convo was supposed to go down," Money admitted. "Can we go somewhere and talk? You here with anybody?"

Lachelle looked away, and then back at Money before answering. She knew they had a lot to talk about. Mimi was going to be the topic of discussion and Lachelle wasn't sure if she was ready to speak to him about how she felt about being a mother to their daughter. Motherhood was a foreign thing to her. But she figured if they didn't address whatever Money wanted to talk about tonight, she'd have to later.

"Yeah, I came with my girl, Jackie. She's up in VIP cakin' wit' some ol' country ass bamma nigga. Let me go tell her I'm leavin' wit' you," Lachelle replied, turning away.

"No, just send her a text message when we get outside," Money insisted. "She'll be lookin' for you once she's ready to leave. And when she doesn't see you, she'll check her phone to call you and see the text you sent her instead."

"You got it all figured out, huh?" Lachelle eyed him skeptically.

"Always," Money replied with a cool nod.

******

"Fuuuck," Money groaned, gripping Lachelle's head tighter as he continued to pump his thick member in and out of her mouth. His thrusts were deep and measured. The slurping sound she was making while on her knees pleasing him was driving him wild. Lachelle's head game was as fierce as he had remembered it. He looked down at the mother of his daughter through hooded eyes. Her naked, cocoa skin was glistening under the room's chandelier lighting. It was skin that was once covered by abscesses and battle scars inflicted by the likes of other fiends, pimps, and prostitutes. But all of those memories were long gone. The only mark she had left on her body to tell the story of her past was that of an ugly keloid on her chest, which started from her left shoulder and ended under her right armpit. Money thought back to the days when he used to kiss that scar during their love making. He used to tell her it was a mark of survival and all great warriors had battle scars; some were on top of the skin while others were skin deep. And for that, she'd loved Money back, all the while keeping her secrets of being an addict and mother of eight to herself.

"Shiiit, La. I wanna fuck the shit outta you right now," Money moaned with his eyes closed and head tilted back on the couch.

"You wanna fuck me, Daddy?" she asked seductively before taking him back into her mouth and teasing his head with her tongue.

"Hell yeah," Money replied as he flapped his muscled legs.

"Mmm, and I want you to," Lachelle countered, as she rose to her feet and straddled him. She ran her hands over his sculpted chest and rested them on each bosom as her eyes met his. She then leaned into him and kissed him sloppily on the lips. When he didn't pull away and slipped his tongue inside her mouth, Lachelle knew she had him right where she wanted him.

"I want you to fuck me in da ass like you used to, Daddy," she said breathlessly.

Without a word, Money lifted Lachelle from on top of him and stood to his feet. He watched her grab the back of the sofa, arch her back, and push her apple bottom up in the air. She was waiting for his long anticipated entry.

Money stepped back a little to take in the breathtaking view, while his member pointed straight at its desired target. Satisfied with the sight before him, Money opened his right hand, spat on it and lubricated his pulsating tool with his saliva. He stepped forward, spread Lachelle's cheeks with his massive hands, and slowly slid into her dark tunnel. The two former lovers let out moans of pleasurable pain as Money pushed himself deeper inside of her. Lachelle's rectum walls wouldn't expand anymore to accommodate his extra large size, making the friction between their muscles ignite a fire of sheer ecstasy.

Money pounded into Lachelle unmercifully until he reached his climax. Knowing it was only the first of many rounds with her that night, he made his way over to the bed to lie down until he was ready to go for seconds. He had no idea how they went from talking about Mimi to how much fun they used to have when they were together. As much as he wanted to hate

Lachelle for all that she put him and their baby girl through, Money couldn't. He never did. He didn't know what it was like to be a fiend. He only knew how it felt to love one.

When she pressed her sweet lips against his, he'd kissed her back. He hadn't kissed another woman since Karma. Money figured he'd question his actions later because at the moment he was comfortable with Lachelle. She wasn't Karma, but just like Karma, she had his child. That meant *something*. Being inside of her and wanting her to stay and lay with him until they could go to that place of no return again, felt all too right. Money was complacent and he was going to stay that way as long as he had Lachelle back, even if it was for one night. *Why?* Because misery loved company. Money was too deep in denial to acknowledge his own misery and that of Lachelle.

Lachelle smiled blissfully as she joined Money in bed. In her mind, she had her one and only true love back. And she'd hold on to him for the days to come because she needed him. Money would make it easier for her not to think about going out and getting her hands on some dope. It didn't matter if she was a recovering addict or not. She was still an addict. Hopefully, Money would be all the drug she needed now.

******

Back up north, Karma was busy helping the staff and her uncles clear the dancehall of any tables and chairs left over from a young woman's *quince*. The party had been a huge success. During the time of the gathering, Karma walked around the crowded room of hormonal adolescents and drunken adults and reminisced about her own *quince*.

Both of her parents had been present; something that was not planned. Her father was stationed in Guantanamo Bay around that time and had expressed his regret for not being there on her special day. Karma, in return, told him that it was okay and they'd celebrate again once he returned home. Receiving a phone call from him that morning had been more than she could ever ask for. She remembered hanging up with him and looking over at her mother. Soleil's face was tight and full of disgust. Karma reassured her that she was fine with her father's absence, but Soleil knew better.

It wasn't until that night when her mother's disposition changed. Karma saw him walk into the room. And like a flash, she ran to him and jumped in his arms. Her mother was down in the wine cellar when he arrived, which made his guest appearance more sweet. And when she returned, still oblivious to his arrival, he walked up behind her and covered her eyes with his hands. Soleil, knowing there was only one person who would ever make such a gesture, spun around and looked up into the eyes of her beloved husband. Karma remembered her father flashing his beautiful, white smile at her. And her mother's own mouth turning into a frown. She turned away from him and made an attempt to walk away, but he pulled her back into him. And it was at that very moment when their song came on, Gladys Knight & The Pips' *Neither One of Us*. Karma would never forget it. She watched her father take her mother's hand into his and lead her onto the dance floor. And whatever issues the two had between them that night were put on the backburner once Gladys began to croon.

Karma couldn't help but notice how engrossed they were in each other. The mixture of pain and pleasure on their faces grew with each word Gladys sung. Her father held her mother so close; one hand holding the small of her back, the other caressing the middle of her spine. Her mother's arms were wrapped around her father's strong neck; her wide hips grinding against his rising manhood. Her body asking his not to leave again. And his begging hers for forgiveness.

Karma remembered watching her father wipe a tear away from her mother's eye before leaning into her and planting a kiss on her lips. It had been deep and passionate and uncomfortable for her to watch. But she did nonetheless. It was a kiss that had reached back into their history of king and queendom and a desperate attempt to reclaim it. Her parents caught the attention of some guests, but their lips never parted. They had been in their own world and it was some sight to behold. It was true, unadulterated love in its rarest form.

It was memories like that one that made Karma miss her father dearly. Even though they spoke on the phone twice a week, it was nothing like having him physically present. In truth, she wanted to keep a close eye on him. During their last conversation, he informed her that he'd been to the doctor and was told his cholesterol was dangerously high. For as long as she'd been alive, his diet had always been poor. Had it not been for her mother monitoring his food intake over the years, he would have surely died a long time ago. But since she was gone now, Karma was left with the responsibility of taking care of him. *How much more could she take?* She had her own son to take care of. *When would she have the time to look after a grown ass man? Niggas ain't nuttin' but big babies*, she'd thought to herself after hanging up with her father. She didn't know how she was going to take care of him. He lived all the way in Upper Marlboro, MD. She would have to figure it out sooner than later.

The birthday celebration began at eight o'clock on the dot the previous evening and ended over an hour ago. It was now three-fifteen and Karma was ready to bid farewell to everyone and lay down for the rest of the day. Unfortunately, the number one rule of being the manager of any establishment was that you had to be the first one to arrive and the last one to leave.

She walked over to the bar and rested against it. She was ready to get out of her pastel pink, paisley-print cocktail dress and matching four-inch high-heeled sandaled shoes. Karma removed them from her worn feet and proceeded to rub them one at a time.

"Karma!" her uncle Victor yelled from the top of the stairway across the spacious room.

"Yes, *Tio*?" she replied exhaustedly.

"Have you seen the keys to the storage room? I don't remember what I did with them!" he exclaimed.

"No, I haven't! Did you check the men's bathroom? You probably left them in there again!" Karma smirked. She couldn't understand why her uncle always asked her about the storage room keys after every party they hosted. He'd have two or three bathroom breaks throughout the night, with the keys in hand, and leave them in there, laying on one of the urinals. The routine was getting old and so was his mind evidently.

"Okay, I'll check! Thank you!" he replied, walking off.

Karma scratched her head and sighed. She was so ready to leave. But she knew her uncle had to find the keys first before she could make a mad dash out the door. As she pressed her back against the counter again, her cell phone began to vibrate on her hip. She'd clipped it onto the satin ribbon tied around the waist of her dress. As she removed the miniature device from its holder, she mouthed the "202" area code to herself. *What state was that? And who in the hell was calling at three-something in the morning?* Karma pressed the ACCEPT button on the phone with her thumb, then placed it to her ear.

"Hello?" she asked with a slight attitude.

"Good evening, ma'am," said the southern, deep-voiced individual on the other end.

"My apologies for disturbing you at this late hour, but I'm trying to locate a Ms. Karma Walker."

"This is she. Who may I ask is this?" she countered with furrowed brows.

"This is Lieutenant Beaumont from the Metropolitan Police Department in Washington, D.C., ma'am."

Karma's heart dropped.

"I'm calling to inform you that we have your father in custody this evening for drunk driving. He was spotted driving in the wrong direction along I-95 by highway patrol, ma'am," the officer stated regrettably.

"What?" Karma asked, trying to wrap her mind around the unexpected news. "Well, is he okay? Where is he? Why--?"

"Ms. Walker, Ms. Walker, please. You're father is fine. I assure you. He's asleep in one of our holding cells. That's why I'm calling you myself."

Karma rubbed the back of her neck as she scanned the room with wide eyes. She was speechless. Her father never sounded intoxicated over the phone. She thought he'd regained control of himself after she berated him about the excessive drinking two Christmases ago. He told her he'd stopped since then and found another way to cope with her mother's death. Standing there with her mouth agape and the cell phone to her ear, Karma let the truth of her father's lie sink in. "Was anyone hurt?"

"No, ma'am," Lieutenant Beaumont assured her.

Karma closed her eyes and let out a sigh of relief.

"If I may ask, what has he been charged with?"

"He's been charged with a DWI, second-degree assault, and resisting arrest. He had a blood alcohol concentration of 1.28," Lieutenant Beaumont confirmed.

Karma's nostrils began to flare. It was one thing for him to have been arrested for drunk driving, but the addition of assault and resisting arrest just added more fuel to the fire. Her father's temper had gotten the best of him yet again. Not only was she going to have to pay out of pocket for his recklessness, but for his belligerence as well. Karma was heated. *Remain calm*, she thought to herself.

"How long will you keep him there?" she huffed.

"Until five o'clock Monday evening. If bail is not posted by five, he'll be sent to Landover."

"Thank you, lieutenant," Karma muttered with closed eyes.

"You're very welcome, ma'am. I apologize once again for the inconvenience. Good night."

Without another word, Karma pressed the END button on her phone and placed it back in its holder on her hip.

"Shit," she said to herself. Things just didn't seem to be working in her favor lately with the men in her life. The only relationship she was certain would come close to withstanding the test of time was the one she shared with Mekhi. But even that notion sounded too good to be true. She knew he'd give her hell, eventually. How Mekhi would turn out in the end was anyone's guess. His father was a rapist and his mother was a murderer.

Karma shook her head in dismay. She needed to talk to her mother. She would know what to do about her father. Maybe she would give her some kind of sign or come to her in her dreams when she finally laid her head to rest.

"I found them, Karma!" Victor yelled from the across the room.

Karma looked up at her uncle and shook her head again. Talking to her mother was definitely what she needed to do. Mother always knew best.

Chapter 6

know, I know. Mommy's sorry," Indigo cooed as she applied antiseptic ointment on Desiree's raw, newly pierced ears. Marguerite shook her head in disapproval as she rubbed her traumatized granddaughter's back for comfort. Indigo had gone against her wishes of waiting until Desiree turned a year old before getting the baby's ears pierced. What was supposed to be a quiet Saturday morning outing, turned out to be a guerrilla war between mother and daughter instead. Indigo didn't know why her mother even bothered to propose she wait until Desiree was *of age* to have the procedure done, knowing good and well she would oppose it.

Like most West Indian mothers, Marguerite spent most of her life telling Indigo what to do, when to do it, how to do it, and why to do it her way. The controlling, no-nonsense, all-knowing attitude had been deeply rooted in her by her mother and her mother before her. And like most West Indian daughters, Indigo had always done the complete opposite of what her mother told her. Unlike Maggie, Indigo was a free spirit and had an open mind about people and the world, which only caused more conflict between them.

"Me told you she too young for dat, Indi," Maggie stressed as she rocked from side-to-side. "Dat was too much pain for she."

Indigo rolled her eyes as she snapped the cap back onto the ointment and threw away a ball of cotton into a nearby trash can.

"She's fine, Mommy. There are babies younger than her who get their ears pierced."

Maggie sucked her teeth in disdain. "Me not talking 'bout no utter babies. Me talking 'bout *our* baby. It's bad luck for a baby girl to have her ears pierced before de age of one. You know dat. Just like its bad luck to take a baby to de cemetery or cut a baby boy's hair before de age of one."

"That's old West Indian superstition, Mommy. No one believes that stuff but you and Papi," Indigo smirked as she pulled the baby's high chair toward the kitchen table. "Desi will be just fine."

"Her will never forgive you for it," Maggie stated seriously.

"She won't even remember it!" Indigo laughed as she took the baby out of her mother's arms and placed her in the high chair. "I think *you're* the one who won't forgive me for it, but what else is new?" Indigo sat down at the table across from her mother and proceeded to open a jar of baby food. Desiree's uncomfortable disposition automatically changed to one of eagerness. She cooed at the sight of the jar of delectable food.

"Her wouldn't have had no pain had you waited, so me could have done it de right way," Maggie poked at Indigo a little further.

"Mommy, enough. Okay?" Indigo spat while scooping up excess food from the baby's chin with a miniature spoon. " No one pierces ears with needles and string anymore, all right? Having it done with a gun was much faster. So can you please just let it go? Desi isn't complaining. You shouldn't be either."

Maggie's eyes flickered as she tried to regain her composure. It was too early in the day to get told off by her child. But she'd asked for it. She wasn't very good at flat out telling Indigo how she felt about certain things. In fact, Maggie never wanted to acknowledge her role in the miscommunication between them. A very proud woman she was indeed. And as a result, Indigo always did what she wanted with no regard to her mother's thoughts or feelings.

There were many things Maggie wanted to experience with her granddaughter that only grandmothers could understand. Just like when Indigo was young, she wanted to experience certain things with her as her mother. But the way history was being written, she wasn't sure if it would ever come to pass.

Indigo glanced over at her mother and noticed the hurt etched on her face. She hadn't intended to shut her down so abruptly, but the woman had a tendency to irk her last good nerve. It was typical for her mother to press her buttons, but she usually just ignored her. Today was an exception. She was on edge. And she'd been that way ever since Karma's rape. She'd been sworn to secrecy and it had begun to haunt her. Five long months she'd been keeping their secret to herself.

Nothing good had come of it. She still had Money as a partner, who had since moved on with someone unknown to her, and was forced to act like everything was fine between them when she went to work. The lovemaking between her and Stuff reached a whole new level that had yet to be defined. When she lay beside him at night, she always found herself at loss for words. So she spoke to him with her body. Indigo supplied Stuff with adulterated, no holds barred sex. And she could no longer have a conversation with Karma without mentioning the crime, which eventually led to a brutally uncensored argument, then non-communication between them for days.

Something had to be done. With her cousin heavy on her mind, Indigo knew what she was about to do would jeopardize their relationship. It would change it forever. But it was a risk she had to take.

"I didn't mean to disrespect you, Mommy. I'm sorry," she said quietly as she continued to feed the baby.

Maggie struggled to fight the smile of relief that was growing along her face. "Dat's all right, baby. Me know me can be a pain in de ass," she replied as she waved her hand dismissively.

"It's not you. It isn't," Indigo responded, shaking her head slowly.

Maggie sensed that something was very wrong. Indigo rarely apologized for ever putting her in her place. She appeared to be struggling with something she couldn't quite grasp. Even though the two barely got along, as a mother, she wanted to relieve her child of any distress.

"What's de matter, baby?" she asked leaning forward. "Tell Mommy."

Indigo looked over at her mother and sighed. The last thing she wanted to do was betray Karma. But her cousin was wrong for wanting to keep something like being raped to herself. It was selfish.

A tear crept down Indigo's face.

"Mommy," Indigo began before sighing and placing the baby food down on the table.

Disliking the drastic change in her daughter's mood, Maggie rose from her chair and pulled it around the table. She sat back down and grabbed Indigo's hand. "Tell I," Maggie replied with concern.

Indigo looked over at her content baby girl before setting her eyes on her mother.

"Mommy, I want to tell you, but..." Indigo began again.

"But what, baby?" Maggie asked while wiping Indigo's tears away. "You can tell I anyting. What me say? *Anyting.*"

Indigo looked into her mother's sincere eyes and inhaled deeply, then released the air of her quietly kept torture.

"If I tell you, you have to promise me you won't say anything to Papi, Stuff, or Uncle Miguel...Uncle L," she stressed seriously.

Maggie's eyebrows furrowed. She didn't like where the conversation was going. Whatever Indigo was harboring didn't sit well with her. And promising not to tell the rest of the family was something she was sure she wouldn't be able to uphold, especially if the news was unfavorable.

She sat back in her chair, crossing her arms at her chest. "Me can't do dat, baby. Me got a feeling what you have to say is not good. And me don't like to make promises me can't keep.

So me tink you should just tell I," Maggie replied in a way only a seriously concerned mother could.

Slightly shaken by her mother's staid tone, Indigo gathered the last bit of courage she had left and finally freed herself from the shackles of her cousin's fear.

"Money raped Karma," she admitted just above a whisper.

Maggie said nothing. She remained seated next to her daughter and allowed the information to register. A pang of fear crawled up Indigo's spine. She couldn't read her mother's face. It was expressionless. Her eyes remained locked with hers as she continued to sit and say nothing.

"Him done fucked wit' de wrong one," Maggie finally said before rising from her seat and making her way toward the wall phone. "No one fucks wit' mine," she went on while staring straight at Indigo. "*No one.*"

Chapter 7

H ey, Ma," Karma said, kissing her mother's headstone while Indigo lay a blanket for them to sit down on. What started out as a weekly ritual for the girls to visit Soleil's grave, slowly progressed to a monthly sacrament. At the beginning, Karma couldn't go a weekend without visiting her mother's gravesite. She needed to be near her some way, somehow. Indigo would accompany her on the trips and they would cry together. The first couple of times they visited, Karma had sobbing fits that left her hyperventilating. Indigo did everything in her power to try to console Karma, but she would only pull away.

As Indigo stood before her aunt's resting place, now thinking back to those first god-awful weekends, she reflected on one of the worst moments of her cousin's mourning—the event that took place at the burial site.

The rainbow and sun shower that graced them upon arriving at the funeral had long passed. The sky had since turned dark and a consistent, cold drizzle hovered over them as they all gathered around the silver casket. Indigo stood directly across from her cousin and uncle; the two holding on to each other for dear life. She, as she did during the service, watched her cousin carefully. Karma hadn't cried at all during the ceremony and Indigo wondered if it was because of shock or because she wanted to be strong for the rest of the family. She hadn't responded to any of the musical selections like the rest of them; not a bopping of the head, an abrupt wail, rocking of the body, nothing. She'd just been very still; her sunshade-covered eyes fixed on her mother's closed casket. When she did move, it was only to wipe her father's fallen tears or to rub his back.

Father Pacella settled at the foot of her aunt's coffin, took out his Bible, opened it, then proceeded to ask everyone to bow their heads. Indigo, still wanting to keep her eyes on Karma, kept her head raised. Father Pacella began to recite the 28th Psalm. And even through that, Karma remained still. Upon completion, the remainder of the family and other mourners raised their heads and watched him make the sign of the cross over the casket for the last time. He then, with one simple nod, signaled the grave diggers to start lowering her aunt into the ground. And as she slowly descended into her final resting place, it happened. Karma collapsed. Indigo had watched her head roll back, but before she could tell her uncle to catch her, Karma was already on the ground. She'd fallen straight back, hitting her head on a small mound of wet, hardened dirt. When she finally came to and was asked if she was all right, she said nothing. She just rose to her feet, looked over at the gaping hole that her mother had disappeared into, and walked away from them all.

~~~~~~

Indigo would never forget that day for as long as she lived. Long after the funeral, the burial and the repast, she still waited for her cousin to break. That day would come on a Saturday morning one week later.

The girls drove up to Rosedale Cemetery an hour after it opened for the day Indigo, who agreed to drive that morning, parked her car along the path that led to the area where Soleil was buried. Karma hadn't said a word to her on the ride over. She just stared out the window. Indigo got out of the car first and waited for her cousin to climb out too as she looked at her aunt's gravesite in the near distance. The dirt hadn't settled much since the previous week. It was still a huge mountain of brown dust. Indigo turned and looked back at Karma. She still hadn't gotten out of the car. Indigo walked over to the passenger side door and opened it. Karma didn't even acknowledge her. Her eyes were fixed on the mounds and mounds of soil her mother lay still under.

"You ready, K?" Indigo asked her cousin, looking into her eyes. They held the same temperature and color as the autumn sky that morning---cold, dark, and gray. Karma's eyes had been robbed of their ocean blue hue and it scared Indigo right to the bone.

Karma slowly blinked and looked up at her worried cousin.

"Yeah, I'm ready," she replied in a whisper. Karma stepped out of the car, closing the door behind her. She and Indigo walked arm in arm toward her mother's grave. Once they reached it, the girls simply remained, neither one of them saying a word. Indigo couldn't help but start to cry. Her body tensed up and her grasp around Karma's arm tightened.

Karma didn't bother to look over at her cousin. She just closed her eyes and wished the pile of dirt set before them wasn't that of her mother's grave. She wished her cousin wasn't crying. She wished it was all a bad dream. But when she finally opened her eyes and saw that none of her wishes were ever going to come true, Karma slipped out of Indigo's clutch and fell to her knees. She ran her fingers through God's tainted earth, held on to a handful of it, and let out the most gut-wrenching scream anyone could ever hear from the pits of a young woman's lost soul.

"Oh, Mommyyy," Karma cried, shaking her head with tightly closed eyes. "My poor mommyyy," she said sadly when she found her breath to speak. Karma repeated those words over and over again until she lost her voice altogether. Indigo didn't know what to say or do. She just stood over her in shock. And when she finally came to, she knelt down beside her cousin, laid her head on her back and gently rubbed it until her sonorous cries became soft whimpers.

That first visit to the cemetery had been one of many difficult trips. But since then, Karma had gotten better, as did Indigo. And instead of them going there to plant or change withered flowers, the girls began to stay and talk to Soleil. The small conversations ultimately turned into bigger ones, keeping the girls at her resting place until they grew tired. Before long, they were bringing food and beverages with them.

Private picnics between the three Alonso-Cruz women were born. And it was at one of those picnics where Karma decided to continue her mother's work in the community. She'd open the restaurant every Sunday, Thanksgiving, and Christmas for the homeless and collect/donate money, toys, and clothes for the women and children of the Family Violence Program (an emergency shelter for domestic violence victims) in Newark and Livingston's St. Barnabas Hospital Cancer Care Center.

******

"Hey, Auntie Sol," Indigo sang as she sat down on the blanket, crossing her legs Indian style. She'd been late picking Karma up as a result of being held captive by the family back at her mother's house. They wanted to know what happened to Karma *exactly* and Indigo recounted what her cousin had told her *word for word.* She didn't know what her father, uncle, and husband were going to do to Money, but she knew it was nothing short of killing him. It had taken her over an hour to calm them down and regain her own composure before driving over to pick up Karma.

She took the plastic bags of White Castle burgers out of her cousin's hands and placed them on the blanket while Karma made herself comfortable across from her.

"It sure is a beautiful day today, Ma. I wish you could see it," Karma said, looking up at the beaming sun. "It's not too hot. It's just right."

"Sure is," Indigo chimed as she handed Karma her three cheeseburgers, french fries, and small Pepsi.

"*Gracias,*" Karma replied with her dimpled grin.

"*De nada,*" Indigo responded, her gap-toothed smile adding to the sun's light.

"You hear that, Ma? Your girls are speakin' Spanish now," Karma laughed to herself. "I know how much you wanted us to speak it on a regular basis. Tellin' us how important it was to embrace our Cuban heritage and all."

"Yeah, Auntie Sol, we finally came around. You should see us in action on the streets whenever we walk past a group of papis and they say something slick. Auntieee, we let 'em have it!" Indigo bowled over with laughter. " You should see their faces when they realize we understood what they said," she giggled. "You know..." Indigo said, looking over at her cousin. "...I never have my freakin' camera when we go out. I should really start carrying it so I can take pictures of their classic facial expressions."

"You are so random," Karma laughed.

"I should though!" Indigo replied, biting into her burger.

Karma looked over at her cousin and shook her head with a smile. Times like these were what she loved the most. And even though her mother wasn't there physically to share the moment with them, Karma knew she was very much there in spirit.

"Oh, which reminds me, when do you want to go to Sears to have the kids' pictures taken?" Indigo asked with a mouthful of food.

"I don't know," Karma shrugged. "Whenever," she replied, sipping on her soda. "We can go on your next day off or durin' one of your breaks if you want. It doesn't matter."

"All right. I'll let you know, then," Indigo smiled.

Silence fell upon them. Indigo took in the sights of the cemetery before continuing.

"So...are we going to talk about it?" she frowned, changing the subject.

Karma placed her newly grown-out hair behind her ears. The asymmetrical bob she'd been donning for the past four months suited her chiseled face well.

"And *it* would be?" she replied facetiously.

"Your conversation with Uncle L," Indigo inquired before popping another burger in her mouth.

"It was short," Karma began in a flippant tone as she placed her empty boxes of food in the plastic bag and took a sip of her soda before speaking again. "I told 'im I'd be down there to bail 'im out Monday morning and he told me it was all a misunderstanding."

Indigo's eyebrows slowly rose. She scratched her forehead in uncertainty. "Maybe it was."

"It wasn't. Trust me," Karma stressed with contempt. "I got a phone call from his commanding officer right before you came and picked me up. He hasn't gone on any of the special assignments they've given him in the last two months," she added, looking over at her cousin despairingly.

"Oh, my God," Indigo replied in concern. "Poor Uncle L. He hasn't been the same since Auntie Sol died. I feel so bad for him. Do you want me to go down with you?"

"No, I'll be all right by myself. I don't want you to be a witness to what the hell I'm goin' to do to 'im when I see 'im." Karma sucked her teeth in disgust.

"Aww, that makes me so sad. What are you going to do?" Indigo asked sincerely as she wiped her mouth with a napkin.

"I don't know. I don't know. He'll fight me if I try to admit 'im into an AA program. And I really don't have the strength to fight wit' his ass anymore," Karma sulked. "Those days are over." Karma sighed heavily. "I don't know what I'm gonna do. I can't make 'im do anything he doesn't wanna do. I don't know."

"You'll think of something, *mamita*," Indigo sang. "I know you will."

"I need 'im to be well, Indi," Karma said while continuing to rub her throbbing head. "I need 'im to be well. He's gonna drink himself to death. I just know it."

"Okay, now you just stop," Indigo replied sternly. "You're going to work yourself up into a state. And you can't afford to do that. You don't know what's going on with him. For all we know he could have a cold or something and had too much cough syrup the night he was arrested. You haven't seen him for yourself and until you do, you just sit there and shut your face."

Karma couldn't help but shake her head in disdain. As much as she wanted to believe her cousin, she knew better. The D.C. police and her father's commanding officer had confirmed her greatest fear---her father had become an alcoholic.

Indigo cleared her throat, bringing Karma back to the present. When she looked back up at her cousin, the expression on Indigo's face told her she had something on her mind, but was uncertain if it should be voiced.

"What's up?" Karma inquired with raised eyebrows.

"What makes you think something is up?" Indigo asked without making eye contact.

"You just cleared your throat. I know what that means," Karma replied, staring through her daunted cousin.

Another loud silence fell upon them.

"Okay," she said before taking a big, long gulp. "Well...I think you should know that...Money's moved on with someone else. I don't know why I think you should know, I just do. I really shouldn't care and neither should you, but--"

"You're ramblin', *mami*," Karma said, cutting her off.

"Oh. I am, huh? Sorry," Indigo replied.

"It's okay. Go on," she said calmly.

"Well, I overheard him talking to some chick on his cell while we were on patrol the other night. He was telling her he couldn't wait to see her and all this other mess that I rather not get into."

"Oh, yeah? Well, good for him," she said without missing a beat.

"You don't feel some kinda way about that?" Indigo asked confusingly.

"No," Karma lied. "Should I?"

Of course Karma was bothered by the news. She hadn't moved on, so what gave him the right to? She had plenty of admirers, more than enough, but she never pursued any of them out of love and respect for Money. *If anything, he should be seeing a psychologist to help him figure out why he raped me*, Karma thought to herself. Then another thought came to her. Money had a penis and she didn't. That was it. How soon she forgot. Men had 'needs' so deeply rooted in the psyche of their penis heads that it shut down the emotional state of their hearts and altered the rational thoughts of the brain in the bigger head. *Why couldn't he just use his hand for relief?* She had been using hers.

Karma made a mental note to speak to him about his new relationship. Because if she found out he had his new girlfriend anywhere near Mekhi, there was going to be hell to pay.

"Yes, you should. Money's got no right to be moving on with *anybody* after what he did to you," Indigo sneered. "He shouldn't even be breathing right now, but--"

"Oh, okay. We're goin' back to this now," Karma huffed.

"That's right. We are going *back to this now*," Indigo responded tersely before she could stop herself. "You've made it very difficult for me to continue to work with him and not be able to say anything to him."

"So it's my fault now you can't work wit' 'im? That's my fault? For real?" Karma asked with wide eyes.

"I didn't say it was your fault," Indigo countered meekly.

"Yes, you did. Because I haven't let you tell Stuff or Uncle Vic or whoeva else you had in mind to handle Money, you're blamin' me for havin' to work wit' his ass. If you don't wanna be bothered wit' 'im, then ask for a fuckin' transfer," Karma spat.

Indigo sighed, shaking her head. She looked over at her aunt's headstone and wondered what she was thinking, watching this fiasco unfold before her resting place.

"Do you have to curse *here*?" Indigo asked, cringing.

Karma ran her fingers through her hair. She knew there was nothing more disrespectful than using profanity at her own mother's grave.

"Sorry, Ma. Indi..." she sighed. " ...look, I didn't mean for it to come out that way. I told you I'll take care of 'im and I will. But I do think you should consider transferring to another department if workin' wit' him is gettin' to you."

"I can't just transfer to another department, Karma. At least not for the department I would want to go to. I'd have to take an exam first," Indigo replied dejectedly.

"Well, take the exam then. It'll be a breeze for you," Karma said genuinely.

"I thought about taking it, but I decided against it. I'm going to retire instead," Indigo replied, eyeing her cousin closely.

"You're gonna retire? All because you have to work wit' Money?" Karma asked in confusion. "You're takin' this a little far now, don't you think?"

"I'm not retiring because of Money, Karma. I'm retiring because of Desi."

Karma tilted her head back a little and stared at her cousin for a moment.

"Are you sure it's not because of Money?" she asked.

"Yeah, I'm sure," Indigo nodded. "I've been thinking about leaving for awhile now. Stuff got on my case about it again the other night."

"Rightfully so," Karma replied.

"Uh, you're supposed to be on my side." Indigo sneered.

"Normally, I would be, but Stuff has every right to get on your case. It's not just you and him anymore. You've got Desi to think about now," Karma replied carefully.

"I know, I know," Indigo sighed. "And that's why I'm leaving. She needs me." Indigo looked away and tried to focus on something, *anything* to get her mind off of the reality of her ten-year career as an officer coming to an end. In those ten years, she never thought about how her safety or lack thereof affected anyone else, especially the family. She made herself not care. She was the law and would continue to be just that until the American flag was hanging half-staffed outside of the 5th precinct on Bigelow Street and her fellow officers were saluting her at her funeral. But after having Desi, she knew she'd be forced to choose. And Desi won. *That's what motherhood was about, right?* Sacrifice. In order for one to move forward in life, she must let go and let God. And even though Indigo was having a hell of a time accepting the new path that had been laid for her, she was going to walk it for the sake of her daughter.

Karma felt a pang in her heart as she watched her cousin's eyes well with tears. She knew better than anyone how much Indigo loved being a cop. She'd spent her entire career fighting to change the stigma behind her occupation and in that same length of time, fighting even harder to earn her father's respect.

"You wanna come work at the restaurant for awhile, until you figure out your next move?" she asked gently. "We could use the extra help."

Indigo turned back to her concerned cousin, blinking back her tears.

"I would if I could, but I want to see how things go with the opening of my dance school," she said with a mischievous, gap-toothed grin.

A look of disbelief veiled Karma's face before a sincere dimpled smile of approval replaced it.

"Are you really goin' to open one?" she asked eagerly.

"Yeah, I think it's time. Dance for me is what track was for you...my passion, my gift. And you know what they say, once a dancer, always a dancer." The girls shared a warm laugh.

"What can I do? It's in my blood. And just because I didn't get the chance to dance with Ailey doesn't mean the next generation shouldn't," she said seriously. "They deserve to. But I need to find a space first. I've got a couple of my old dance buddies on stand-by to be instructors. I've got my license, the money, and Jose's going to be the contractor behind it. All I need is a space," Indigo nodded. "I'll keep my eyes open," Karma replied excitedly.

"I know you will," Indigo giggled before composing herself.

"I can see Desi bouncin' around that place now in her little tutu," Karma laughed.

"That's the plan," Indigo admitted sincerely. "I'm going to name it," she began with her hand in mid-air. "The Soleil Alonso-Walker Dance Academy."

Karma leaned forward, opening her arms to welcome her cousin in for a heartfelt hug. Indigo met her half-way and received it without hesitation.

"She would have loved that," Karma whispered in her ear.

Indigo slowly pulled away and checked her cousin's face for tears. She watched a couple of them fall before wiping them away with her thumbs. "I haven't told the rest of the family yet. Only you and Stuff know."

"I'll be right by your side when you're ready to tell 'em," Karma replied through a strained grin.

"Thank you," Indigo replied. "So now that we've settled that. When are you going to start running again?"

Karma smirked and rolled her eyes in response to her cousin's insinuation. "Mm-Mm," she said, rising from the blanket.

"*Mm-Mm*, what?" Indigo asked seriously while following suit. "I'm serious, K. Why don't you start running again? You're faster than Johnson, Headley...all of those female sprinters out now. I bet you anything you could break Flo-Jo's records if you wanted to."

"I don't know about all that," she replied while folding her end of the coverlet.

"Trust me. *You could.* All you gotta do is make that call to Kersee," Indigo urged, locking her eyes with Karma's.

"It's not that simple," Karma admitted.

"Why isn't it?" Indigo asked in confusion.

"Well, for one, I haven't spoken to the man in over a decade. And two, I haven't been on a track longer than that," Karma grinned.

"Write him a letter first to open up the lines of communication. And as far as a track goes, Rutgers has two of them----an outdoor and an indoor. Get yourself a membership card and an I.D. to use the tracks and you'll be good to go," Indigo said evenly.

"You got it all figured out, huh?" Karma chuckled.

"Of course I do. Just think about it, okay?" Indigo stressed with pleading eyes.

"We'll see," Karma replied with a yawn. "Mm, excuse me."

"Didn't get much sleep last night?" Indigo asked with a mischievous smile.

"Not really," Karma admitted.

"I wonder why," Indigo teased.

"Um, no. Whateva you're thinkin', you're wrong," Karma cringed, pointing her finger at her cousin.

"You sure about that?" Indigo asked suspiciously.

"Yes. I am," Karma replied seriously.

"So your new friend 'Val the Vibrator' didn't keep you up last night?" Indigo queried.

"Okay, this conversation is over," Karma stated as she placed the blanket under her arm.

"You know he did. If it makes you feel better, I have one, too," Indigo shrugged.

"Okay, this conversation is definitely over now," Karma stressed before turning toward her mother's grave. "Véale *la semana próxima, Ma*," she whispered, kissing the headstone once again. *"Besaré Mekhi para usted. Adórele para siempre,"* she smiled pitifully.

Karma turned and walked away.

"Miss you, Auntie Sol. Don't worry, I'm still working on her," Indigo confessed, hugging her only aunt's gravestone before turning away herself and jogging to catch up with Karma. Indigo grabbed her cousin's muscled arm and fastened it with her own.

"You okay, *mamita*? You know I was just playing, right?"

"No, you weren't," Karma said, cutting her eyes at Indigo.

"You're right, I wasn't. But I would like to know if you're okay or not," Indigo asked genuinely concerned.

"Yeah, I'm all right," Karma smiled weakly, looking back into her concerned cousin's eyes. "I just miss her that's all. I keep tellin' myself she's in a much better place and to accept it.

But every time I look at Mekhi, he just reminds me that I'll never really be able to explain to him how beautiful a person his grandmother was. He'll never know 'cause his sorry ass black bastard of a grandfather took her away from 'im." Just the thought of having referred to Jimmy as her son's grandfather made Karma's blood boil. Indigo took notice of her cousin's sudden change in demeanor and proceeded to rub her arm in comfort.

"Forget Jimmy. You took care of him a long time ago. Don't go back there," Indigo warned.

"I'm not. I'm cool," Karma reassured her as they made their way out the cemetery. They stood at the corner of High and Washington Street waiting patiently for a funeral procession to go by when Indigo spotted him across the street in the parking lot of the Star Tavern, the same parking lot she'd parked in.

"Oh, no," Indigo said more so to herself than to Karma. Even if she wanted to avoid what she knew was about to happen once Karma looked across the street, she wasn't going to be able to. Karma had been doing so well keeping her temper under control and in the next few moments, that was all going to change. Indigo hoped Karma was too engrossed in the procession to have heard what she said. But she heard it nonetheless.

"*Oh, no* what?" Karma asked, looking at Indigo's side profile in bewilderment.

When Indigo didn't look back at her or part her lips to answer her question, Karma followed her cousin's eyes to what they were transfixed on across the street. And what she saw almost knocked the wind out of her. Money was handing over their son to a woman who was holding Mimi's hand. She watched him kneel down and tie the shoelaces on one of Mimi's sneakers, then stand back up and kiss the unfamiliar woman on her cheek. And when his lips parted from her face, she placed her own repeatedly on Mekhi's plump jaw.

"What the fuck?!" Karma screamed, snatching her arm from around Indigo's. Cars beeped their horns at her as she ran in between them, but her stride never broke. Indigo ran after her, holding her hands up to the drivers of the oncoming cars.

"Karma! Karma, wait! No!" Indigo yelled.

Hearing Karma's name shouted over blaring car horns forced Money to look in the direction of all the commotion. He wasn't sure if he'd heard correctly, but when he saw her and Indigo jogging over to where he, Lachelle, and the kids were, Money knew all hell was going to break loose.

"I'd appreciate it if you would give me my baby," Karma fumed, glaring into Lachelle's back. It was taking everything in her not to snatch the girl's head back and start beating the black off of her.

Lachelle turned around and sized Karma up, her face fixed in a cringe. She looked familiar, but she wasn't sure if she had a run-in with her before or not.

"Ya baby?"

"Did I stutter? My muthafuckin' baby," Karma spat with her hands on her hips.

"Hi, Mommy Karma!" Mimi squealed, pulling away from her mother and running over to Karma. She wrapped her chubby arms around her caretaker's muscled legs and smiled.

"Hi, baby," Karma answered the little girl, never taking her eyes off of the unfamiliar woman.

"*Mommy Karma?*" Lachelle asked as she squinted her eyes in an effort to try to grasp the familiarity in Karma's face. When she found it in her light eyes, Lachelle remembered she asked the woman for some money the day Money kicked her off his stoop. Lachelle's hard stare soon turned into a devious one. Karma was the woman Mimi always talked about and Money never wanted to discuss. He'd told her about the unfortunate events that led up to their demise the night they hooked up in Atlantic City, but he never spoke her name again. That is until night fell and Money said Karma's name over and over again in his sleep. It was something Lachelle never spoke to him about, but she knew he was still in love with the woman. And for that, she hated Karma.

"I don't believe we met," Lachelle lied. "I'm Lachelle, Mimi's mother."

A grimace of disbelief spread across Karma's face. She looked over at Money, then back at Indigo who was covering her mouth with her hand. Karma turned her eyes back at Money and shook her head. Out of all the women he could have moved on with, he'd chosen his daughter's mother. The man had taken back a crack ho. Karma knew Money had officially lost his mind, especially when she saw him allow the fiend to kiss all over their son from across the street. Her *remain calm* mantra was now a distant memory.

"Oh, no, we've met," Karma confirmed with wide eyes. "Which reminds me, did you eva find that spare change you were lookin' for?" she asked smugly.

Knowing what Karma was referring to and wanting to beat her at her own slick word game, Lachelle coolly replied, "I did, actually...right between Money's legs last night."

That was the last thing Karma wanted to hear from the likes of Lachelle. She knew the trick was lying. She was going to say anything she could to get a rise out of her, but Karma wasn't going to give her the satisfaction. Her issues were with Money, not with this cracked out whore.

"Why doesn't that surprise me? My son," she nodded with an attitude.

Lachelle handed Mekhi over to his mother without hesitation.

"Come 'ere, Mimi," she beckoned in a light voice. Mimi, noticing the tension between the two women, looked up at Karma in indecision.

"Go on, baby girl," Karma instructed sweetly, pushing her gently toward her mother. Mimi walked over to Lachelle and leaned against her as she tried to figure out what was going on between the adults.

"La, do me a favor and take Mimi inside. I need to talk to Karma for a minute," Money finally said.

Lachelle was hesitant to oblige. She saw the way Money stared at Karma throughout their bitter exchange. He had been undoubtedly mesmerized by the woman's presence. And the gaze made Lachelle uncomfortable. His eyes had told Karma he was sorry for ever hurting her in the first place, which left Lachelle questioning her place in his life. She was his woman now. She had been the first and she would be the last if she had anything to do with it. Even though such thoughts were pleasant ones, she would have to step back into reality and seriously ask herself if fighting for Money's love, attention, and pockets was worth her time.

"All right, Daddy. Don't be out here too long, though. We still gotta movie to catch," she reminded him.

"I know. I won't," Money replied uneasily.

Lachelle cut her eyes at Karma, then reset them on Money and smiled sexily before taking Mimi's hand, turning away, and sashaying into the pizzeria.

Lachelle needed a fix. Her mouth watered at the thought of getting a hit of crack. She saved face outside because she knew there was little chance of her and Money making it as long as Karma was still around. Money had disrespected her right in front of their daughter. She needed her fix. It would calm her nerves. It took any pain she had away, burying it deep down inside of her in a place that couldn't be seen or touched. Lachelle had to get her hands on something *tonight*.

Once Lachelle and Mimi were out of view, Money moved toward Karma with his arms outstretched.

"Don't fuckin' touch me you no good piece of shit," she snarled. "Indi, go put the baby in the car," Karma demanded as she shoved the baby in her cousin's arms.

"Come on, Karma. He's not worth it. Let's just go," Indigo pleaded as she rubbed Mekhi's back.

"Do what I said, Indigo! I'm not askin' you, I'm tellin' you! Take the baby and get in the fuckin' car!" Karma screamed, causing Indigo and Mekhi to flinch. Indigo didn't bother to argue with Karma. She was in her infamous state. So Indigo walked off to the car with the baby in arms without further dispute.

"Karma--" Money began.

"Karma, nothin'! Daddy? What kinda pimp-ho shit is that?"

"Karma--" Money began again.

"No, Money! No! How dare you have my son around that bitch! A fuckin' fiend?" Karma growled.

"Come on, Karma. Don't be like that. She's been clean for eight months now. I wouldn't have had her around Mekhi if I didn't think it was okay," Money admitted with desperate eyes. He knew good and well he was wrong for having the baby around Lachelle. One, she wasn't Mekhi's mother and two, he should have told Karma about Lachelle's return.

"What the fuck you mean *don't be like that*? Don't be like what, nigga? A mother concerned about her only child? I don't give a fuck if the bitch has been clean for eight minutes, she has no right to be holdin' and kissin' all over my son!" Karma could feel the heat in her body rising. She was so close to punching Money in his mouth again she could taste it.

"He's my son too, man!" Money fired back. "I mean, what the fuck is your problem? She ain't done shit to him or to you, for that matter, for you to be spazzin' the fuck out right now!"

"You defendin' da bitch now?" Karma asked incredulously. She couldn't wrap her mind around Money's sudden need to defend Lachelle. The woman left him to raise their child by himself without ever looking back. And now she was back in the picture, doting over the two people she left in the wind. What made matters even worse, she had taken Karma's place and Karma was fit to be tied. "Oh, okay. You must be fuckin' her den if you defendin' her, right? You fuckin' her, Money?"

"Come on, Karma. What kind of question is that?" Money asked in embarrassment.

"An honest fuckin' question. Now answer it. Are you fuckin' her?" she pressed.

Money looked down at her as he chewed on his bottom lip. He hesitated before answering.

"You can call it whatever you want."

Karma's own lip began to quiver. He hadn't even tried to lie. In the beginning, that was one of the things she loved most about him, his honesty. But standing there under his sad, slanted brown eyes, she didn't know what was worse, a man who was remorseful for his wrongdoings or a man who wasn't. There wasn't much of a difference between the two. A man of regret still, in fact, did wrong.

"How long?" she asked just above a whisper.

He didn't say a word.

"How long, Money?" she repeated in a shaky voice while looking up at him.

He looked away, never parting his lips.

"She's not the first since the break-up, is she?"

Money looked back down at her and exhaled a heavy, tormented breath.

"Did she or did she not fuck you and your daughter over?" Karma continued matter-of-factly. "You know what? Don't even bother answerin' that since you don't feel the need to answer any of my questions. But help me understand this. Every time you see me, you tell me how much you love me and wanna make things right between us. But how can you let shit like that fall from your lips when you layin' up wit' that bitch every night? How can you stand here and know that, Money? You didn't even have the fuckin' decency to tell me that you moved on and *with her*."

"I know I didn't and I'm sorry for that. But every time I try to talk to you, you walk away from me, Karma. You won't let me get close to you. And I just want you to let me back in. She doesn't mean shit to me. None of 'em do. That's my word. You can keep treatin' me the way you've been treatin' me, but it's not goin' to change the fact that I still love you. That I still want to work things out and make it right between us again," Money said with great sincerity.

"Oh, please, Money. Please. Spare me, okay? You don't love me. You don't. 'Cause if you did, you wouldn't have replaced me with her or any of the other bitches you're fuckin'. You wouldn't have replaced me at all. If you loved me, *I* would be the one in your bed at night, not her. If you loved me, you wouldn't have raped me. If you loved me, you would be gettin' help for what you did to me. You don't know what love is," Karma scoffed. "But I'm sure your crack ho doesn't have a problem showin' you the true meanin' of the word since she equates it with bein' on her knees. Of course, that's if she doesn't get caught back out there and gives it all to that glass dick she left you and your daughter for."

"That's a real fucked up thing to say," Money said through a tight jaw.

"No, it's just a real thing to say," Karma replied with a slight nod. "Once a fiend, always a fiend. Everybody knows that. So you better watch her. 'Cause if you don't, she's gonna hurt you and Mimi far worse than she did before. And the pain is gonna be unimaginable. I won't even be able to help you this time around," she confessed. "She stays away from my son or you don't see your son. The choice is yours." Karma stressed with a pointed finger before turning her back and walking away. Once she reached Indigo's car, she realized she forgot something. She turned on her heels and proceeded to walk back in Money's direction.

"Gimme dis fuckin' bag," she snapped while snatching the baby's diaper bag off of Money's shoulder.

Money didn't move. He watched Karma make her way back to the car, jump in, and speed off out of the parking lot until she, Indigo, and Mekhi were no longer in sight.

He was so confused. Lachelle had come back into the picture and blown his mind. Her sex was fierce and her heart seemed to be with him and Mimi. She'd blinded him with her sobriety and her desire to want them to be the family he'd always wanted. But she was no Karma. Lachelle didn't hold a candle to her. But she was *loving* him the way Karma should have been. Unfortunately, Money had not yet discovered that people and things weren't always what they appeared. Everyone and everything had a representative.

Chapter 8

Mimi sat on the floor of her father's living room dressed in her cape-less Wonder Woman costume, watching a track and field meet on the big screen television. She'd become obsessed with the sport after attending the Penn Relays with Karma last year. The little chocolate drop sat wide-eyed and Indian-style before the electronic monstrosity. Her head and deep brown eyes turned slowly as they followed the runners down the blue and white straightaway. Mimi was mesmerized by the sight. She'd expressed her love for the sport to Karma, telling her she wanted to be a track star when she grew up. Karma subtlety smiled at the eager child and told her she could be whatever she wanted to be when she grew up.

Mimi missed Karma. Ever since her mother had come back into the picture, she saw less and less of her shero. She began having crying fits that neither her father nor mother could control. Mimi would find herself crying until she wore herself out and fell asleep. She needed Karma. Karma gave her baths with bubbles in them and put that pink lotion on her pudgy body that made her smell good. Karma always put nice clothes on her and put barrettes in her hair to make her look pretty.

Karma sang her to sleep and kept the monsters away. Most importantly, Karma taught her how to pray and never left her alone to say them by herself.

Mimi craved Karma. Her need for the woman she wished was her real mommy was far greater than the dependency she had for crack as a newborn baby. Lachelle did none of the things Karma did. *Weren't mommies supposed to?* Mimi didn't understand the concept of the word "hate," but she did understand the concept of the word "mommy." And Lachelle was not a mommy. So, Mimi refrained from referring to her as such and continued to call Karma by it instead.

She didn't understand what purpose Lachelle served. She heard the noises the woman and her father made late at night. Mimi figured Lachelle's purpose in her father's life was to make sounds come out of him. *But what purpose did she serve in her five-year-old life?*

Lachelle treated Mimi so badly when Money wasn't around. She wouldn't play with her. Anytime she spoke to the child, she cursed her and never called her by her name. She'd speak ill of Karma in her presence and often threatened her little life if she thought about telling Karma what she said. Lachelle hadn't put her hands on Mimi, but she'd come close during one of the little girl's tantrums. The only thing that stopped her was the thought of Money. She had to play her cards right because she was still trying to prove to him that she wasn't the same woman who left them to fend for themselves.

Lachelle walked into the room barefoot and dressed in nothing more than one of Money's football jerseys and a pair of panties. She plopped down on the plush leather couch, leaned forward, and emptied the contents she had in one of her hands onto the glass coffee table. Money left for work hours ago, which gave her the perfect opportunity to call her old dealer and tell him she was willing and ready to do whatever he asked of her to get his best product in her system. He gave her a price; she told him she had the money. She gave him the address and he delivered the goods within an hour. She gave him a blow job after he arrived. He gave her an extra vial before he left to meet another customer.

The run-in with Karma earlier had stirred something in her so deep, she saw nothing but red for the rest of the day. It was bad enough that prior to the pizzeria debacle, she had a run-in with Evelyn while she and Money had gone to pick up the kids. Money's mother, unaware that she was even back in the picture, expressed her disapproval of the relationship to Money. Evelyn showed no regard to Lachelle's feelings as she cursed her and Money in the main entryway of her home. It was quite a show for the neighbors that morning. Money had to practically threaten the woman in order for her to hand the kids over to him. He told her if she wanted to see her grandchildren as often as she did now, she'd better give them to him or else today would be the last day for a long time. Lachelle remembered the look on Evelyn's face when he said it. It was that of disbelief mixed with fear. It was a look that said the man that stood before her was not her son and if she was getting the worst of his fury, then the woman he'd chosen to stand beside him now would get a taste of it also.

Evelyn, with much hesitation, handed the kids over and watched the foursome drive off into the world. *What other choice did she have*, Lachelle thought to herself as she looked back at the upset woman in the rear-view window. The kids were Money's. And even though Evelyn hadn't informed Karma about the event that had taken place, the thought of the possibility of that happening never crossed Lachelle's mind. But it crossed Money's. And he made sure she knew he was having second thoughts about whatever it was they were doing.

Lachelle licked her lips as she began to cut the powdered white substance into three long lines with a photograph she found of Mimi and Karma upstairs in the child's room. Mimi looked over her shoulder at her mother, curious about what she was doing with the stuff that looked like her favorite Pixy Stix candy, a treat that Karma hated for her to have. Her curiosity grew even more once she saw the evil grin that spread across Lachelle's face as she ripped the picture in two.

Mimi rose from the floor and made her way to her mother. Oblivious to her little girl's presence, Lachelle rolled up a piece of the photograph, pressed her index finger down on one of her nostrils, and snorted the first line of cocaine into the other. She jumped back and quickly began to pinch her nose as she waited for the drug to take effect.

"Chelle, is that candy?" Mimi asked with a quizzical look on her round face.

Lachelle ignored her as she leaned back into the couch and smiled at the sudden euphoria that had taken over her being.

"Chelle," Mimi repeated while patting the heavily drug-induced woman's leg. "Is that candy?"

"No," Lachelle responded dazedly. "Get away from me," she demanded as she weakly pushed Mimi away from her.

Mimi stumbled some before catching her steps and turning away. But before she did, she looked down at the tabletop and noticed that her favorite picture of her and Karma was torn.

"That's miiine," she whined as she pointed to the destroyed image.

Lachelle ignored the child once again as she went to snort the second and third line of coke.

"I'm telling my nanny," she exclaimed as she snatched the unrolled photo off the table and sprinted toward the steps. Lachelle's slanted eyes popped open. And before she could comprehend how quickly she had just risen, she was on Mimi's heels. She caught her on the steps by one of her ankles. Mimi kicked and cried, clawed and screamed for her mother to let her go, but Lachelle had the grip of death on her.

Mimi felt her tubby body bouncing off each step as she descended toward her mother. The picture she loved so dearly had long slipped out of her little fingers and floated onto the floor. And just as her mother's hand raised high into the air, ready to strike her unmercifully, there was a loud, aggressive knock on the front door.

Puzzled by the noise, Lachelle lowered her hand and looked down at her trembling, hysterical daughter beneath her.

"Shut up," she hissed.

Scared for her life, Mimi did as she was told. Lachelle felt herself beginning to sweat. She didn't know who was outside waiting for her to let them in, but she knew they'd probably heard all the commotion. The knocking sounded again, reverberating off the walls. Lachelle slowly rose from her knees, shuffled over to the door, and opened it.

"Game over, Lachelle," a tall, Caucasian man with slicked back hair said. He was standing in between another Caucasian man with bad acne and a short Hispanic woman who had a smirk of satisfaction on her face.

Knowing exactly who the trio were, Lachelle turned quickly and started to run toward the back of the condo, only to be tackled by the pock-faced male and female bounty hunters.

Slick-back glanced proudly over at his comrades before cautiously approaching Mimi and picking her up into his arms. He spoke to her calmly and brushed her tears away with his massive fingers. Once she settled down, he asked her what happened.

"Chelle broke my picture of me and Mommy Karma. So I have to call my nanny now and tell her," she said plainly. "You come with me, okay?"

Chapter 9

ndigo, you gotta talk to her for me," Money pleaded as he plopped down on one of the six benches in the precinct locker room.

"Now, why would I want to do something like that?" she asked with an apathetic look on her face. The last thing Indigo wanted was to be kept at the precinct longer than she had to tonight. It was a quarter after eleven. She and Money's shift was over and she was ready to get home to her husband and daughter.

"Because she'll listen to you," Money replied honestly.

Like Lachelle, he hadn't expected to run into Karma earlier. The image of him not being able to answer any of her questions because he'd been too much of a coward kept playing over and over in his head. The hope he'd seen in her eyes as she looked to him for resolve reminded him of the same hope the women he'd been with since Karma possessed. But their hope was much different than hers. Those women hoped they'd be *the one* to take Karma's place. But Money knew she was already *the one* and would forever be. They hoped they could save him from whatever it was he was running from. But Karma was his only saving grace, her and God. But his actions had already turned her away and he just knew they'd done the same to God.

The hope he'd seen in her golden brown eyes earlier was a desperate hope. She wanted to hear him tell her he hadn't been with anyone else. She wanted to hear him tell her that the business with Lachelle was just that---business. She wanted to know how he could abuse her with the same piece of himself that he was caressing Lachelle with. The extension of his better self, his lineage, the part of him that planted a seed in her garden, consummating their union as man and woman. She *needed* to hear him say all of those things, but he hadn't. And when Money watched Karma struggle to keep her heart from breaking in front of him, he loved her so much more for showing him that she was a much better person than him.

"No, she won't. And I'm not going to make her," Indigo replied matter-of-factly. "Besides, she's already got enough to deal with right now. The last thing she needs is you adding to her stress," she said with a smirk and the raise of her perfectly arched eyebrow. "Oh, wait. You've already done that."

Indigo could feel the heat rising within her. How dare this man ask her to speak to Karma on his behalf. *Was he out of his everlovin' mind?* She never did understand why people challenged the strength of family. This man raped her cousin and had the audacity to sit there and ask her to apologize for his misdeeds. Indigo admired God more now than ever as she stood before Money, putting her uniform and equipment in her duffle bag; because only He could forgive someone for incessantly backsliding.

As far as she was concerned, Money had no regard for anyone but himself. And that was fine with her because she had no regard for him either.

"But you're my partner," Money said desperately as he rose from the bench.

Not for long, she thought to herself.

"And she's my cousin," Indigo snapped, forcing Money's eyes to flutter.

"We took an oath, Indigo. Doesn't that mean anything to you?" he asked while leaning against one of the lockers.

"No. I can't say that it does," Indigo continued packing without making eye contact.

"Are you kidding me?" Money cringed. There was so much animosity between them now. He knew he messed up, but she was supposed to be the understanding one out of her and Karma, the forgiving one. She always found the good in people. But as he looked down at her, he saw that her greatest attribute had vanished. He wasn't sure when it happened, but it was gone nonetheless.

"No, I'm actually quite serious," she replied as she finally looked up at him.

"Well, why doesn't it?" Money asked.

"Why don't you ask yourself that question the next time you look at yourself in the mirror," Indigo hissed as she placed her bag on her shoulder. She moved forward to step past Money, but he caught her arm, gently pulling her back toward him.

"What the hell is that supposed to mean?"

Indigo looked down at Money's hand around her arm, and then met her sharp, dark eyes with his. He slowly released her arm.

"You know *exactly* what it means. Our job is to serve and protect, not to lie and cheat. And *certainly* not to rape."

Money froze right where he stood. Indigo knew what he had done. Immediately, his mind began to race. If she knew, then the rest of the family had to know too. But then he thought against that notion. Had the rest of the family known, he was sure they would have approached him about it months ago.

He thought back to what Karma told him. She said she hadn't told anyone. Then again, he told her he'd never hurt her and had done it anyway. And now, in that institutional blue-colored room with the metal cobalt lockers and stripped wooden benches, he stood before her cousin who knew who he truly was---his father's son.

"Parks," a young officer called from the entryway of the locker room.

Money snapped out of his state of shock and gave the rookie his side profile.

"What, Santos?" he asked over his shoulder.

"Captain wants to see you," he replied.

"Captain? For what?" he asked, facing the young man completely.

The officer shrugged his shoulders.

"Don't know. I'm just the messenger."

"A'ight, man," Money replied as he faced Indigo again.

The rookie nodded before ducking out of the doorway.

"She told me she didn't tell anyone," Money finally uttered to a stone-faced Indigo.

"And you believed her?" she asked with an incredulous smile. "My cousin tells me everything, Money. *Everything.*"

"I didn't mean to r--, I didn't mean to do that to her," he replied, shifting his weight from one leg to the other. "I swear to God I didn't."

"It doesn't really matter now, does it? She's moved on and so have you...in your own disgusting way," Indigo said as she looked him up and down.

"Indigo--" Money began.

"Just keep moving, Money. Do what's best for the both of you, but make sure when you do, you walk softly," she said with the raise of both eyebrows.

"Another one with a riddle," Money sighed heavily as he waved his hand dismissively at her. He was so engulfed in his defeat that he didn't hear or feel his cell phone vibrating.

"That wasn't a riddle," Indigo said as she looked down at the trembling device on his hip. "Your phone's vibrating."

Money looked down at his hip, snapped the phone from its holder, and read the name on the face. His mother was calling.

"Fuck!" He sucked his teeth and placed the phone back in its receptacle. He would have to call her back later.

"Walk softly," Indigo said again before giving him one last glance and moving past him right out the door.

******

Karma settled herself and the baby down beneath the coolness of her father's cotton sheets and comforter. She'd cried tears of fury on the ride back to the house. Indigo tried her hardest to console her, but couldn't do much to comfort her. Karma had reached her breaking point. As soon as they pulled up to the house, she jumped out the car, snatched the baby out of Desi's car seat, slammed both front and back doors and stormed into the house without looking back. Indigo didn't bother going after her. She just watched helplessly from behind the wheel.

It only took Karma twenty minutes to pack her and Mekhi's things. Originally, she wasn't going to leave for her father's until Monday morning, but the encounter with Money had forced a change of plans. She spent the first hour on I-95 on her cell with Evelyn who called to tell her about her own confrontation with the couple that morning. She reassured Karma she disapproved of the relationship, but Karma was too deep in her rage to be relieved. If there were any chances of her and Money getting back together before today which, of course, she hoped for but wouldn't admit, they didn't exist anymore. She told Evelyn she'd be turning her business and standard cellular phones off for the weekend and would speak to her once she returned to New Jersey. The last two hours of her three-and-a-half hour trip were spent in silence. Mekhi had slept the entire way down, leaving her alone with her thoughts, her eyes dry and her hands trembling.

When she and the baby reached her father's one-story bricked mini-mansion, all Karma could do was shake her head in disillusion. She felt like the weight of the world was on her shoulders. *How did she not know Money had moved on? How did she not know her father had become an alcoholic? Had she*

missed the signs from them both? And how did she suddenly
become responsible for them---two grown ass men?

Karma pressed the OPEN button on the garage remote that
was attached to her sun visor before stepping out of the car. She
moved to the back to pick up her hushed baby boy, then entered
the confinement of her father's house. When she walked inside
through the garage, the first thing she noticed was the rancid
smell of rotten food and liquor. The smell was something
similar to the contaminants of a garbage dumpster and a bar.
Karma immediately searched the wall for the light switch. It
was unusually dark in the house, especially at six o'clock. The
sun was still high in the eighteenth hour. Karma hoped the
darkness was a result of closed blinds. But when she finally
found the light switch, she flipped it a couple of times and
cursed aloud as the darkness remained.

Mekhi stirred in her arms as she proceeded to walk the rest
of the premises. There was trash on the floors in almost every
room. Empty liquor bottles and beer cans were spewing out of
the trash cans throughout the house. The kitchen sink was full
of dirty dishes, many with mold growing on them. The landline
phone had no dial tone. When she reached the master bedroom,
she found dirty clothes and used sheets thrown all over its floor
and on the floor of the private bath. Fortunately, Karma was
able to find a clean sheet in the linen closet to lay the baby
down on before she allowed the reality of her father's suffering
to hit her.

When Mekhi was settled on the coverlet in the middle of
the king-sized bed, Karma took hold of her father's cross, rested
it on her back, and let her legs give way beneath her. She

collapsed onto the floor, her back against the foot of the bed and did the only thing she could do---cry. She cried long and hard.

"Why'd you have to die, Mommyyy?" she asked through heavy sobs as the rays of the setting sun peeked through the room's blinded windows. "Whyyy? I don't know what to dooo," she said with the palms of her hands pressed against her wet eyelids. "Why'd you leave meee?"

It had taken her five hours to clean the entire house and handle her father's unpaid electric, phone, internet, and cable bills. She bleached the house from top to bottom. She dispensed all of the rotten food inside and outside of the refrigerator, the trash, and empty liquor and beer bottles into giant black garbage bags, placing them alongside the exterior of the house. All molded dishes were thrown out as well. All dirty clothes were placed in hampers and laundry bags.

As she lay beside Mekhi, watching the flame of one of many candles she found in her father's closet dance a silent ballet, Karma hoped the disarray of her father's home would begin and end there. If his inner and outer self were anything like his domicile, she was going to have her work cut out for her.

In a time like the present, a normal person would get down on their knees and pray to God above for guidance and understanding. But Karma simply lay her head down on her pillow, closed her eyes, and asked her mother *"Why?"* again. It was just so unfair. *God* was so unfair.

If only she would read the letter her mother wrote to her two years ago. She'd then realize that 'why' *always* had answers. It had her *mother's* answers.

Chapter 10

'm going to have to suspend you, Parks," Captain Pagano said regrettably to Money as he leaned back in his leather double-armed swivel chair. "Indefinitely."

Money's facial expression drastically changed from hopeful to grim.

"I swear I didn't know, Captain," he said with a frown.

"Let me get this straight, Parks," Captain Pagano began as he leaned to one side of his chair. "You've known this woman for a few years. You have a child by her and discovered she was an addict while she was carrying your child. She told you she'd been sober for the last eight months, but you had no idea she'd just been released from Rikers two months ago for solicitation and had a warrant out for her arrest for probation violation?" he asked through hooded eyes.

"That's correct, sir," Money admitted honestly.

Captain Anthony Pagano, a third-generation Sicilian, former NYPD officer, and proud NPD police captain, sat back in his chair and looked at his best officer distrustfully. He shook his head as he closed his hazel eyes thinking about Money's future and that of the department. The last thing the precinct needed was the indiscretions of one of their own getting out to the public. The residents of Newark already hated them and everything they stood for.

He ran his aged, olive-colored hand over his meticulously trimmed mustache and sighed. He'd received a disturbing phone call from Internal Affairs about the arrest of a wanted prostitute who hadn't been hesitant to give Money's name to anyone who would listen. Pagano asked the official on the other end of the phone if he'd been given the correct information by the young woman. The official assured him that he had. Pagano, visibly hot and bothered by the news, sent for Money. Now, the two men were sitting across from each other, trying to understand what Money had gotten himself into.

"I thought you were engaged to Alonso's cousin," he stated with a quizzical look.

Money looked away briefly, then set his eyes back on his confused superior.

"I was, sir. But she and I are having problems right now." He began to chew on the inside of his cheek. "We've been separated since January."

Captain Pagano shifted in his chair once again. He studied Money closely. The young man sitting before him, in his damp office on a dreary Thursday evening, was a broken man. He was a man who'd made a huge mistake by falling victim to misery, his own and that of a drug-addicted prostitute.

"Are you sure you didn't know this..." he looked down at the paper laying on his desk in front of him. "Lachelle Wilson had a warrant out for her arrest?"

"I swear to you I didn't, Captain," Money replied with heavy eyes.

Captain Pagano leaned forward, resting his wrists on the edge of his desk and thought about his next choice of words carefully.

"You're the finest officer I have, Parks," he confessed. "You haven't given me any problems since you've been here. Your colleagues speak very highly of you. The level of respect they have for you is quite admirable. You meet your quotas every month, but..."

"But you have to suspend me indefinitely anyway," Money interrupted him by saying.

Captain Pagano nodded slowly.

"This is some bullshit, sir, and you know it!" Money screamed while jumping up from his chair.

"Sit down, Parks," Captain Pagano instructed as he looked up at the irate young man.

"Naw, fuck that, Cap! You know this is some bullshit, man! I told you I didn't know anything! She never said shit to me! I'm not guilty of anything!" Money fumed.

"Sit down, Parks!" Captain Pagano blared as he jumped up and slammed his hands on his desk.

Money glared back at the white-haired man and decided against doing as he was told.

"That's an order!" Captain Pagano continued.

Money remained.

Pagano squinted his eyes and thought he recognized something in Money. It was a twinge of fearlessness. He was standing on the other side of his desk as a man who had nothing left to lose. His woman was gone and so was his job. And a man who had nothing was a very dangerous one.

Pagano straightened his back and held his arm out with his palm facing upward.

"Hand over your badge and your gun. Clean out your locker."

Money held his eyes with his boss's. He slowly reached down to his sides and removed the requested items from his hips. He placed them on the desk, his eyes still sharing time and space with Pagano.

"You are guilty of housing a fugitive and having intimate, physical contact with her. She's a repeat offender and she had every intention of dragging you down right along with her, Parks."

"Can't I be pardoned, sir? I mean, I knew her way before she even became a prostitute, fugitive, and whatever else she's living as now?" Money bellowed with hopeful eyes.

"How do you know she wasn't all of that before you met her, Parks?" Pagano implied. "You said you didn't know she was an addict when you two became involved years ago. How do you know she wasn't a woman of many trades then? Drug addiction, prostitution, probation violation...it all goes hand-in-hand, son. She didn't become an invalid over night."

Money ran his hand over his stoned face as he looked away.

"I'm going to write your departure as a leave of absence instead of an indefinite suspension, Parks, because I believe you." Money breathed a small sigh of relief. "But I will not allow you to return until this all blows over. And I can't promise that it will be immediate. Take this time to reassess your life. Try to work things out with Alonso's cousin. Go away for a little while. Do whatever you have to do to get your shit together, you understand me?"

"Yes, sir," Money replied curtly. "Is there anything else?"

"You're on leave with pay," Pagano stated as he sat back down in his swivel chair.

"May I go now?" Money ran his tongue across his top row of teeth.

"Yes. You're free to go," Pagano smirked.

Money turned, snatched open the door, and left without uttering another word. Captain Pagano leaned back in his chair, closed his eyes once again, and shook his head. This was a tough job, but someone had to do it.

~~~~~

Money shook his head and chewed on his bottom lip as he walked out of the precinct with his duffle bag on his shoulder and his pride clutched in his tightly balled fists.

After he returned to the locker room, he'd decided to return his mother's phone call. She picked up on her end so quickly that the first ring hadn't even been a complete one. Money's ear was practically deafened by Evelyn's hysteria. He could hardly understand what she said. She talked a hundred miles per hour, her words were running together, and her cries could only be described as shrieks.

Money waited for her to take a breath, and when she did, he calmly asked her to compose herself and tell him what happened. When she finally did, he was informed about Lachelle's arrest. He, in return, told Evelyn he was well aware of what happened and she was the least of his worries. His only concern was Mimi. Evelyn reassured her son that his daughter was okay, but went on to ask him if he was *aware* that Lachelle had been mistreating Mimi throughout her stay with them or that she was speaking ill of Karma to her. Money admitted he had no knowledge of such behavior from Lachelle because Mimi never said anything to him about it. Evelyn countered by saying the child was too afraid to. She proceeded to inform her son that with the accompaniment of one of the bounty hunters, she'd taken her grandbaby to University Hospital to be checked for physical and sexual abuse. Mimi was cleared for the sexual abuse, but confirmed for physical abuse. Photographs were taken of her bruised ankles and carpet burned knees by the physician who had a right mind to call DYFS, but didn't because of corroborated testimonials given by Mimi and the bounty hunters.

Money's blood pressure immediately shot up after hearing about the harm that had been brought upon his daughter at the hands of her mother. He suddenly became light-headed and sat down quickly on one of the benches as he continued to listen to his mother. Once she finished, she said to Money, "None of this mess should have happened tonight. You had no business going back to that girl and getting caught up in her foolishness. And because you did, your daughter was hurt behind it. Now, I don't know what's gotten into you, but you better get it out of your system. Mimi needs her father right now. And she needs him to bring her mother back. And I'm not talking about Lachelle. I don't know what it is that you said or did to Karma, but you need to fix it. You have a little girl over here who's crying for her. Not for you, *her*. And I know they're the same damn tears

Karma's been shedding for you *and* this child. Fix it." She hung up right after her final demand.

Having been unable to park his car in the precinct's parking lot as a result of overcrowding, Money was forced to park on a street four blocks away. He'd been pissed when he had to walk the lengthy blocks to work and was even hotter now that he had to walk them again.

His mother's recount of the evening's events replayed in his head. The more he thought about what Mimi had been through, the more he regretted ever looking Lachelle's way in Atlantic City. She could have killed Mimi as a result of the heavily drug-induced state she had been in. And Money was sure she would have if the bounty hunters had not shown up at the apartment. *What had he been thinking hooking back up with her?* Lachelle didn't have custody of any of her children. She hadn't been in a rush to get reacquainted with Mimi or even inform him about her sobriety after her release from rehab. Karma had been right. *Once a fiend, always fiend.*

Money was so engulfed in his thoughts as he drew nearer to his block, he didn't notice the two pair of eyes watching him from a Lincoln Town Car parked directly across the street. As he approached his Chrysler 300, his eyes grew wide at the sight of it sitting on the ground. All of his tires had been slashed and his hubcaps had been stolen. Money ran over to his baby, dropped his duffle bag, and proceeded to examine the damage that had been done to his wheels.

"Goddamnit!" he screamed into the warm, night air. He became so overwhelmed with rage, he began to punch the light wind blowing against his defeated frame. With his eyes closed tightly and his fists boxing the shadows of the evils that destroyed his car and those that lived within him, Money didn't hear the quiet footsteps of the person who walked up behind him. He didn't see who the left hand that snapped his head back belonged to or the right hand he grabbed to try to keep the knife that it held from slicing his throat. He didn't have the voice to scream because it was flowing onto his hand, mixing with the warmth of his streaming blood. Panic set in. Money held on to his throat for dear life as he spun around to see his attacker. Expecting to see a young thug or a gang banger or a desperate fiend to accuse, he instead peered back into a familiar pair of eyes that showed no remorse---only revenge and redemption.

"Now, we're even."

Chapter 11

With Mekhi on her left hip, Karma stood at the picture window overlooking downtown D.C. in the Traffic Safety Unit of the Metropolitan Police Department awaiting her father's release. It was only a quarter after nine and already eighty-four degrees outside. The weatherman stated that temperatures were going to reach a high of ninety-eight degrees by noon.

The humidity had hit Karma like a ton of bricks when she awakened around six, so she knew the news anchor hadn't lied. She decided to dress for the weather and wear a light, green floral sundress with white flip-flops. The dress complemented her bronzed complexion and accentuated the green specs surrounding her irises. She dressed Mekhi in a brown, blue, and white striped cotton onesie with khaki cargo shorts. Brown sandals would have completed his outfit, but Mekhi kicked them from his feet every chance he got. So Karma just gave up and placed them in his diaper bag.

She arrived at the MPD around nine with the expectation of not being harassed by D.C.'s finest. But due to the attention her natural beauty and solid figure automatically drew, she never had a chance. Besides, it wasn't common to see a black woman with light eyes and dirty blonde hair carrying a brown baby with blue eyes on her hip in the Metro area. Her walk and her talk screamed 'visitor.' Always polite, she told the interested officers that she was involved with her son's father, but was flattered.

Luckily, she hadn't had to wait long to speak to someone in the Traffic Safety Unit about her father's discharge. As a government official, her dad was considered a special case, and only the Chief of Police handled special cases. So at the insistence of the officer at the main desk, Karma was forced to speak to the man in command. To her surprise, he'd been an old fishing buddy of Lorenzo's. He reassured her that once she and Lorenzo walked out of the building, her father's record would be nonexistent. She, of course, would still have to pay his $3,500 fine, which was comprised of the DWI, arrest resistance, and assault charges. Karma knew the only reason she was left to pay the outrageous fine was because she turned down the chief's invitation to dinner. He'd turned spiteful in the blink of an eye. The man was married, thirty years her senior, and a friend of her father's. *What in the hell did she look like getting involved in something like that?* As far as she was concerned, she didn't need any favors from him or anyone else for that matter. Whether her father's record was going to be expunged or not, it wasn't going to change the fact that he was an alcoholic. Or that this, to her astonishment, was his second DWI offense. She had not driven down to D.C. in search of a new man for her life.

Remain calm, she told herself as she tried to ignore the chief's change in behavior. She took a deep breath, released it, then calmly asked him how long it would be until her father's release. He told her clearance would take fifteen minutes and continued by urging her to take Lorenzo as far away from D.C. as possible. Karma had rolled her eyes and frowned at him before turning away and settling before the massive windowpane. It reminded her of the one she always saw in her dream...that damn dream.

She didn't know how she got to that house, who owned it, who lived there, or where it came from, but she ran inside of it anyway. It reminded her of the house in the Nightmare on Elm Street movies, but she didn't care. She had to save herself. She was running from "it." She could hear "it"close on her tail. "Its" breathing was heavy and "it" was calling out to her. She felt like a mouse in a maze in search of its cheese. Every which way she turned, she reached a dead end. Doors to unforeseen rooms were locked and screaming for help would play into "its" master plan for her. She needed to keep up her pace just in case she bumped into "it" and "it" caught her. If she could stay swift, "it" would only be able to hold on to her for a brief second. Focus. She could hear "its" heavy breathing in the distance. The echo was deafening. She could hear "it" salivating at the mouth, fiending for her flesh. She had to find refuge.

She began to run again. Her shredded nightgown flew behind her like a waving flag. She struggled to keep what was left of it closed to conceal her bare, heavy chest. Her insides had begun to swell from the beating she'd taken from "it" earlier. Earlier in the day, the year, the relationship...she wasn't quite sure. She'd lost all track of time. The blood that had been running down her legs from her battered womb was still fresh and wet. "It" had tried to love her to death. And when she refused to let it," she ran as an act of not hating "it" enough. She needed to cry out, but who would hear her? Who would get to her before "it" did?

No sooner than the thought of crying out crossed her mind, she found a door that was ajar and ran into the room it housed. And in that room, a glass wall was set before her. On the other side of the glassed obstruction, she saw her family. Her husband was sitting at the head of the table, her daughter was sitting to his right, her oldest brother was to his left, her sister-in-law was sitting beside him, while her niece was sitting beside her daughter, and her other brother was walking around the table serving the food. They were all so happy, engaged in entertaining conversation. There was no door connected to the glass wall, so she didn't know how they were going to be able to help her. She just knew she needed to be where they were, so she began to bang on the window. She banged on it because her life depended on it. Her tears were choking her back, so she couldn't find her voice to scream. She just continued to bang on that window until the palms of her hands began to blister. She banged on it until she noticed her call for help was falling upon deaf ears. They couldn't hear her. The window was soundproof. She started to wonder if they could even see her. The conversation hadn't stopped among them and all of their eyes remained on each other.

She needed to find her voice. Her tears had become her enemy. They were keeping her life from being spared. So, she found the little strength she had left, took a deep breath in, and released her only daughter's name in a cry. And she screamed for her until she saw the chill run down her child's spine, forcing her to finally look her way.

When Karma's eyes met her mother's, everything around her stopped. She couldn't get out of her chair quick enough. She could hear it hitting the floor as she ran toward the window. Her mother's face was the way she remembered it on the night she discovered her body. The only difference was it still had its color; the blood was still running through her veins. Her eyes were clear and golden.

She screamed for her mother and banged back on the window just as hard. She was screaming for the family to come and help her, but they were frozen in time. When she turned back to face her mother, she saw "it." The monster was walking up behind her smiling "its" wicked, crooked smile.

Karma tried to warn her mother by pointing to the presence behind her, but Soleil was too hysterical to follow the gesture. And just when Karma was going to try to warn her mother again, " it " came up behind her, grabbed a handful of her thick hair, and bashed her face maliciously into the window. Karma watched in horror as her mother's blood oozed out of her nose and mouth from the violent impact. Soleil's battered and worn body slid aimlessly to the floor. Karma couldn't take her eyes off of her. But when she did, she saw the monster staring back at her smiling. And Jimmy was smiling from ear to ear with satisfaction. He didn't take long with finishing what he had started and began to beat Soleil unmercifully as Karma watched helplessly.

Karma fell to her knees and begged her mother not to leave her. Soleil just stared back at her with blood-streaked tears falling from her eyes and mouthed "I'm Sorry." Her body created a rhythm with the floor beneath her as the vicious kicks and blows from her jilted lover continued.

"Mommy...don't leave me...please, don't...leave me," Karma would find herself whispering in her sleep.

She screamed, "I Love You" back to her mother over and over again as she watched her drift off into a deep sleep. The sunlight in her honey brown eyes grew dim and glossed over with an eclipse of death. Before she knew it, she was gone.

The ringing of a telephone in the office brought Karma back to the present. She blinked back tears as she refocused on the state of her father. Never in a million years did she think she'd be bailing him out of jail. For the thirty-plus years her parents had been together, her mother was successful in keeping him out of the place. But she was gone and so was his self-control. Even though he used to tell her stories about his former " bad boy" days growing up, Karma thought he, as a person, as an *adult*, would progress as he got older, not regress. But what she realized, as she remained at the picture window in the Traffic Safety Unit of the Metropolitan Police Department, was that adults had the tendency to behave worse than children.

"Baby Doll," a low, exhausted voice called from behind her.

Karma turned around to meet the face from which the worn voice had come. And when her eyes settled on the voice's six-

foot-two frame, her intended response of "Daddy" got caught in
the depths of her throat. Lorenzo stood inches away from her
with a woolly-beard, sunken face, and wrinkled clothes. He
held his suit jacket and tie in the crux of his bent arm as he
stared back into her glossed eyes. He couldn't stand the sight of
the tears that were holding her captive, so he looked away in
shame and waited. He waited for her to speak...to move...to
respond. But Karma simply stared, eyes wide and filled with
terror.

She couldn't believe the sight she was beholding. Her father
appeared to have lost twenty or more pounds, his cheeks were
hollow, the hair on his face had grown out completely, making
him look like a mountain man, and the hair on his head that she
swore couldn't grow was sprouting. She didn't realize it, but her
mouth was slightly agape. Had Mekhi not started "talking" to
the man as he approached them, Karma would have stayed in
her trance.

She watched the man whose arms she used to fall asleep in
so many a night as a little girl reach out and touch the hand of
her little boy. She watched her son watch the man kiss it, then
smile from its familiarity. The man smiled too. It was a sad
smile, but a beautiful one nonetheless.

******

Karma closed the driver's side door of her Acura before
settling down behind the steering wheel. Lorenzo followed suit.
She placed the key in the ignition and turned it just enough to
generate power for the windows to be rolled down. She turned
the key back toward her before running her hands up the helm.
She was in no condition to drive. Her father and son were going

to have to wait until she collected herself. The grand maple tree she had parked under was providing more than enough shade for them to be cool.

She held on to that steering wheel with all of her might, her eyes still teary and staring straight ahead. She couldn't bear the sight of her father, so she just listened to his presence.

So many thoughts were running through her mind. So many emotions were pulling at her heart strings. *How did she let his misery slip from beneath her radar? How did she not know this man was deliberately trying to kill himself?* It had been going on for a year and a half and she never knew.

Karma was so angry with herself. She was supposed to know her father better than anyone else in the world---including him. But she'd dropped the ball somewhere. And now she had no other choice but to intervene before it was too late. *But what if it was already too late?* She closed her eyes and slowly began to shake her head from side-to-side. This load was too much to bear. She couldn't bring her mother back for her father to love again. She couldn't close the distance that had grown between them, keeping them miles apart and in different time zones. She couldn't tell him that it wasn't his fault that her mother was dead, because she believed it was. She sniffled back her tears as she continued to shake her head.

"I was thinking. We should go to the Tidal Basin later and sit by the water like we used to when you were a little girl," Lorenzo said, breaking the silence between them. He looked over at Karma in search of a response, but she didn't give him one.

"If you don't look just like your...like your mother today, then I don't know what," he continued with a pitiful smile. "They should have never called you. They weren't supposed to call you," he admitted as he briefly turned his attention to a couple getting out of their car and making their way to the police station. He cleared his throat.

"I'm not an alcoholic," he said, averting his eyes to his restless hands.

Karma clenched her jaw and continued to shake her head before opening her mouth to speak.

"Well...," she began. "I have a receipt in my purse for a $3,500 fine that I just paid for that says otherwise." She looked over at him finally, eyes clear and full of desperate hope again. And she waited for him to admit he had a problem, instead of denying it.

Lorenzo cringed after hearing the paid cost for his freedom. It was highway robbery, but it was all based on politics. He felt Karma's eyes on him. She could see right through his lie. *How could he tell his daughter he'd been this way since that dreadful September night? Or that being this way was the only way to get to her mother again?* The bottle was his vessel. It was the only thing that was going to close the gaps of time and distance between them. His guilt was driving him. And the more guilt-stricken he allowed himself to be, the closer he was to getting to the other side. Once he made it over there, he could make up for all the lost time and space spent away from his beloved. He didn't have a problem. He had a solution. And he knew Karma wouldn't understand.

"I want you to come back to Jersey with me," she said, breaking his train of thought. "And stay for good."

Lorenzo pulled his eyes away from his hands and met Karma's serious glare.

"You need help, Daddy," she continued with tears brimming in her eyes once again. "You're tryin' to kill yourself. I know you are. But I'm not gonna let you."

Damn, Lorenzo said to himself as he took a big gulp, digesting his daughter's words. He and Soleil hadn't raised a fool.

"Because you see, there's no chance of you goin' where Mommy is if I let you die like the drunk I know that you're *not.* She's gone," she continued seriously. "Accept it."

Damn, he said to himself again. She truly did understand. *And how could she not?* She was staring back at him with his wife's eyes. His baby doll was indeed her mother's child.

Chapter 12

Saturday afternoon. Evelyn sat at her son's bedside with his cold hand in hers. She'd been holding vigil at his side since last Thursday night. The moment she opened the door and peered back into the eyes of two distressed police officers, she knew something terrible had happened to Money. The loved ones of police and military officers know that when their fellow uniformed men show up at your home, the news is never good. Evelyn immediately thought Money had been shot and killed in the line of duty. She hadn't been prepared to hear that his throat had been slashed. She called Hawk hysterical and told him what had been done to their "precious boy." He, in return, told her to drop Mimi off at a neighbor's house, then meet him at the hospital.

When brother and sister reached University Hospital, a nurse informed them that Money was in emergency surgery. The two were then escorted to the emergency waiting room. They would wait the longest twenty minutes of their lives before hearing the status of their pride and joy. Dr. Robert Davis, the Chief Trauma Surgeon at University, would emerge from behind the doors leading to the operating room where Money had fought for his life.

"His left jugular vein and carotid artery were severed," he began. "Whoever slit his throat had every intention of killing him. And they would have had they cut much deeper and carried the knife over to the large carotid on the right side of his neck."

Evelyn felt herself slipping away after hearing that. She started to sweat profusely as she grabbed on to her brother to keep from sliding out of her chair onto the floor. Sitting in that cold, heavily disinfected waiting room, she felt her whole world crash down on her. As a mother, she was supposed to protect her child. And, if anything, she was supposed to go before him, not the other way around. If she'd been able to save him from his father's hands, then she knew her own would make him whole again. They had to.

"Well, how deep did they cut him?" Hawk asked irritably.

"They cut him deep enough for him to have lost consciousness after seven minutes," Dr. Davis answered calmly. "Usually, when the jugular is severed, a person loses consciousness within five minutes. But because his carotid was incised as well, it took two minutes longer."

"Lord, have mercy," Evelyn whispered with tears cascading down her face.

"As I was saying about the carotid artery on the right side," he continued. "It is much larger. It's located under the angle of the jaw where one can feel his or her pulse. It's most accessible by cutting it between the trachea and the sterno-mastoid muscle. But if one throws his head back, the carotids are moved under the sterno-mastoid muscles and limits damage to the trachea or larynx. Money's head was, indeed, thrown and held back. And as a result, the incision to his left carotid and jugular was more aggressive than that of his windpipe, right carotid and jugular. By the appearance of the defense wounds on his fingers, the attacker struggled to cut him much deeper than he wanted."

"How is he?" Hawk asked while rubbing his lined forehead.

"The surgery was successful. We performed an end-to-end anastomosis. Now, what that is, is a procedure where we join the severed arteries or veins together to regain the continuity of blood flow to the brain after resection," Dr. Davis replied. "He's in stable, but critical condition. His pulse rate will fluctuate throughout the night. It is a common effect of neck trauma that victims have after surgery. It will eventually stabilize once the blood regulates itself." Dr. Davis cleared his throat before going on.

"We've got him heavily sedated and under heavy observation in the ICU. I assure you, Mr. and Ms. Parks, that my staff is giving Money the best care possible. Had he and the police officer who found him not held his neck together, he wouldn't have survived."

Evelyn closed her eyes and threw her hand over her mouth. She heard enough. She heard everything except if he was going to live through the night.

"Can we see him?" she asked, staring the doctor straight in the eyes. "I want to see my son."

"Of course, Ms. Parks. But I want to warn you, your son will not appear the same way you are used to seeing him. Due to the large amount of blood he lost, his head and neck have swelled five times their natural sizes. He's hooked up to a number of machines...one being a ventilator. I want you to prepare yourself," he stressed sincerely.

Nothing could have prepared Evelyn for what she saw laying motionless in that bed hooked up to never-ending wires and tubes, especially the one protruding from the inside of her son's mouth. Tape and gauze were the only things holding it in place. The thought of that one particular tube supplying breath for him caused her heart to skip a beat. She blinked back tears as her eyes continued to roam her son's still body. She noticed a blood stain beginning to grow and spread along the bandage covering his wound. There wasn't a soul alive who could have prepared her for the sight of his engorged head. She imagined she was looking at her son the same way Mamie Till-Mobley must have looked at Emmett...helplessly, furiously, beautifully pained. When her eyes settled upon the face that shared her grandchildren's, she lost her breath. And when her brother looked over at her, he watched her eyes take refuge in the back of her head. Evelyn would see nothing but blackness thereafter.

She let the sound of his stabilized heartbeat on the monitor above his head bring her back from that dreadful Thursday night. She took a deep breath in and released it as she looked over at her sleeping son. Money had been moved to a recovery room since then. His condition had changed significantly over the last couple of days. He was awake and alert and breathing on his own. His head and neck were slowly getting back to their original sizes and he was trying to speak.

Evelyn tried to get in touch with Karma for the hundredth time, but had no luck. Both of her phones were still off. She wished she'd turn them back on because she already left ten voicemails and even more text messages. Deep down inside she knew the only reason Money wanted to speak so badly was to ask her about Karma's whereabouts. If there was anyone he was going to fight to live for, it was her. Evelyn knew she, herself, and Mimi were only half of his reasons for living. He needed Karma more now than ever before. He needed her forgiveness.

Hawk walked in, placing his cell phone back in its holder on his hip. He briefly looked over at his nephew before meeting his sister's tired eyes.

"Her phones are still off," he expressed as he walked over and sat down in a vacant chair adjacent to Money's bed.

"I know. No one can reach her. Indigo's been calling her...her aunt....Captain Pagano," Evelyn replied wearily.

"When did she say she was coming back?" Hawk asked while stretching out in the chair.

"She didn't. She just said she'd call me as soon as she got back. I know her father isn't doing well. He got into a little trouble down there. Lord, have mercy. I hope he's all right," she said once she realized how much stress Karma must be under. "Jesus Lord, help us! That poor child! She already has enough on her plate. She doesn't need this," Evelyn uttered through fresh tears. "Lord knows she doesn't need this right now."

Hawk quickly rose from his seat and went to his panic-stricken sister. He let her fall into him and cry. He held her close, rubbing her back.

"Karma's going to be all right. She's strong and so is Money. They're both going to be fine. You hear me?" he asked, looking down at his distraught sister. "Just fine."

As much as he meant it, Hawk sincerely hoped the outcome of his nephew and niece's future was going to be a positive one. Because the way things were playing out, it was anyone's guess if the two were going to survive this ordeal. He could only imagine how Karma was going to react once she found out about Money.

******

Karma sat on the floor of her father's bedroom, packing the last of his things while he and Mekhi slept soundly on his couch a few inches away. He had one SFP-90 Internal Frame Woodland Camouflage backpack, one USMC Digital Camo duffle bag, one single strap canvas duffle bag, and two plastic clothing bins full of clothes. Everything was separated by style and fabric; every piece rolled in the typical military burrito-fold. She was fully aware of how anal her father was about orderliness. The man couldn't stand seeing anything out of place. Although, it was apparent he'd lost his sense of order over the course of the year and a half she'd been away from him. Nevertheless, she was there to get him back on track. It was going to be an uphill battle, but she hoped Indigo and Evelyn would offer their much needed unconditional love and support.

Packing had almost taken up to two hours. The only man Karma knew who had as many clothes as her father was Money. But even he had luggage to place them all in. Lorenzo only had military equipment. Karma made a mental note to buy her father luggage as soon as JC Penney's had a sale.

She placed the top on the second container as she rose to her feet. She, Lorenzo, and Mekhi were scheduled to leave for Jersey tomorrow morning around 10:00 a.m. They'd gone and picked up his truck from the pound right after their talk in the MPD parking lot. She wanted to speak to her father's real estate agent earlier that day as well, but she'd been informed by the agent's secretary that he was out of town and wouldn't be returning until the end of the month. The kind woman assured her that she would relay the message to him.

As Karma snuck a peek at her napping men, she realized she forgot to turn her phones back on and check them for messages. She had been so engrossed in her father and his poor living that she hadn't called anyone back up north. She pushed the container aside, lining it up with the rest of the luggage before making her way across the hall to the guest room she and the baby had been occupying for the duration of their stay. She retrieved her purse from the closet's doorknob, took a few steps over to the bed, then sat down on the edge of it. She flipped both phones open, pressed the power buttons on each, and waited for them to charge. It didn't take long for the consistent sound of dinging to fill the room and grab her attention.

Karma looked back and forth from one phone to the other in alarm. The number of messages continued to rise. In the end, she had twenty-four voice messages and sixteen text messages altogether. Unsure of which phone to tap into first, she opted for the one she used for standard conversations. She pressed the button with the text message symbol on it and began to scan through them all. Every message was either from Indigo or Evelyn. All of them scribed: *Karma, call me back, it's an emergency, Karma, please call me ASAP*, or *Karma-911*. Karma quickly logged out of her messaging application and called Indigo on speed dial. She went through the text messages on her business cell while she waited for Indigo to pick up. The text messages on her business phone read the same exact thing; all of them from her cousin and Money's mother.

"Karma?" Indigo said on the other end of the receiver.

By the sound of Indigo's voice, Karma knew something was terribly wrong. Her cousin, whose voice was usually light and pleasant, was uncharacteristically small and cheerless.

"Indigo, what's wrong?" she asked anxiously.

Indigo immediately began to weep. Karma, taken aback by her sudden response, rose to her feet.

"Oh, my God, Karma...I'm so sorry," she sobbed.

"Sorry about what, Indigo?" Karma asked, now beginning to pace the carpeted floor. "What happened? Tell me what happened."

Indigo's cries rose.

"I caaan't. I just...I...I didn't mean to tell them."

"Tell *whom what*, Indigo?" Karma asked in annoyance.

"What did you do? Tell me what you did!" Karma gripped her phone.

"M-Money..." Indigo began.

"What about Money?" Karma replied. Her face twisted with vehemence.

"They...he..." Indigo wept furiously.

"*They, he, what*, Indigo?" Karma screamed into the phone. "What the fuck happened to Money?"

"He...he cut his throat," she finally admitted.

Karma stood in the middle of her father's guest room, gripping her phone tighter and trying to comprehend what she just heard. The horrified look that spread across her face was almost identical to the terror that settled there the night she found her mother beaten beyond recognition. Tears began to well in her eyes as they pulled themselves over to the figure standing in the doorway. Lorenzo was staring back at her in concern. He watched her two ghetto sunsets become two lunar eclipses in a matter of seconds.

"I'm so sorry, Karma. Please forgive me. I didn't mean to tell them," Indigo continued. "I swear I didn't."

"*Them...who*?" she heard herself slowly ask.

Silence ensued.

"Answer me!" Karma shrieked into the phone.

"The family," Indigo confessed. "I told the family," she sniffled. "He's at University Hos--"

Karma threw the phone at the wall, cutting her cousin's words and their relationship off---indefinitely.

Chapter 13

Evelyn stepped out of Money's room into the hallway, quietly closing the door behind her. It was going on seven o'clock. Visiting hours would be over at eight-thirty. She knew Karma was probably flying up the turnpike, trying to make it before she was turned away for the night. The two finally got in touch with each other three hours ago. Karma called from her business phone and Evelyn filled her in on everything. She couldn't help but fall apart on her end as she listened to the hysteria in Karma's voice.

"I should have been there," Karma cried over and over.

All Evelyn could do was reassure her that at the time, she was where she was supposed to be. She had to remind Karma that her father's well-being was just as important as Money's---far more.

"The worst is over, baby," Evelyn said, restoring confidence in the young woman. "Just get here as soon as you can...and safely. He's waiting for you."

******

Lorenzo pulled up to the emergency entrance of University Hospital in his Ford Expedition. Karma insisted she drive her car and he follow in his, but Lorenzo told her she was in no condition to operate any vehicle. The two went back and forth about each other's unstable state. Karma expressed her distrust in her father's inability to drive them down the street, let alone back to New Jersey. And Lorenzo stressed that her hysteria would kill him, her, and the baby before his hangover would. With that said, he ended up driving.

"I'll be right up after I find a place to park," he said as he put the truck in park.

"No, Daddy," Karma replied as she unbuckled her seatbelt. "You don't have to. Can you just take the baby home and put him to bed for me? I'll catch a ride home with Mother Evelyn or somethin'."

"You sure?" Lorenzo asked in uncertainty.

"Yeah," she answered while retrieving her house keys out of her pocketbook. "Here," she continued as she passed them to her father. "I lost the spare and I haven't had time to get a new one made. Can you leave the door unlocked for me?"

"Of course. Just go. I'll be waitin' up for you until you get home," he said sweetly.

"K," she said before giving him a quick peck on the cheek and hopping out of the truck.

Lorenzo waited until she was out of sight before pulling off. He thought about Money and how much he genuinely liked the young man. He wanted to believe that Money's attack wasn't personal. But after hearing Karma's account of how the man's tires and throat were slashed, he knew it had indeed been deliberate. Lorenzo figured it must have been a disgruntled criminal Money had locked up once before. There was no telling who the culprit was.

He hadn't been briefed on the events that took place between his daughter and Money. Karma purposely left her father in the dark when it came to certain aspects of their relationship. Lorenzo still didn't know that Money raped her or that the rape was the real reason behind their break-up or that he'd gotten back with Mimi's mother and been suspended from his job for doing so or that Jimmy was his father. According to Karma, Money had been putting his job before her and the kids and she'd gotten fed up with it. Lorenzo believed her. The story sounded all too familiar to him. It was the same one Soleil told years ago. The only difference between the two was that the elder's story had been true.

******

Karma stepped off of the elevator and made her way down the corridor to Money's room. Room: 1023. She mouthed the numbers to herself as she walked hurriedly past each room. The numbers ascended as she continued down her path. Before she knew it, she was standing before the love of her life's alcove. Karma placed her hand on the knob and turned it. As she gently pushed the door open, Money's figure immediately came into view. He appeared to be sleeping peacefully on his back beneath a crisp white sheet. His head was slightly turned, facing the window.

As Karma walked toward him with quiet steps, she took in every detail of her family's revenge on his body. From his swollen head to the puss oozing out of his stapled, distended neck; she collected, stored, and locked the image before her in her mental database. She wouldn't forget this sight for as long as she lived, just like she wouldn't forget that of her mother's.

She walked up to Money's bedside and began to rub his face. He stirred under the touch of her fingertips. She held his face in her hand as she slowly bent down and kissed his cheek softly. His eyes opened and smiled at her once he realized he wasn't dreaming. The love of his life was indeed there next to him. She'd traveled miles, minutes, hours, and seconds to be at his side.

"Hey, baby," she whispered with a concerned grin. "I missed you."

Money struggled to wet his mouth. He gathered as much saliva as he could and swallowed.

"I missed...you too," he managed to say in a raspy voice. "I'm sorry...for...everything...I put...you through. I'm sorry," he stated as a tear fell from his eye.

In the year-and-a-half she and Money had been together, Karma never saw him cry. She noticed how he tried to hide the sadness he carried behind his nonchalance during the time he wasn't speaking to his mother. But even then, he never shed a tear.

As she leaned against him, she recognized that he and the baby looked exactly alike when they cried. And as far back as Karma could remember, she had always been the type to start crying when she saw someone else doing so. After having Mekhi, it seemed like that part of her had become more sensitive. She couldn't bear to see her baby cry. And now, as she stared down at his father, she knew she was one sigh away from sharing Money's tears.

"I know, I know," she cooed while wiping his tear away. "Don't cry, baby. It's okay. I forgive you."

A rush of tears followed. Money had been waiting to hear those words from Karma the very moment he started messing up eight months ago. He fixed his lips to say something else between sobs, but she cut him off.

"Money, baby, you have to stop crying. You're gonna choke," she urged through her own tears. "It's all right. Everything is gonna be all right."

"But--," Money continued.

"I already know," she confessed, wiping her wet face.

Money questioned her with his eyes as he began to control his breathing.

"And I swear on my mother, I'm gonna make them pay for what they did to you."

"No," Money replied with tightly closed eyes. "Don't. I don't...want...you to."

Karma pulled away from him. She looked down at him in puzzlement.

"Money, they tried to kill you."

"I know...that," he cringed as he took another breath and released it. "But I can't...blame them...for it. Because I...probably...would have...done...the same thing."

"You can't be serious," Karma smirked in disbelief. "You're not in your right frame of mind right now. You can't be. Because if you were, you wouldn't be talkin' like this."

"I know...what I'm sayin', Karma," Money countered seriously. "I mean...what they did...to me...is nothin' short...of what you did to...Jimmy...when you walked in....on him rapin' your...mom. He had...it comin'. Just like...I did."

"You are not your father," she stressed through angry tears.

"I'm as much... my father...as you are your...mother," he expressed before closing his eyes for a brief moment.

"You don't mean that," Karma said just above a whisper.

Money reopened his eyes and held his gaze with Karma's.

"Yes...I do." He wet his mouth again before continuing. "I've had...a lot of...time to...think while I've...been here."

Karma braced herself for the worst.

"And...I think...we should stay...separated for...a little while...longer."

Karma sat beside Money stunned. He'd surprised her yet again. His ability to do so had yet to fail him. She traveled all that way to be at his side. And even though he was grateful to her, he'd still taken it upon himself to make a decision on the future of their relationship without consulting her first.

"How long is a *little while longer*?" she asked in confusion.

"I don't...know," he shrugged. "I'm still...real fucked up...over what Lachelle did...to Mimi. And this," he said in reference to his condition.

"You think they're gonna come after you again?" Karma asked sincerely.

Money hesitated before speaking. He knew if he even thought about rekindling his relationship with Karma, her aunt and uncles would make his life a living hell. *And what about the way they would treat her?* Money knew they'd try to hurt or break her in some way. He just wasn't sure how much more harm they could do. After all, they sat back and watched her mother die a slow, horrible death, a death that could have been prevented.

"No," Money replied honestly.

"Because they're not. I can promise you that," Karma said matter-of-factly.

"I'm not...scared...of them...or...for my...life...if that's what...you're thinking. I just...don't want...to bring anymore...of my...shit to your...door. I need to...work some...things out with...myself...and with Jimmy. I don't trust...myself...with you. And...the last thing...I want to do...is hurt you...again." Money sighed.

He was exhausted. He wanted to say so much more to Karma, but talking as much as he had winded him. He loved her with all of his heart and soul, but he couldn't risk losing himself in her presence again. The arms of his father's demons had too much of a hold on him, and he was scared that he'd hurt her far worse than before. The pain she suffered from the rape and his dealings with Lachelle and the other women would be nothing compared to what he'd do to her while in his current mental state.

He'd been given a second chance at life, and he didn't want to screw it up. There were issues he needed to resolve with himself and his father. The sooner he found and spoke to him, the sooner he'd be freed from the mental and spiritual prison he felt he'd been living in since birth. He could not let Mekhi fall victim to his or Jimmy's sins. Now was the time to break the cycle.

Karma looked away, blinking slowly. Tears cascaded down her flushed face as she tried to find the true reason behind Money's sudden revelation. A part of her believed that he was scared for his life and didn't want to take the risk in rekindling their relationship. The other part of her told her to stop trying to convince herself of such an idea.

The last thing she wanted Money to believe was that he was his father. Now, it was no secret that the two shared many traits; from their complexions to the shape of their eyes to their violent tempers and possessive ways. But Karma knew he was a much better man than Jimmy. Of course, she and Money had their share of arguments and she told him he was just like his father, but she said it out of hurt and anger. Yes, he made the mistake of not telling her why he'd become distant after Mekhi's birth. But when he finally did and she thought about his reasons, she felt bad for him. He wanted to be everything his father wasn't.

"Stop lookin' for your father," Karma said unexpectedly.

Money looked up at her with furrowed brows.

"What? Why?"

"Because you're never gonna find 'im," she admitted with a dead stare.

Money studied her cold eyes long and hard. They were the empty eyes of a person who'd seen and been through too much too soon. Her response to his confession unsettled him a bit. It was random and had been delivered so unemotionally."I don't...believe in the...word...*never*," he said hesitantly.

"Well, in this particular case, you should," Karma urged as she rose from the bed and began to gather her things.

"Where...you goin'?" Money asked as he watched her prepare to leave.

"Home," she whispered painfully. She leaned back down toward her love and placed a gentle kiss on the side of his swollen mouth. She stared at him pitifully for a moment before speaking again.

"Trust me when I tell you, you'll never find 'im, Money. You can't find someone who's already been found," Karma stated before pulling away with a small, sad grin and walking toward the door.

"What...you sayin'...Karma?" Money asked suspiciously. He was so intrigued and baffled all at the same time by what she *wasn't* saying, he had to sit up.

Karma stopped at the door. She gave him her side profile while she thought about what she was going to say next. She couldn't let him see her eyes because if she did, he would undoubtedly see the truth of the sin she committed.

"I'm sayin'...you're a little too late," she calmly threw over her shoulder before walking out.

"Karma!" Money called behind her in a strained voice. "Karma!" he struggled to yell again before he started to choke.

Chapter 14

Monday mid-afternoon. Karma sorted through the multicolored envelopes strewn across her desk in her office at the Orange condominium. This building was her last stop before she went home to tend to Lorenzo and Mekhi. She hadn't spoken to Money since their reunion. She walked out of his room without looking back, her final words sending him into a mental and emotional whirlwind. She heard him call her name over and over again until he fell into a coughing fit. But she never turned around. She didn't dare go back to that room. Coughing fit or not, she didn't have the nerve to explain what she meant. She hadn't planned on saying anything about Jimmy until Money started going on and on about needing to find him.

Karma had been ready to mend their relationship and start anew. Money, on the other hand, had been too caught up in wanting to cleanse his tainted blood. Mending their relationship was the last thing on his mind. Karma felt that it should have been the first. Money owed her that much. He owed them both.

Karma kicked herself for making such a horrible mistake. Her mouth had always moved faster than her brain when she was angered by something. She swore to Hawk that she'd never say a word to Money about killing Jimmy. But Money had come out of left field with his declaration about him being his father and her being her mother. He was the second person to insinuate that she was her mother---the face of domestic violence, not the superwoman she loved and worshipped from 1980 to 2003, the pre-Jimmy era.

She bumped into Evelyn on her way out the main emergency exit/entrance after the confrontation. Evelyn, noticing the distressed look on Karma's face, stopped her and asked her what the matter was. The only thing Karma could think to do in that moment was mutter an apology and tell the concerned woman she had to go. Karma rushed past her out the door and into a cab.

On the ride home, she called Hawk and told him what had been said between her and Money. Hawk became upset upon hearing the news of his nephew's quest to find his father and told Karma not to worry. He instructed her to cut off all communication with Money until he devised a plan to dissuade Money from looking for Jimmy any further. Hawk's goal was to force his nephew to forget what Karma had said to him in the hospital. How he was going to do that, he didn't know and neither did Karma.

As she listened to Hawk's steady voice on the other end of her phone, she began to have second thoughts about evading Money. She asked herself over and over again how long she was actually going to be able to hold him off. He was as stubborn as they came. And Karma was well aware of his persistent nature. After all, his persistence is what got her pregnant. So, fully recovered or not, he was going to find the strength to be wherever she was and make her explain herself.

******

Money was discharged from the hospital and moved back in with his mother. And just like Karma predicted, he'd been trying to reach her since yesterday morning. She, of course, had been avoiding his calls. It didn't take long for him to get the hint, so he got his mother involved and used her as a messenger. Karma, in return, politely asked the woman to stop relaying messages to her from her son. Then, she went on to tell her that the only matters left to discuss between them was their son, Mimi, and her (Evelyn). She didn't want to hear about anything else. Evelyn, ever so understanding, obliged to Karma's request and the messages from Money ceased.

Karma had to put Money and their issues in the back of her mind for now. She had to handle the rest of her business today. It was rent collection day and she was ensuring checks were received from tenants. She'd already been to her property in Newark and the one in Montclair. Orange was her last stop and she was almost finished with the task at hand.

Karma hated the rent collection process. It was long and tedious. She had to go through every single envelope and make sure all checks, money orders, and hard cash were in their full amounts. If they weren't, she would have to either telephone those tenants or go to their apartments personally. The last thing she wanted to do on collection day was ride the elevators and walk down endless hallways for hours on end.

Now, of course, she excused those who told her in advance that their rent wouldn't be paid in full on the due date---the fifteenth. She, in return, would comprise a payment plan for those individuals. She understood how hard times were for everyone currently. The country was still in a deep recession. And from the looks of things, it was going to be awhile before a succession ensued. As far as those who gave her no notice or the excuse of *"I forgot,"* Karma gave them until midnight to pay up. She had little tolerance for anyone's nonsense today. The two most important men in her life were waiting for her at home.

Karma continued to mark off the last set of names of paid tenants when the sight of her cousin's name gave her pause. She sifted through the pile of envelopes in search of Indigo's payment, but came up empty handed. Karma sucked her teeth in disgust. She wasn't sure if Indigo had honestly forgotten the rent was due as a result of all that was going on between them or that she purposely didn't pay it, knowing Karma would have to contact her in order to retrieve it. Whatever her reason, Karma wasn't ready to confront Indigo or anyone else in the family for that matter.

Indigo had been trying to get in touch with Karma since she "hung up" on her, but Karma hadn't returned any of her calls. And when the guilt-ridden woman came by the house, Karma simply ignored her knocking, ringing of the bell, and calling of her name.

Karma could have easily approached her cousin and the rest of the family after seeing Money at the hospital, but she thought against it. She hadn't been to the restaurant since the day before she left for D.C. and had no intentions of returning until September at the fundraiser, which was three months away.

While Karma was pregnant with Mekhi, she had an epiphany one night. September was Ovarian Cancer Awareness Month as well as the month of her mother's birth and death. Since Soleil had been an ovarian cancer survivor and held fundraisers each year at the restaurant for St. Barnabas's Cancer Care Center, Karma thought to give the fundraiser a name and add on another cause to the function in her mother's memory.

Thus, the Soleil Alonso-Walker Ovarian Cancer and Domestic Violence Gala was born. One half of the proceeds would go to St. Barnabas and the other half would go to the Family Violence Program. Karma would officially change the date of the function to September 7th, the anniversary of her mother's birth and death. She would wait until after she had the baby to host such a bittersweet affair. Now, here she was a year later with the baby already eight-months-old. Yeah, she'd wait until the gala to see the "family." They weren't important right now; rehabilitating her father was.

She huffed at the thought of having to call her cousin, but she did it anyway.

After four rings, Indigo's voicemail picked up. Karma immediately hung up. There was no need to leave a message. *She's probably not pickin' up on purpose*, Karma thought to herself as she rose from her chair and exited her office. She locked the door behind her before making her way to the stairwell. She didn't even give the elevator a second glance.

Seconds later, she was knocking on her cousin's door.

"Who is it?" A masculine voice asked from behind the wooden structure.

Karma didn't respond. She just stood there scratching the back of her head impatiently. She was slightly relieved that Stuff was the one answering the door instead of Indigo. *Slightly.* He was family now too, by law, which made him just as guilty as her cousin, aunt, and uncles. Knowing how Stuff felt about her, there was no doubt in Karma's mind that he hadn't taken part in the attack on Money.

The turning of the doorknob and locks sounded before the door swung open. A look of surprise scrawled across Stuff's face before it quickly disappeared. Karma's look of abhorrence had completely wiped his brain of any thoughts of smiling at her or extending a welcoming hand. He knew about the confrontation she and Indigo had. He told his wife not to tell her cousin anything, but the guilt had been too heavy for Indigo to bear. She'd gone and told her anyway and now Karma had completely disconnected herself from the family.

"The rent is due," Karma snapped.

"Damn. Good aftanoon to you, too," he replied semi-seriously.

Karma sighed heavily.

"The rent," she reiterated, extending her hand out to him.

"I ain't got it," he countered honestly.

"What'chu mean you *ain't got it?*" she asked smugly.

"Yo, what I jus' say?" he replied, shrugging his shoulders. "I ain't got it. Indigo does."

Karma pursed her lips as she sighed heavily again.

"What? It wasn't in ya mailbox or nothin'? She ain't slip it unda da door?" Stuff asked genuinely.

"No, she didn't," Karma responded with attitude.

"Well, she said she was goin' to before she lef' dis mornin'."

"Well, she didn't. So I'd appreciate it if you would tell her that I want it in my mailbox *tonight*. She has until midnight," Karma stated sternly before turning away.

"Ay, yo, you need to come up off of dat bullshit you on, Karma," Stuff spat at her back. "Real talk."

"What?" Karma asked abruptly turning back to him.

"You heard me," he said unmoved by her nasty attitude.

"Nigga, don't worry about what the fuck I need to be comin' up off of. My needs don't concern you," Karma expressed while moving back toward him.

"Well, my wife's do. And bein' dat you da reason why she's all fucked up, not eatin' and shit, cryin' herself to sleep at night and--," he stopped himself. "She only told 'cause she loves you, Karma....and you know dat."

"No, I'll tell you what I know. The only reason why she's all fucked up is because she fucked *herself* up," Karma frowned. "All dat cryin' and not eatin' shit don't mean a damn thing to me. If anybody should be cryin' themselves to sleep at night, it should be me," Karma continued, pointing to herself. "Fuck her tears."

"No, fuck dat half-dead, pussy ass nigga you lovin'," Stuff fired back, stepping out into the hallway and into Karma's personal space.

"No, fuck you, nigga!" Karma shot back. "Who I love is *my* fuckin' business! Not yours! Not Indigo's...*no one's!*"

"Ay, yo, listen to yaself, right now, girl!" Stuff stressed. "Dat nigga *raped* you! And you standin' here sayin' you ain't da one to blame for ya cousin's misery! Her fuckin' feelings don't matter? What kinda fucked up shit is dat?"

"She had no business tellin' you!" Karma seethed. "*Any* of you!"

"And he had no business rapin' you and fuckin' dem otha bitches. But he did! So what'chu sayin'?"

A loud silence befell.

Karma could feel the tears welling up in her eyes. In all the years she and Stuff had been friends, they'd never had a serious argument. And here they were standing face-to-face ripping each other new ones.

"Niggas come and go, sis. You *know* dat shit," he said calmly. "And you know you can have any nigga you want. *Any* nigga. Now, I undastand he's Mekhi's father and y'all got a history and all dat. But so fuckin' what? Dat nigga still ain't shit. And I'm tellin' you, *right here, right now*, to leave his punk ass alone."

Karma let Stuff's words fall upon both *hearing* ears before speaking again.

"I don't have to leave 'im alone. And you wanna know why, Stuff? Because he's leavin' *me* alone," she admitted, looking up at him desolately. "Yeah, dat's right. He doesn't want my ass," she said curtly. "You satisfied now? You and the rest of those *maricons* got what you wanted," she disclosed tearfully.

"No, we didn't," Stuff smirked. "'Cause dat nigga's still breathin'."

Taken aback by his sardonic response, Karma took a step back and searched Stuff's face for remorse. There wasn't any there.

"Did you do it?" she asked in a trembling voice. She held her glassy, dimly lit eyes with his. "I need to know."

"Nah. I ain't do it," he replied truthfully. "He'd be dead had I done it. I just watched."

Karma breathed in deeply, registering and accepting Stuff's admission. She nodded her head as she made a mental note. *One of her uncles had done it, but which one?*

"You have until midnight," was all Karma could muster up to say before turning and walking away.

Chapter 15

Money sat upright in his bed with Mimi snuggled comfortably against him. The two were watching her favorite Disney movie, *The Little Mermaid.* It was on the five-year-old's favorite part; the scene where Sebastian the Crab and his fellow sea creatures sing the infamous *Kiss the Girl* song in Prince Eric's ear so that he could break the spell cast upon Princess Ariel. Before Money's "accident," he would sing the song to Mimi in a Sebastian-like voice. Tonight, the tables were turned. Mimi was singing it to him instead.

Money smiled as he carefully bopped his head to the catchy tune. He listened to his little girl sing along with the animated crustaceans and laughed when she even sang the adlibs. It was moments like this one that Money cherished the most. And it was these moments that took his mind off of Karma and what she said to him about his father. She hadn't taken any of his calls since then and he had questions he needed to ask. He made a couple of attempts to drive over to her house, but had been cut off at the path each and every time by his mother.

Evelyn would make him march himself back up the stairs and get back into bed. When she asked where he thought he was going, he told her to see Karma. All the weary mother could do was shake her head in dismay. She would tell him that he was in no condition to walk or drive anywhere. And it wasn't right for him to pop up at the restaurant or the house unannounced; it wasn't his place to do so anymore.

Evelyn, barefoot and donning a pastel pink cotton robe, entered the room with gauze in one hand and doctor-prescribed medication in the other. She caught Money's wary eyes as she approached the bed.

"Don't give me that look," she said earnestly. "I would let you change the dressings yourself, but you're too heavy-handed. And I don't want you to make matters worse," she continued as she settled beside him on the bed.

"Karma never complained about my hands," Money countered with a mischievous grin. His voice had changed drastically as a result of the permanent damage that had been done to his throat. He'd gone from having the velvety-textured voice of Money Parks to the strained whisper of Harry Belafonte overnight. And he would have to live with the new part of himself for the rest of his life.

Money slightly lifted his head for his mother so she could tend to his wound. Evelyn frowned as she began to remove the faintly stained bandage from her son's neck. The swelling had gone down immensely and the leakage of blood and puss had slowed down as well.

"No, she didn't," she replied while applying the ointment on his neck with her fingertips. "She never complained about anything. Not even about that little temper of yours."

Money looked back at the knowing eyes of his mother and swallowed hard.

"Hopefully, these staples won't leave a nasty scar behind. I'm praying you take after me in the skin department and not your father. He was prone to keloids," Evelyn said as she placed and secured the new dressing on Money's neck.

"He was?" Money asked in hesitancy.

"Was he ever. You'd think a man with skin as pretty as his would heal beautifully, but that was hardly the case," she informed him. "He'd get a keloid from a paper cut."

"Damn," Money replied.

"Oooo, Daddyyy. You said a bad wooorrrd," Mimi chimed.

"You're right. You're right. I'm sorry," he said before turning his attention back to his mother.

"Does it feel okay? I didn't wrap it too tight, did I?" she asked in concern.

"No, it's fine," Money reassured her.

"Okay," she said, flashing a sad grin. She studied Money for a moment before grunting in displeasure. "My Lord. Whoever did this to you did some job," she sighed.

"Come on, Ma. Don't get yourself all worked up," Money pleaded while giving her a chary glare.

"I'm not. I'm fine. Really," she smiled painfully. "I just...I haven't seen a wound like this since the seventies," she admitted. "Your father...he cut a man's throat like that once."

Money sat up a little. He wanted to hear this story. Of all the conversations he and his mother had over the last couple of months pertaining to his father, she hadn't mentioned anything about any men falling victim to his wrath. Money only knew of his father's fury inflicted on women.

"He and I were over in the City at a club called The Garage. It was a Saturday night and the club was filled beyond capacity. I had this beautiful white mini turtleneck dress on with matching go-go boots. Nails were done, hair, diamonds in my ears, on my neck, wrists, fingers, everywhere. I was sharp, you hear me? And your father...your father was as clean as the Board of Health. He had on this khaki suit with a gorgeous white, gold, and khaki satin striped tie, with white gators on his feet and a matching white fedora on his head. He smelled good and looked even better that night. Anyway, he and I were trying to move through this crowd of people to get to the bar. And while we were making our way over there, this *man* grabbed my behind. And I'm not talking about a pinch either." She chuckled. "This was an all-out grab and squeeze type thing. Well, you know I grabbed the negro's hand, tried to pry it off, started to curse him out...everything. He still wouldn't let go."

"Was the nigga drunk?" Money asked with furrowed brows.

"Far from it," Evelyn said, shaking her head. "That's what made it worse. So, anyway, your father saw what was going on, grabbed the fool's hand and started to curse him out worse than me. The guy, of course, tried to laugh off the whole, what he called a *misunderstanding*, but it was too late. Your father pulled out this switchblade and cut him. He sliced him from one side of his neck to the other." She grimaced. "There was screaming and then a chair was thrown. Fights broke out everywhere. Your father had to practically drag me out of there because I was still in shock over what he'd done. And I remember, as we got closer to the exit, looking back at the man he'd cut. And when I spotted him through the crowd, he was grabbing his neck, trying to keep it attached to his head," she said before pausing. "When we got home, he beat me for wearing that white dress. Even though he'd been the one who'd bought it for me and told me to wear it, it made no difference. Everything that happened that night had been my fault. That's what he told me."

Money sat wide-eyed, registering the story in his head. He wasn't sure if he wanted to ask the next question, but did anyway.

"Did he live?"

"No," Evelyn replied, shaking her head regrettably. "An article had been written in *The Star-Ledger* the next day about the mêlée and murder. But even after reading it, your father didn't believe the man had died. So just to make sure he was truly dead and gone, we went to his funeral."

Money cringed in response to his mother's confession.

"What?"

Evelyn couldn't help but cringe herself.

"You heard me." She cleared her throat before continuing. "We arrived at the church about twenty minutes before the service was scheduled to begin. Your father wanted to make sure we got there early so he could have an uninterrupted moment with the man. The funeral directors were setting up the flowers and the lighting when we stepped inside the church. Once they finished doing what they had to do, he grabbed me by the arm, and pulled me down the aisle to view the man. Now, you know me, baby. I hate to be anywhere near dead bodies. So you can imagine how I felt standing up there trying not to look at that man." She sighed before going on. "Anyway, your father threatened to break my arm if I didn't look at him, so I did. He told me to get a good look at him because that's where I'd be if he ever had to kill another nigga over me. And then he did the unthinkable. He bent down, unclipped the tie that had been attached to the man's shirt, then unbuttoned it so he could see the scar he'd left him with. He made me look at it afterwards and it was...it was an image that haunts with me 'til this day. And that's why I pray that your neck will heal better than his."

As Money looked into his mother's eyes, he knew she'd really been speaking about more than just his neck healing. She'd been beaten and battered by the man she loved and feared at the same time, but had no traces of his fury on her body. The scars his father left behind on her were buried beneath the skin. And each scar pulsated through her veins with each beat of her heart.

******

Karma held on to the end table in the foyer with her left hand while clutching her heart with the right. She'd been stricken with the worst heartburn she ever had the moment she reached the front door. The searing pain shot through her chest every time she moved. As she stood motionless in the dimly lit hallway, waiting for the gas to dissipate, she made a mental note to cut back on the Cajun gumbo her father had made last night for dinner. Karma had been helping herself to the pot more than she knew she should have been. Her self-control had gone out the window. And she wasn't sure if she'd eaten so much of the delicious stew because it was the best she ever had or because it had been a source of comfort. Money, like her mother, left a void in her and she'd needed something to fill it.

"Daddy?" she called weakly.

Karma could hear water running through the pipes in the wall. She figured her father was preparing a bath for the baby. It was going to be a challenge calling for him again, but she had to try. She just hoped her voice would carry over the water.

"Daddy!" Karma yelled; her face fixed in a cringe.

"Baby Doll?" Lorenzo shouted back from the second floor. He walked to the top of the stairs with the baby in his arms and listened for any movement below. He saw that the light was on in the foyer, but didn't see Karma. "Baby Doll, you down there?"

Karma took a deep breath in, then released it.

"I'm by the..." she began before sucking in some air. "...by the door," she continued faintly.

Lorenzo, immediately detecting the abnormality in his daughter's voice, scurried down the stairs and met her in the vestibule. He noticed her completely bent over the table and clutching her chest. Not knowing what the hell was going on, he put the baby down and began to panic. He'd already lost his wife and by the looks of things, he was about to lose his daughter as well.

"What's the matter?" he asked as he reached for her flushed face. "Talk to me, Karma. What's the matter?" he pressed while holding her face in his hands.

"I need some water," she whispered. "Gas."

"Are you sure? Are you sure it's just gas?" he asked with furrowed brows.

Karma nodded.

"Okay," Lorenzo said before trotting down the hall to the kitchen.

Karma listened to her father move about in the kitchen. She was so grateful he was there. No matter how she felt about him then or now, she was thankful for having a father at all. Growing up, she had a lot of friends who called one too many men "Daddy." Their mothers had what looked like boyfriends for every month of the year. And even though Lorenzo had been out of her life more than in, she still considered herself lucky.

Since their return to Jersey, he'd been a great help around the house. He fixed a lot of things that Money cared not to have repaired. The refrigerator was always stocked. The house was clean and tidy. He cooked breakfast, lunch, and dinner. He did it all. Karma hadn't lifted a finger since he'd been there and was loving every moment of it. He told her that she had enough on her plate with the restaurant, condos, and the baby. He'd take care of the house. It was his pleasure. So, Karma let him be.

But what gave her peace and allowed her to sleep at night was the fact that he hadn't had one single drink since coming back. Not one. But she still kept a close eye on him. He had every reason to relapse. The hit on Money's life and move back into the home he used to share with her mother were the first of many Karma could think of. She had to stay on her Ps and Qs because he cried at night. She heard him in passing one evening. He'd cried hard and said her mother's name over and over again. Karma, unsure of what to do, just pressed her ear against the door, closed her eyes, and listened. She dared not enter the room. There was nothing she could do for him. Not that night or the ones that followed. He needed this time to mourn. And there was no greater rehabilitation or cause for sobriety than the truth of their reality.

Lorenzo returned to the foyer with a glass of water in hand.

"Here, baby," he said, handing it over to Karma.

"Thank you," she replied before taking a swig of the warm liquid.

Mekhi, recognizing there was something wrong with his mother, grabbed on to her pant leg and pulled himself up. He looked up at her and gurgled, then began to blow spit bubbles.

Lorenzo watched Karma closely as he rubbed her back and waited for her to empty the glass.

"You left the water runnin' upstairs," she managed to say before taking another guzzle.

"Shit," Lorenzo proclaimed as he ran back up the stairs to turn the water off.

Another minute passed before Karma's indigestion finally dissolved. Karma, finally able to move, shook her head and smiled as she stood up and drank the last of the contents in the glass. She placed the glass on the table, then bent down and picked up her eager baby.

"Hi, Pooh," she cooed as she kissed him repeatedly on his cheeks. Mekhi, in return, held on to his mother's face and giggled. "I missed you," she sang.

Lorenzo walked back down the stairs and took in the sight before him. He was so proud of the woman Karma had become, the devoted mother, which many other young women struggled to be. Soleil had done one hell of a job with her. He couldn't deny that.

He placed his hand on her cheek again and began to rub it with his thumb.

"You all right now?"

Karma looked up into her father's warm, concerned eyes and smiled.

"Mm-Hmm. Thank you."

"You sure now?" he asked warily.

"Yes, Daddy. I'm sure," she chuckled. "It was just a little indigestion. I had too much gumbo."

"Well, how much have you had since last night?" he inquired.

"Too much," she jested.

They both shared a much needed laugh.

"It's too spicy, isn't it? You never could eat anything too spicy," Lorenzo stated.

"No, it was fine. I just had too much of it."

Karma set the baby on her left hip and picked up the empty glass with her right hand. She proceeded to walk down the hall into the kitchen where she placed the cup in the sink.

"How was your day? He didn't give you any problems, did he?" she asked in all seriousness.

"My day was fine. And, no, he didn't give me any problems. He was the perfect little man," he replied endearingly.

"Well, good. I'm glad to hear that. Because, you know, this one right here has his moments," she frowned. "He can be a handful."

Lorenzo chuckled.

"Well, he got it honest."

"Shut up, Daddy," Karma smirked.

"What?" Lorenzo shrugged with a broad smile.

Karma waved her hand dismissively at him before moving to the living room.

She walked over to the phone and began to check it for messages.

"Did I get any calls?"

"Yeah, one. Victor," he admitted.

Karma turned toward her father and raised one eyebrow.

"Oh, yeah?"

He's got some fuckin' nerve, Karma thought to herself.

"Yeah, he wanted to know how you were holdin' up. He said he and the rest of the family have been tryin' to reach you since last week, but haven't had any luck. I told him you were fine. You were just using this time to get yourself together. And as soon as you were ready, you'd call them all back."

"Thanks, Daddy," Karma managed to say through tight lips. Victor had some nerve calling the house "looking" for her. He tried to kill her son's father and was acting as if he had no hand it. She knew better not to call him back. There was no telling what he'd say to her over the phone. And if she knew him like she thought she did, he would try to make her feel bad for not thanking them for what they did to Money on her behalf. *Over my dead fuckin' body,* Karma said to herself.

"I'm gonna take 'im upstairs and give 'im the bath you were preparin' 'im for," she told her father as she headed toward the stairs.

"Okay. Well, I drained the water out of the tub already," he informed her. "So you're goin' to have to refill it."

"Am I really?" she asked facetiously over her shoulder.

"Aww, hell. Leave me alone," he huffed in embarrassment.

Karma laughed all the way up the stairs until she disappeared behind the confines of the baby's room.

Lorenzo continued to move about downstairs in the family room before the ringing of the doorbell halted him. He walked out of the den into the foyer, looked through the peephole in the door, then opened it. There, with her little girl sleeping in her arms, was Indigo. Lorenzo hadn't seen his niece since his wife's funeral. But even then, in spite of the circumstances, she didn't look the way she did now.

"Hey, Uncle L," she said through a sad, gap-toothed grin.

Lorenzo, in shock, closed his gaping mouth and opened his arms for a hug. Indigo walked into it without hesitation and remained there for a moment.

"Lady Bug," he whispered lovingly. Lorenzo gently pulled back some to get another look at her. He moved his hands to her face and studied it for some time.

"Is Karma home?" she asked in a tiny voice.

"Yeah, yeah. She's home. She's upstairs giving Mekhi a bath," he replied, still shocked by her daunting appearance. "I'll go get her for you."

"Thank you," Indigo said meekly.

Lorenzo welcomed her in and closed the door behind her before jogging up the stairs to fetch Karma. Indigo, knowing the house rules, removed her flip-flops and set them by the door. She then made her way into the den and laid the baby down on the couch. She sat beside her and gently rubbed her back as she waited for her cousin to come down.

Indigo could hear footsteps descending the stairwell and immediately stood up to greet her cousin. Karma walked into the room and grunted the moment her eyes settled on Indigo. Suddenly, Karma felt an overwhelming amount of pressure behind her eyes. When she realized the rush of water that was beginning to flood them, she immediately looked away. And as hard as she tried to keep the tears from falling, they did anyway.

Karma hadn't expected to see Indigo in such a state. She had dark circles around her eyes. Her hair was limp and dull. Her beautiful face was no longer full and glowing. The weight she gained from having Desi was gone. She had on black baggy sweats and sneakers, which made her look even thinner. Her cousin looked sick. And if Karma hadn't been informed by Stuff earlier that day about the lack of food and sleep Indigo had in the last couple of days, she would have thought otherwise.

As hard it was for her, Karma refocused her eyes on Indigo. Indigo, having not moved at all from the spot in which she stood, held Karma's glossy gaze. Seeing her cousin standing across the room with tears streaming down her beautiful bronzed face crippled Indigo's being even more. Before she could catch herself, she was crying right along with her.

"Karma, I'm so sorry."

Karma remained; her face strained with both anger and hurt. After the argument with Stuff, she had a lot of time to think about what was said. She had been totally wrong on her part, especially in regards to not caring about Indigo. Stuff, on the other hand, had been right. Everything he said about Money was true. He wasn't shit. And a man like that would only continue to hurt her. It was all he knew how to do. It was all he was supposed to do.

On the drive back home, Karma had been able to think long and hard about what she really wanted. And even though the list had been a short one, it had consisted of things that were necessary for her to have so that her and Mekhi's future would be a bright and abundant one. When she went over the list for the second and third time in her head, Karma realized she hadn't put Money on it at all. None of her present or future plans involved him. So she took that as a sign that it was officially over between them. She was going to move on with her life without Money. But first, she had to achieve the first goal on her list---mending her relationship with her cousin.

"You promised me," she cried. "You promised."

Indigo began to sniffle back her tears and the snot that was running out of her red nose.

"I know I did. And I'm sorry. But I just...couldn't sit back and watch history repeat itself through you and him. I just couldn't. So, I told. You were about to walk down the same

path   as   Auntie   Sol   and   I   had   to   stop
you...someway...somehow."

"You gave me your word," Karma said, storming over to
her unmoved cousin.

"And you gave Auntie Sol yours," Indigo countered.
"Remember?"

Karma looked away.

"No? Well, let me refresh your memory. And I quote, *'If
that's what you call love, then I don't want it. I don't want to
know it. I don't want to fall into it.'* End quote," Indigo spat.

Karma looked back at the young woman she shared the
same bloodline with and shook her head in despair. Indigo had
gone from pitiful to irate in the blink of an eye. Really looking
at her now, Karma realized her cousin had taken on the weight
of her world and carried it on her back for the last five months.
How heavy a load that must have been for her to bear on her
own. Indigo loved her that much to do such a noble thing. How
inconsiderate she had been. Even though she didn't agree with
the decision Indigo made to involve the family in her business,
Karma understood it.

"That wasn't a promise. That was spite," Karma sniveled.
"Promises don't hurt people like that. And that's *exactly* what I
did to her that morning," she said breaking, down into heavy
sobs. "And I tried, Indi. I tried to take it all back later."

Indigo, momentarily stunned by her cousin's unexpected
breakdown, outstretched her arms and brought Karma into her.
She held on to her tightly and waited for her to hug her back.
And when she finally did, Indigo closed her eyes and sent a
silent prayer up to God.

"I know you did. I know you did. It's okay," she reassured her in a soothing voice.

"I didn't mean to hurt my mommy. I didn't mean to hurt you," Karma cried. "I'm so sorry, Indigo," she expressed in hiccups.

"It's okay, *mamita*. It's okay," she cooed through her own heavy weeping. "You made a mistake," she said tightening her hold on her. "We all make mistakes."

Lorenzo, having heard the girls' crying from upstairs, stood at the top of the stairs with one hand holding the back of his neck and the other gripping an empty bottle of beer.

"Then God forgives us," he whispered under his breath. "He forgives us," he repeated as he looked down at the bottle of sin in his hand.

Chapter 16

She looked out into the crowd of beautiful brown, white, red, and yellow faces and flashed her dimpled, white smile. Standing behind a wooden podium before a forty-foot television screen with a video montage of her mother playing on it, Karma took in the incredible sight before her. She, donning a floor-length royal blue beaded crisscross matte jersey gown with rhinestone straps that wrapped the surplice bodice and pleated Empire waist, silver sandaled stilettos, and a newly cut and spiked do, was an exquisite spectacle herself. Her bronzed skin glistened under the room's dim lighting as she waved back at a couple of people she hadn't seen in awhile. She could hear Mekhi "talking" and squealing over the silence she commanded upon stepping behind the mahogany wood podium.

Her sunlit eyes brushed over the faces of her father and son, Indigo, Stuff and Desi as well as her aunt and uncles, who she hadn't spoken to since she'd been there. Also in attendance were Money's mother and daughter, his uncle and his wife, her mother's former doctors and nurses, members of the family's church, regular customers of the restaurant, staff members from the women's shelter, and a reporter and photographer from *The Star-Ledger*. Karma was so overwhelmed with emotion, she had to briefly bow her head and close her eyes to regain her composure.

"Good evening, everyone," she said once she found the strength to speak.

"Good evening," replied the guests.

"You all look so beautiful," she continued through another broad smile.

"So do you, baby!" a woman hollered back.

"Thank you," Karma blushed. "I'm not going to make this long. I, along with my father and the rest of my family, just wanted to thank you all so very much for coming out tonight and joining us in raising money for these two causes and celebrating my late mother's life. It warms my heart to see all the people whose lives she touched and those who touched hers," she said before pausing. She could feel the tears welling up in her eyes again. Not knowing what else to do, she just smiled and shook her head in uneasiness.

"Mmm," she grunted through her evident pain.

"Take your time!" a man shouted from the back of the room.

"It's all right, baby!" a woman yelled after him.

A thunderous applause erupted thereafter. Karma, taken aback by the crowd's reaction, looked back up to see hundreds of smiling, glossy eyes staring back at her. She grunted to herself again.

"If my mother were here today, she would be moved to tears," she uttered in a trembling voice. "In the last eight years of her life, she hosted her Breast and Ovarian Cancer Awareness Gala here---two causes that were very important to her, one more personal than the other because she'd battled it and won. But never in those eight years was this room as packed as it is tonight," she expressed in amazement. "My mother, as I am right now, would be full. She would also be fifty-four-years-old today." Karma inhaled deeply, before releasing her breath and continuing. "I'd be lying if I told you these last two years without her haven't been hard because they have. Some days are better than others. But the days that aren't, I find myself struggling to do the simplest things, like getting out of bed in the morning. But I do, eventually, because I know I have to continue to live and be the mother she was to me to my own son. Or at least try to be."

"Speak, chil'! Speak!" a female voice bellowed from the crowd.

"And trust me, those are some hard shoes to fill," Karma chuckled to herself.

The guests joined in with their own heartfelt laughter.

"But they're hers. And I don't mind walkin' in 'em," she smiled painfully.

"Go 'head, now! Tell the story!" another woman cried.

"She's not here to celebrate with us tonight. Not physically. But I have no doubt in my mind that she's here right now with us spiritually. So, once again, on behalf of myself and my family, thank you all for coming."

And with that said, Karma smiled graciously at the mass of handclapping people before her and walked into the proud arms of her father and son. The angelic hoo-hooing of Jennifer Hudson filled the crowded room as she took her baby boy into her arms and kissed him lovingly on the cheek. He, in return, laid his head on her shoulder and closed his eyes; for he didn't want to be in anyone else's arms. He needed and wanted his mommy's. And she was there to give him just that.

Hours passed and Karma, who had spoken to and taken pictures with just about everyone in attendance, sat at the family's appointed table and watched the remaining guests tear up the dance floor. She, herself, had stepped in the name of love with her father, became a victim all over again with Mekhi, salsaed to the *quimbara* queen with Indigo, followed Mimi's lead under the soca boys' direction, and boogie woogied her way across the room during the electric and cha-cha slide alongside Evelyn. And although she'd enjoyed herself immensely, there was nothing like watching the enjoyment of others.

Her father had since gone home with Mekhi as Evelyn had with Mimi and Stuff with Desi. Karma looked around the room, admiring the remnants of the night's success. The teal and pink ribbon-shaped balloons were still filled with air and dancing along the ceiling of the hall. The many tables, covered with deep purple tablecloths, continued to shimmer under the waving tiered candles that were set upon them. The lavender cloth napkins that the silverware was lain across now were strewn over empty plates and wine glasses.

She was not the only member of the family who had stayed behind. Indigo was among the many on the dance floor. Her uncle, Miguel, was manning his station at the reception table, making sure guests received their parting gifts.. Each person walked out of the restaurant with a gift bag containing a program of the night's events, pamphlets about Breast and Ovarian Cancer Research/Awareness, two booklets with the history of St. Barnabas Hospital's Cancer Care Center and the Domestic Violence Shelter of Newark, and a black one-size-fits-all T-Shirt with a black and white photo of Soleil on the front of it and the lyrics to the late Celia Cruz's classic, *Azucar Negra* on the back. The words, *Please Help Us Find a Cure and Stop the Violence*, were written beneath the song. It had been Indigo's idea to have the shirts made. Karma had been reluctant to approve the proposal, but once they were made and she saw how beautiful the outcome, she apologized to her cousin for ever doubting her.

Karma crossed her legs and, with her elbow resting on the table, rested her head against her closed fist. She thought about how her mother hadn't been the only one absent that night. Money and her aunt, Maggie, had also been no-shows. She invited Money to the affair since they were on speaking terms again; had been for the past two months. And during that time, the pair had gone out to lunch and dinner a couple of times. Karma accompanied Money to a number of follow-up doctor appointments. They'd even shared a number of passionate kisses. Nothing more, nothing less.

By no means were they a couple again, but one looking at them from the outside in would undoubtedly beg to differ. The hospital incident hadn't been a topic of discussion between them yet, but Karma knew it was only a matter of time before it would.

She covered her mouth as she yawned and tried to figure out why he hadn't showed. Karma assumed Money decided to stay home because he thought he would have been disrespecting her mother's memory by being there. But as far as her aunt was concerned, she had no clue.

Indigo, finally taking a break from dancing to catch her breath floated over to the table and plopped down in a chair beside Karma.

"Woo," she said, retrieving a cloth napkin from the table and wiping herself down with it. "That was fun."

"Tired?" Karma jested.

"Never," Indigo replied with her signature gap-toothed smile. "I just came over to tell you...," she breathed heavily. "...that Dr. Bridges is about to leave."

"Oh, okay," Karma countered, rising from her seat."Where'd you put her gift basket?"

"Downstairs in the wine cellar," Indigo replied.

"Okay," Karma smiled before turning and making her way down to the wine cellar.

She and Indigo made a gift basket earlier in the day for the person who donated the most money. And because Dr. Bridges presented the family a check for a whopping $500,000, the creel full of exotic fruit, wine, and cheese was going to her.

Karma opened the wooden door to the subterranean vault and cursed under her breath once she saw that it was already occupied by her uncle, Victor. She hadn't seen or spoken to him since the summer, so the chance encounter proved to be an uncomfortable one.

He took a quick glance over his shoulder before refocusing his attention on the inventory.

"I didn't know anyone else was down here. I'll just come back," she uttered while doing an about-face.

"That was a beautiful speech you made tonight," he said as he continued to scribble on a sheet of paper that was clipped to a clipboard.

"Thank you," Karma replied hesitantly, her back still facing his.

"Your mother would have been proud," he went on to say.

Karma didn't respond.

"You made us all proud tonight," he said, setting the board down on the counter beside him. He turned around and faced her back thereafter. "But what I don't understand is why this is the first time we've seen you in months. All summer we tried to reach you, but you never called any of us back, except Indigo, of course. But I still don't understand why that is. Because you know, she had just as much to do with Money's "accident" as the rest of us did."

With those words, Karma spun around and locked eyes with her uncle for the very first time in two years. And as she peered back into his cold, dark, empty eyes, she saw him for what he truly was---another nigga in the devil's army.

"You did it," she growled with furrowed brows; her eyes, two blazing infernos.

"He asked for it!" Victor hollered back.

"It was none of your fuckin' business!" Karma spat back.

"You are my business!" he replied, pointing his finger at her. "You have always been my business! From the day you were born!"

"You had no right, *Tio*," Karma stated, shaking her head in dismay. "I'd already broken up with him after it happened. I took care of it."

"No, *I* took care of it," he countered.

Karma dropped her head and ran her hand across the nape of her neck. She was at loss for words. The man had no remorse for what he'd done. His self-satisfaction was almost sickening. *But hadn't she felt the same complacency after killing Jimmy?* As Karma stood there before her uncle with her head hung, she wondered who he was actually angry with.

"He didn't mean it," she said just above a whisper.

"What did you say?" he asked, walking up to her slowly.

Karma lifted her head, meeting his eyes again.

"I said...he didn't mean it."

A smile of disbelief grew along Victor's aging face.

"You're just like your fucking mother," he sneered.

"And you're just like yours," Karma seethed back. "You think you did me some kinda fuckin' favor by tryin' to kill him, *Tio*? Well, you didn't. 'Cause the one who you should have killed was Jimmy's ass," she said turning away, walking toward the door again.

"Why? He didn't kill your mother! She killed her own fucking self!" Victor screamed at her back.

Karma spun around again and walked swiftly up to her uncle, invading his personal space.

"What?"

"She went against our word. She chose that Negrato over us," he said before

"You call her stayin' with him against her will a choice?" Karma asked in disbelief.

Victor smirked.

"She was afraid for her life, *Tio*! She had no choice! What the fuck do you not understand about that?! She *couldn't leave him*! You see what happened when she tried!" Karma trembled with rage.

"She had a choice after he hit her the first fucking time!" Victor snorted.

"Did she?! Because if I remember correctly, you said something real fucked up to her when she came to you right after it happened!" Karma inquired knowingly.

Victor clenched and unclenched his jaw.

"Right?" she asked. "You remember what you said, don't you?"

Victor clenched his jaw again.

"No? Okay, then...I'll tell you what you said. And I muthafuckin' quote, *'Bien, hermana de bebe, esto es lo que sucede cuando usted jode monos.'* End quote. You remember now, *Tio*? I know you do," Karma frowned, looking up into her uncle's expressionless face. "And I know that you know she was never right after that," Karma informed him. "Never!"

"I meant it then and I mean it now. She should have never given him or your father the time of day," Victor admitted. "She should have stayed with her own fucking kind!"

"My father is not a bad person! He's made some mistakes, but it's not because of his race! And the last time I checked, your wife was black and so was your daughter, granddaughter, and niece!" Karma scolded.

"You're not black *men!*" Victor insisted.

"All black men aren't bad, *Tio!* Just like all Cuban men aren't bad! For Christ's sake, the president is a black man!" Karma countered.

"I didn't vote for him," Victor shook his head.

"Okay, so what about the Castro brothers?" Karma asked.

"What about them?" Victor shrugged.

"Are they not Cuban men?" she prodded.

"Yes, they are," Victor replied.

"Do you not detest them?" Karma went on to ask.

"Yes, I do," Victor nodded. "What's your point?"

"My point is you make no fuckin' sense, *Tio*. You hate black men, but you also hate the former and current president of your parents' birthplace...Cuban men. Your mother *and* your father, both, were of African and Cuban descent. You named this restaurant...what? *Afro-Cubana.* So what does that say about you, *Tio*? I'll tell you what it says. It says that you're a muthafuckin' monkey, too," Karma declared with tight lips.

Victor looked down at Karma and inhaled deeply before releasing a silent breath.

"Your mother had no loyalty. *None whatsoever* to this family," he fumed. "And for that...she got exactly what she de-"

Victor's declaration was interjected by a glob of spit that had flown out of Karma's mouth onto his face. He closed his eyes and ran his hand along the wet trail, wiping it off before reopening his eyes and setting them back on his irate niece.

Karma stood face-to-face with him, crying and trembling. In the last two years, she tried to forgive her uncle, wholeheartedly, for leaving her mother to fend for herself; and in the last three months trying to comprehend why he would go to the extremes of killing Money for her and not Jimmy for her mother. She didn't have to ask herself why anymore or even forgive him now because she finally knew the truth.

Her uncle, Victor, who she once loved so very much, was now officially dead to her.

"I didn't understand it then, but I do now. You were the tree she was always talkin' about," she whispered.

"Tree? What tree? What are you talking about?" Victor asked indignantly.

"The tree, *Tio*. The one that could never grow straight because it was born twisted. My mother used to always say that to herself after speakin' to you."

"Well, *mami*, your mother and I share the same roots," he countered smugly.

"That may be so, but she was no weeping willow like you. She was a cherry blossom...beautiful and full," Karma replied proudly. She quickly pulled the gift basket she'd been looking for off the shelf to the left of her and stormed out of the room without looking back.

Stunned by his niece's actions and stung by her words, Victor stood there in the confines of the vault and sighed. He was, without a doubt, just like his mother. He could admit that. But he just couldn't understand why Karma refused to admit she was just like hers.

Chapter 17

What took you so long?" Indigo asked Karma as she approached her with the gift basket in arm.

"I couldn't find it," she lied. "Somebody put it in one of the storage chambers." Karma looked around for Dr. Bridges, but saw her nowhere in sight. "Where is she?"

"She left," Indigo replied. "She got a page from the hospital. So I told her you'd bring it by her office sometime tomorrow."

"Okay," Karma sighed, placing the heavy basket on a table. She looked around the hall again and noticed Dr. Bridges hadn't been the only one who left while she was in the wine cellar. The DJ even packed up and departed for the night. The only people remaining in the empty room were her, Indigo, and the waiting staff who were moving about, clearing tables.

Karma rubbed her forehead, thinking about her next move.

"I'm gonna help clean up," she decided.

"Okay. I'll be right back to help you as soon as I find out why that one...," Indigo pointed to her mother across the room. "...is just now making an appearance."

Karma frowned as she watched her cousin walk away from her and move in the direction of her aunt. She wondered where

Maggie had been during the event, but thought against asking her cousin about the woman's whereabouts.

Karma turned her back to her aunt and cousin and proceeded to remove her shoes from her throbbing feet. She'd been in those high-heels all night and released a sigh of relief the moment her feet touched the cold, hardwood floor. Karma was just about to bend down and pick up a program from off of the floor when she heard Indigo call her name from across the room. She turned in the direction of her visibly disturbed cousin and made her way over to where she and her aunt were.

When Karma reached them, she looked at them both with quizzical eyes.

"What's the matter?"

"Look at her face," Indigo instructed.

Karma, confused as to what she was talking about, looked over at her aunt and studied her face for a moment. And when her eyes finally settled on the sombre woman's swollen and busted mouth, she damn near lost her breath.

"What happened to your mouth, *Tia*?" Karma asked while gently taking her aunt's face into her hand and examining it.

"Answer her, Mommy," Indigo demanded.

"Me had an accident is all," Maggie replied nonchalantly.

Karma stared into the eyes of her aunt and took a deep breath. She'd heard that excuse before from the lips of her own mother. And when Soleil tried to convince her of having such an "accident," she didn't believe her either.

"Did *Tio* do this to you?" Karma asked, her eyebrows knotted together; nostrils flaring.

Before Maggie could answer, Karma was already flying out of the room with an empty champagne bottle in her hand. Mother and daughter stood at each other's side, dazed and confused, and just watched the back of Karma's dress wave behind her like a flag.

As she turned the corner, Karma thought about what her uncle had said down in the wine cellar. *"She got exactly what she deserved" replayed* over and over again in her head as she darted around another corner. She thought she discovered the truth about her uncle's disconnection from her mother when they spoke. But as the image of her aunt's battered face flashed before her eyes, she kicked herself for not digging deeper into his meaning. He was a woman beater, himself, and she'd never known it.

Victor never saw it coming. He was climbing up the stairs from the basement when he heard footsteps moving hastily in his direction. Before he could comprehend what was happening, his shirt collar was grabbed and the sound of a bottle shattering across the side of his face was heard. He violently pulled away from the hand that had him in its clutch and found himself briefly covering his bloody face before falling backwards down the steel steps. He hadn't been on the floor for a whole second before the attacker was on top of him, cutting his face with the neck of the bottle. He heard the screams of his wife and daughter at the top of stairwell.

"Stop, Karma! Stop!" one hollered from above.

"You're going to kill him!" yelled the other.

He heard them descend the stairs thereafter and try to pull Karma off of him. But their strength was no match for hers. She was in a maniacal state, a condition he'd triggered. He tried to open his eyes to see who else was witnessing his thrashing and saw a number of the servers huddled in the doorway. Blood began to trickle into his eyes, blinding them. But he managed to get a glimpse of his brother pushing through the crowd and making his way down the steps. Miguel shoved Maggie and Indigo to the side and attempted to lift Karma from Victor's aching body, but failed terribly. She accidentally cut his left forearm during their scuffle, causing him to fall back onto the steps and writhe in pain.

And then, just like that, it all stopped. She wasn't on top of him anymore. When Victor opened his blood-filled eyes to see who managed to get her off of him, he saw Money carrying her back up the stairs. She was kicking and screaming profanities at them both. With the hellish fight she was putting up, he thought, for sure, the young man was going to lose his balance and fall down the stairs, landing right on top of him with Karma in his arms. But Money kept a strong grasp on the banister and continued to scale the steps until they were no longer in sight.

Victor lay motionless on the cold concrete floor, his wife kneeling and crying beside him. He was slipping in and out of consciousness, wishing that he never tried to take Money's life. It had been a good idea at the time, so he thought. But it wasn't as good as Money's, who thought enough of him to try and save his.

Chapter 18

aptain Pagano bounced back and forth in his high-back leather swivel chair as he read through a two-year-old cold case file. In the ten years he'd been captain of the 5th precinct, he never had the misfortune of coming face-to-face with the son or daughter of a murder victim whose case was still unsolved. And he surely never had the displeasure of having the son or daughter brought in for a second degree aggravated assault charge. But he had tonight. The daughter of Soleil Alonso-Walker was in one of the precinct's bathrooms scrubbing the blood of her uncle off of her body.

When one of Pagano's officers came to him and told him who they had in custody, he almost defecated on himself. The last time he'd seen or spoken to Karma was the night her mother was killed. He knelt down before her, took her trembling hands into his, and promised her that he would do everything in his power to find Jimmy. But the promise had been nothing more than an empty assurance; because he knew finding a man who left little to no traces of himself behind was practically impossible. If Pagano wasn't confident in anything else, he was confident in knowing that the family's perception of him and the precinct would eventually change for the worse once they realized Soleil's case would ultimately fall to the wayside. He wanted to tell them why she was going to become yet another victim of the system, but had too much pride to say anything. He had too much pride then to look Karma in her eyes and tell her he'd failed her and her mother. And he had just as much now. But it was time to explain himself and finally give her the apology she and Soleil deserved. An apology that was long overdue.

******

Karma took the beige towel into her hands and began patting her face dry with it. Under Captain Pagano's instruction, she was escorted to a bathroom to cleanse herself of any incriminating evidence from the night's previous events. She'd been shifting her weight on a cold, concrete bench in a holding cell when an officer came to get her. As uncomfortable and damp as the makeshift seat was, she'd melted in its solid arms anyway. Under the special circumstances, she had not been entitled to a phone call. But luckily, there had been enough witnesses at the restaurant to phone her father on her behalf.

Karma looked back at her reflection in the mirror before closing her eyes and trying to recount all that had taken place. Money took her back up to the ballroom in an attempt to calm her down. Indigo followed behind them, as did a number of the waiting staff. Those in attendance stood around, with cell phones to ears, watching her struggle to escape the arms of the man who loved her so. Money, clearly confused by what occurred between her and Victor, wanted clarification. But she'd been too busy fighting him to give him an answer. All she wanted to do was run back down to the basement to finish her uncle off. But Money wouldn't let her.

She'd been so deep in her rage that she went deaf and hysterically blind. She barely noticed Indigo standing before her, trying to settle her down. She didn't remember seeing the police and medical technicians enter the dancehall. She didn't even recall the questions the police officers had asked her. But she did remember Money's declaration of disapproval when she told them the attempt on her uncle's life had been premeditated. Her emotionless confession led to her arrest and the restrain of Money by his fellow officers as she was put in the backseat of a patrol car. She heard Money calling her name from the sidewalk, but she kept her eyes forward. She didn't look out the window and acknowledge him until she heard the cries of her aunt. She watched the battered woman walk alongside the stretcher her uncle lay motionless on. His face, hands, and arms were all wrapped in gauze. Karma couldn't help but smile to herself as she watched the medical crew wheel him past the car. She wasn't sure if he was still alive or not, but she smiled nonetheless at the work she'd done on him. It wasn't long before her uncle, Miguel, appeared with his arm wrapped in a tourniquet. His face was fixed in a cringe and his footing was off. Her smirk faded as she watched a paramedic and her cousin assist him into the back of the ambulance. She hadn't meant to hurt Miguel. He'd just gotten in the way and was unfortunately cut in the process. She didn't know either one of her uncles' prognosis when she was sitting in the back of that police car and she still didn't know standing in that precinct bathroom.

Karma reopened her eyes and sighed at the irony of her current situation. She'd been charged with second-degree aggravated assault, a charge she was quite familiar with. It was the same charge she received three years ago after attacking Jimmy with a telephone. She'd been brought to this same precinct, placed in the same cell, and was seated in the same spot. And while she awaited her fate, her heart and mind united as one and decided that she was not going to feel sorry for what she'd done to her mother's killer. As far as her uncle was concerned, she did what she thought was right at the time and was prepared to take full responsibility for her actions; even if it meant doing time in prison. *What about Mekhi?* Karma had forgotten all about her son. He needed her and she needed him even more. She'd never spent more than two days away from her little boy. And even then, she would always call Evelyn or Money three times a day to make sure he was all right.

She felt a migraine coming on. She closed her eyes and shook her head in dismay as she placed the tips of her middle and ring fingers on each temple. She began to rub them in a slow, circular motion. *How the hell was she going to get herself out of this mess?* She had no uncle to save her this time. She'd silenced him. And for all she knew, for good.

"Fuck!" Karma exclaimed.

"You know, you should really try to refrain from using language like that," the attending officer said to her from the doorway.

Karma lowered her hands from her head and sighed heavily. She opened her eyes and acknowledged the officer in the mirror with furrowed brows and tight lips.

"And why is that? Did I just break the law again or somethin'? You gonna charge me with usin' profanity in the presence of a police officer or some shit?" she asked haughtily.

The officer let out a hardy laugh.

"No. I just don't think ladies should swear," he replied with a warm smile.

"Well, did you ever think that maybe I'm not a fuckin' lady?" Karma said curtly, turning around to face him. "Did that ever cross your mind?"

"No, I can't say that it did," the officer responded honestly.

"Well, I'm sorry I have to be the bearer of bad news," she countered, turning back around to face the mirror and sink.

"You don't know who I am, do you?" he asked with his hands in his pocket.

Karma lifted her head and studied the features of the short Hispanic man who was speaking to her from the entryway. She scanned his baby face and short, muscular stature with her eyes. She took in his curly black hair and thick matching eyebrows; the length of his eyelashes and how they appeared to be too heavy for his lids; his thin, pink lips that housed a set of teeth that shared their white space with red gums; each meeting the other in the middle of every single tooth. Karma had no clue who the officer was.

"No, I'm sorry. I don't," she shrugged. "Have we met before or...?"

"No. No, we haven't," he smile warmly again. "I've just seen you in pictures and heard a lot about you from Parks when he was here. He was always talking about you," he confessed sweetly. "I'm Santos. Officer Angel Santos. I'm the one--"

"--who found Money layin' in the street," Karma said, completing his thought.

"Yeah," he professed, bowing his head humbly.

Karma turned back around to face the man who'd given her man a second chance at life. Had it not been for Santos, Money would be dead. Karma smiled at the idea of the young officer's mother naming him "Angel." What a wise woman she was to have given him such a befitting name.

"Angel," she murmured to herself. "You saved his life," she went on to say, looking at him from across the room with tears in her eyes.

Officer Santos lifted his head and locked his eyes with hers. His face was flushed with subtle embarrassment.

"I was just doing my job, ma'am," he admitted modestly.

"A job that my mother would say God only assigns to a chosen few," Karma confirmed.

Chapter 19

'll have her call you as soon as I get her out of here," Money said into the speaker of his cell phone as he entered the Registrant Booking Department of the police station.

"Thank you, Money. I appreciate it," Lorenzo replied on the other end.

"No problem, Mr. Walker," Money continued as he moved toward the service booth. "Call you back in a few."

"Okay," Lorenzo said before disconnecting on his end of the line.

Money closed his phone and placed it in his coat pocket.

"What's good, Jackson?"

A tall, gangly young man with a black eye patch covering his left eye turned around to face the voice that had spoken to him. A smile grew along Officer Ahmad Jackson's face as soon as his "good" eye focused in on the man that was standing before him.

"Parks?" Officer Jackson exclaimed as he and Money clasped hands and gave each other a half hug. "Damn, man! How long has it been? Like five months or some shit? A year?"

"Oh, you think you funny, huh?" Money laughed.

"Hell nah, nigga. I don't think shit. I *know* I am!" Jackson teased.

Money shook his head and chuckled.

"Still a cocky muthafucka."

"Nigga, I know you ain't talkin'. You Howard Rollins lookin' muthafucka," Jackson countered with a wide smile.

"Fuck you, a'ight?" Money laughed.

"Fuck you too, nigga. Shit," Jackson mocked. "And what'chu doin' here anyway? Ain't you still on leave?"

"Yeah, I am. But I had to come through and pick up somethin' that belongs to me," Money confessed.

"Oh, word?" Jackson asked in great interest.

"Yeah. My, uh, lady was brought in about an hour or so ago," Money admitted. Officer Jackson's eyebrows went up as he repositioned his eye patch.

"Ya lady wouldn't be dat fine ass blonde they brought in here, would it? Da one dat was covered in blood?" he queried.

Money ran his tongue across his top row of teeth before sucking them in impatience. The last thing he wanted to hear was this one-eyed fool talking about how fine Karma was. *This nigga's got one more time,* he thought to himself.

"Yeah, that would be her. Last name's Walker."

"You one lucky muthafucka, Parks," Jackson jested semi-seriously. "One lucky muthafucka."

"I know this," he replied sternly. Money and Jackson stared each other down; Money daring Jackson to say another word. He was never a fan of E & J---envy and jealousy. He never drank it and surely never associated himself with those who welcomed the duo's company. Money knew an envious man when he spoke to one and Ahmad was definitely a green bastard.

The stare down finally ended with Ahmad blinking first, then looking away.

"How about you do me dat favor now and look her up in the system so I can get her the fuck outta here," Money insisted.

"I got you, soldier," Jackson surrendered peacefully as he brought the computer keyboard toward him and began to type the last name in the system. "Walker," he muttered to himself. A split second later, a list of names showed up on the monitor. Officer Jackson placed his right hand on the computer mouse, clicked the down scroll arrow on the screen, and skimmed through the hundreds of "Walkers" that were listed. It wasn't long before he found Karma's name.

"Karma Walker?" Jackson asked.

"Yeah," Money confirmed.

"A'ight," Jackson replied as he continued to scan through the database for her set bail.

Money ran his hand over his goatee as he waited to hear the financial fate of his love. He let his eyes scan the room, taking in every detail of its freshly painted institutional green walls, paper-filled desks, and electronically over capacitated processing center. The beeping of the door separating the incarcerated from the free sounded, capturing Money's attention. He saw a white, aged hand push and hold the door open for another being. He blinked once and after resetting his eyes, he watched Karma emerge with Captain Pagano right behind her. The two were smiling warmly at each other, which confused and irritated Money even more.

Karma saw Money first. Her smile quickly faded as soon as she noticed the annoyance on his face. She knew that look all too well and didn't want it to reach his eyes. Once his rage met his eyes, there was no snapping him out of his demon-like state. She breathed a little easier once she realized his irritation hadn't left the contour of his mouth.

Karma leaned into Captain Pagano and whispered something in his ear. He, in turn, nodded in response as his eyes traveled over to where Money was.

"Money," he called with his arms open wide.

"Captain," Money replied austerely.

Captain Pagano made his way around the kiosk and met his number one officer face-to-face. He placed his hands on each shoulder and squeezed them.

"How are you, son?" he asked sincerely.

"I'm good, Captain," Money answered honestly. "I'm as good as new."

"Good enough to come back?" he asked with an ancient grin.

Money, taken aback by the enquiry, furrowed his brows and searched his boss's eyes for mocking. There was none.

"What about the whole Lachelle thing? I mean, I'm still on leave for that, sir," Money informed him.

"The curtains on the Lachelle situation have been closed for some weeks now, Money. You're cleared. I was going to call you and tell you as soon as I knew your status," Pagano beamed. "So what do you say?"

"I'm good to go, Cap," Money replied seriously with his chin up and chest poked out.

"I hoped you'd say that," Captain Pagano patted Money's solid cheeks. "You gotta good woman there, Money," he continued seriously.

"Thank you, sir," Money countered humbly.

"And...beautiful," Pagano added.

"Thank you," Money blushed.

"We messed up, son," Pagano confessed. "I'm man enough to say it. We messed up. You read me?"

Money looked past his commander and sighed as he took in Karma's pain ridden face from across the counter. He knew what his captain meant.

"Yeah, I read you."

"Well, then, let's go into my office and fix it," Pagano professed; his hands back on Money's shoulders.

******

Money opened the passenger side door of his mother's 2005 Honda Accord for Karma and watched her get settled into her seat before closing it. He walked to the other side of the car, got in, and settled behind the wheel. He put the key in the ignition, turned it, and let the sedan come alive. The car purred as he reached for a button that would activate the heat. Money pressed it and set the temperature to a comfortable one.

He looked over at Karma and studied the discomfort on her face as she tried to find warmth in his wool pea coat. He'd spent twenty-five minutes in Captain Pagano's office discussing the impending state of Karma's affairs. The captain decided that exonerating her record would be fitting. He didn't know Victor personally, but after hearing about the history of malevolence the man had tried to spread throughout his family, he concluded that his brother-in-arms got exactly what he deserved that night.

Karma shivered as she wrapped the coat around her. She'd spoken briefly to her father upon release. He informed her that her uncle, Miguel, received over fifty stitches for the gash on his arm. He'd been discharged from the hospital earlier in the evening and was home. Victor, on the other hand, was laid up in the intensive care unit of University Hospital with over three-hundred stitches in his face, hands, and arms. Lorenzo told her that had she cut him any deeper, she would have severed his facial nerve and caused permanent paralysis. Karma, in return, closed her eyes and sighed in distress. Her father went on to ask her what caused her to do such a thing to her uncle and she told him. Of course she left out the part about Victor trying to kill Money because he raped her. Infuriated by what she recounted to him, Lorenzo screamed and cursed on the other end of the phone. It wasn't long before Karma could hear Mekhi crying in the background. She insisted that he get off the phone and tend to the baby. She reassured him that they would discuss it more once she got home. And without argument, he complied.

"You hungry, baby?" Money asked, gently rubbing the nape of her neck with his thumb.

Karma briefly closed her eyes under his touch. She missed his strong, gentle hands against her skin. He undoubtedly had the magic touch. He knew just how to touch her and where. If she wasn't careful, she was going to end up on her back by dawn.

"No," she replied in a soft, broken voice. "Just tired."

"You sure? 'Cause we can go by White Castle or somethin' and get you somethin' to eat if you want," he said sincerely. "I mean, I don't mind. Really."

"Thank you, but I'm not hungry. I just wanna go home, take a hot shower, and go to sleep," she replied wearily.

"Okay," Money surrendered. "Well, would you mind us going by there anyway, 'cause *I am* hungry," he asked with pleading eyes.

Karma looked over at the beautifully imperfect man sitting beside her and smiled through her own imperfect self.

Chapter 20

They were drenched in sweat, trying to catch their breath. Her heavy chest was pressed against his; her left hand holding his black satin face, her right hidden beneath the pillow his head lay upon. She remained on top of him, straddling him; their hips conjoined. She dare not move. She needed her body to accept and retain the flow of love he'd poured into her. The fullness of him inside of her had brought her hours of pleasurable pain. Tears were shed, smiles were shared, "Sorries" and "I Love Yous" were declared. She slowly opened her sun-kissed eyes and locked them with his. She was crazy to have given herself to him after all he'd done to her and all that he'd put her through. But she was with him, nonetheless, in her mother's bed. If the others found out, they would surely kill her *and* him. But she didn't care. She'd done what was asked of her. She'd submitted to the will of her name.

He looked back at her and silently thanked the Holy Father for his second chance at love. He'd worn down his knees to pray many a night to have her back in his arms. And now here she was looking down at him with so much peace and completeness in her eyes, he couldn't help but tighten his grip around her waist. He never wanted to let her go. And he had no intentions of doing so. She'd made love to him for hours, leaving a trail of kisses and an echo of her sultry voice calling his name at the lobes of his ears. He'd always admired her stamina. She was the only woman he knew who could give and take just as much as him. She did not rush when loving him. And for that he was grateful.

She pulled her right hand from beneath the pillow and gently grabbed the other side of his chiseled face. She closed her eyes as she leaned into him. Her lips found his and her tongue slipped into his moist, warm mouth. They danced once again. He ran his hands up her glossed back and held the back of her head in his hands. He never wanted to know what his life would be like without her in it again. So he kissed her the only way her knew how---slow, long, and hard.

******

Indigo sat on the windowsill in her father's recovery room, overlooking the city. The sun was high and blinding. She hadn't visited him since the night he was admitted to the hospital. After finding out what went down between him and Karma, she stayed away. It was too hard for her to visit a man who she honestly didn't know. God only knew how long he'd been abusing her mother. In all of her twenty-nine years, she'd never seen a blemish, let alone a bruise, on her mother's beautiful, midnight-black body. Indigo didn't know how to process the years of lies and deceit. She couldn't digest it. She thought long and hard about where her relationship with her father would stand going forward. It would exist in a place that was, in fact, non-existent. He'd done the unthinkable, the unforgivable. And as a result, he'd lost her forever.

She was only there this morning out of respect for her mother. Maggie asked her to come. Mother and daughter hadn't spoken much since the incident. Indigo was too hurt and disgusted to speak to her mother and Maggie was so deeply engrossed in Victor to care.

Had it not been for Stuff harassing her earlier in the day to meet with her mother and get some answers, she would still be at home in the bed asleep. But there she was, in that room, sitting five feet away from the man who she'd spent her whole life trying to please. She'd strived to be and do more than enough for him. But in the end, any and everything she did was never good enough. She was never smart enough or talented enough or driven enough in his eyes. She'd simply been his little girl. And even now, at twenty-nine-years-old, she was still just that---a little girl who wasn't enough in her daddy's eyes.

Indigo listened to her mother's careful footsteps behind her. She'd gone into the bathroom to fill a small basin with water. She had intentions of washing the crust out of her husband's eyes and from the sides of his chapped mouth. Indigo gradually turned around and watched her mother dip a wash cloth into the basin, wet it, then ring it out before applying it to her father's bandaged face.

"Indigo, me got a tube of Vaseline in me purse. Can you get it out for I, please?" Maggie asked as she continued to tend to her heavily sedated husband.

Indigo glared into her mother's back for a moment. *Was she serious?* She didn't want any parts of making her father comfortable.

Maggie, noticing Indigo had not moved from the window, placed the wash cloth back into the basin before turning around to meet her daughter's eyes.

"Are you not going to get it for I?" she asked in confusion.

"No," Indigo replied, shaking her head.

Maggie sucked her teeth in disgust. She sat the basin down on the tray connected to Victor's bed and made her way to the closet to retrieve her pocketbook.

"You're a wicked, wicked gal," she uttered in a whisper. "Me want you to know dat. You have a responsibility to he."

"He is not my responsibility. He's yours," Indigo snapped.

Maggie spun around with wild, reddened eyes and fixed her face into a cringe. She placed her hands on her wide hips and tilted her head to one side.

"Me beg your pardon?"

"The only responsibilities I have are Stuff, Desi, you, and Karma," Indigo continued stone-faced.

"You say she name in I presence?" Maggie asked in disbelief.

"Yes. Now, you say it," Indigo said as she folded her arms at her chest. "Say her name, Mommy. She has a name."

"Me don't give a shit about she name. Me curse da day her was born," Maggie spat.

"Say her name, Mommy," Indigo pressed a little more.

"No," Maggie countered. "Her don't deserve dat much respect." Maggie continued as she removed the top from the Vaseline and traveled back over to her husband.

Indigo watched her mother rub the lip moisturizer on the tip of her middle finger and apply it to her father's small lips. She shook her head in disbelief as she turned back to the window and rested her hands against the windowsill.

A loud silence ensued.

"How long has he been abusing you?" Indigo asked, breaking the silence between them.

Maggie let out a heavy sigh as she took her seat next to Victor's bed.

"Did Auntie Sol know? Did Uncle Miguel?" Indigo demanded, turning back toward her mother.

Maggie remained sitting with her eyes closed and her back facing Indigo. She took one of Victor's cold hands into hers and began to massage it.

"Answer me, Mommy! I deserve to know!" Indigo exclaimed.

Maggie reopened her eyes and focused on her husband's heavily wrapped, discolored face.

"Dere are tings dat happen between a man and he wife sometimes, Indigo,"

Maggie threw over her shoulder. "Private tings dat da man, he wife, and God are only capable of taking care of. No one is to sever dat bond."

"Is that why you're so angry with her? Because she interfered?" Indigo asked in uncertainty.

Maggie remained silent.

"We wouldn't even be here right now if he hadn't gotten sloppy and punched you in your face," he informed her mother. "You should have known better than to show up at the restaurant with your face all messed up like that. You knew she was going to be there. She's the last one to leave. *Always*. So I guess now my question is, why did you even show up, knowing good and well she was going to flip the hell out when she saw you?"

"Me showed to speak to your daddy. Me was hoping dat me could avoid being seen by you and she," Maggie confessed. "Me took a vow to love, honor, and cherish he, Indigo. For better or for worse...for richer or poorer...true sickness and in healt'......for as long as we both shall live. Me also took a vow to obey he. And when me don't...him remind I in him own way."

"His way is the wrong way, Mommy," Indigo professed with tears in her eyes. "You're not some...animal. You're a human being. You're his wife...his equal."

"Him loves I. Me am sure of dat. And you need to be sure of dat too," Maggie replied. "Your auntie and me are not da same. And dat's who your cousin saw when her looked in me face. Me didn't need no savin', cuz me never asked for she help."

"That may be, Mommy, but she did what she did because she loves you. And you may not think that you and Auntie Sol are the same...but you are. The only thing that ever separated you from her was that ring on your finger," Indigo confirmed.

Maggie looked down at the diamond eternity band on her ring finger and bit the inside of her mouth.

"Did you know that he told her Auntie Sol got what she deserved?" Indigo confessed. "Did you know that, Mommy?"

A wave of silence washed over Maggie again. She was well aware of what Victor said to Karma. He'd spent that whole day professing his disapproval of the gala. He'd said things about Soleil that were so vile, it made Maggie's stomach hurt. She didn't understand how Victor could speak so ill of his sister. His ranting and raving eventually got to her and she ended up telling him how wrong he was. A screaming match between them ensued. And Victor striking her with a closed fist ended it.

"He said that about his own sister. So what makes you think he wouldn't say the same thing about you?" Indigo asked. She moved toward her mother and knelt down beside her. She rested her delicate hands on her lap and looked up into her deep, dark brown eyes. "He could kill you if he wanted to, Mommy. You will be where Auntie Sol is if you don't leave him...today."

A tear fell from Maggie's eye as she looked into her only daughter's and reflected upon the thirty odd years she spent as her husband's punching bag. She'd set aside her dreams of becoming something so much more than just a wife, nurse, and a mother a long time ago. He'd stolen her identity, not just as an individual or a woman, but as a rare black pearl from the depths of the Caribbean Sea.

She wouldn't know where or how to start anew without him. But she needed to ask herself a question: *"Am I willing, ready, and able to?"*

"I don't want to be where Karma is, Mommy. I don't want to ever know her pain. If something ever happened to you, I'd die. I would just...die," Indigo professed.

How could a mother deny her only child of herself after hearing such a plea?

Chapter 21

Money pulled up to Pak Tokchol, a pool hall on Bloomfield Avenue in Montclair, in his new Chevy Tahoe. His uncle called him earlier in the day, stressing that he needed to speak to him. Money couldn't imagine what was so important that the two had to meet all the way in Montclair. He was eating breakfast with Karma, Lorenzo, and the baby when Hawk called. He had no intentions of going anywhere for the rest of the day. His plans were to spend it with Karma and the baby. He wanted to propose to her again by nightfall. But his uncle's unexpected call broke his train of thought, swaying him in another direction. And that was probably a good thing because he needed to work up enough nerve to ask her again. Even though he knew she loved him more than anything, it didn't mean she was going to take that big step with him again.

Money stepped out of his pearl white SUV, closed the door behind him, and made his way into the pool hall. The smell of nachos and beer hit his nose immediately. The hall was half the size of a warehouse. There were sixteen tables spread around the room with Tiffany lamps hung above each one. Framed photographs of famous Italian actors, athletes, and entertainers donned the brick layered walls. High squared wooden tables with matching stools were set on one side of the hall while leather booths were set on the other. There were a few white and brown faces scattered around the dimly lit space. A handful of them were sitting at the bar across the room drunk and talking loud.

Money, waiting for his eyes to adjust to the darkness, searched the room for his uncle. It wasn't long before he spotted him exiting the men's bathroom and making his way to a booth. Money followed suit.

"Wassup, Unc'?" he asked with a broad smile.

Hawk looked up and returned the gesture.

"Money."

He rose from his seat and embraced his nephew in a full hug.

"Thanks for coming, son," he continued.

"No problem, Unc'," Money said as he and Hawk separated. "Everything all right?" he asked in concern.

"Things could be better," he confessed.

Money tilted his head back slightly, furrowing his brows.

"Come on. Let's have a seat," Hawk said, sitting down.

Money reluctantly removed his coat and placed it down on the seat beside him as he sat down and got comfortable. He grabbed a bottle of Heineken out of a bucket of ice that was set in the middle of the table, opened it, and took a swig.

"So what's up? What did you need to talk to me about?" he asked.

Hawk sat across from Money and took a long, good look at him. He'd raised the boy from birth. He'd been the one who taught him how to tie a tie. The one who schooled him about women and showed him how to put on a condom correctly. He'd been the father his nephew never had. The one he longed for but never voiced.

He'd thought long and hard about what he was going to tell his nephew this afternoon. He discussed it with his wife and she expressed her disapproval of his decision. She believed that it was in his and Karma's best interest to leave well-enough alone. Hawk took Sarah's sound advice into consideration, but he knew better than to follow it. As far as he was concerned, she didn't understand Money like he did. She didn't know about the young man's persistence. When he had his mind set on something, he did everything in his power to get it. What she also didn't understand was that the news Karma brought to him after her argument with Money in the hospital left him unnerved. Money wasn't going to rest until he found his father. So Hawk decided he was going to put Money's mind at ease.

"I wanted to talk to you about your father," Hawk finally uttered.

Money inhaled deeply, then exhaled.

"What about him?" he asked before taking another swig of his beer.

"I hear you've been looking for him," Hawk admitted.

Money slowly set his beer back down on the table. He looked back at his uncle skeptically. *How did he know I was looking for my father,* Money thought to himself. He'd only told one person about his quest. And that one person was Karma.

"Where'd you hear that from?" he asked in disgust.

"A little bird told me," Hawk replied calmly.

"Is that right?" Money asked with a smirk.

"Right it is," Hawk voiced in an even tone.

"Would that little bird have blonde hair and hazel eyes by any chance?" Money asked smugly.

"Maybe," Hawk counteracted.

Money smiled in disbelief.

"Unbelievable," he said, shaking his head.

"I agree," Hawk replied as he pushed his beer to the side.

"What's that supposed to mean?" Money asked with furrowed brows.

"What do you think it means?" Hawk queried coolly.

A loud silence fell over the two men.

Money sighed heavily as he wracked his brain, trying to figure out why Karma had taken it upon herself to tell his uncle about his expedition. He knew the two were close, but he didn't believe she should have made such a drastic move, especially without his consent.

"Are you upset?" Hawk asked, hushing the silence.

"Should I be?" Money enquired.

Money ran his hand over his goatee as he thought about his next choice of words.

"Look, I don't want you to think I don't love or appreciate you for raising me, Uncle D. I do. I wouldn't be the man I am today had it not been for you," Money confessed. "But--"

"But what?" Hawk interjected.

"I don't know who I am," he admitted. "I mean...yeah, I gotta glimpse of myself in him when I saw him at Mrs.

Walker's birthday party, but there was so much more there that I didn't see. I got questions, Unc'. Questions only he can answer."

"Money," Hawk began.

I need to know why I'm the way I am, Unc'. Why I do the fucked up things I do," Money continued. "Why I become this...monster...who puts the fear of God in my mother and in my woman." Money looked away briefly before setting his eyes back on his uncle. "Mekhi has that same muthafucka in him, Unc'. I see it every time he cries. And I'm not talking about when he's tired or hurt. I'm talking about a cry that he lets out when he's mad as hell. This little nigga trembles, Unc'. Okay? His fuckin' eyes turn a darker shade of blue and shit," Money shook his head. "Karma can't do anything with him when he gets like that. I can't. Mama can't. Nobody," he sighed. "And I know there's a way to get this muthafucka out of our systems. There's gotta be. But I can't do anything about it until I talk to Jimmy. 'Cause I know he's got the answer."

Hawk sat back and recounted everything Money said. He was quite familiar with his nephew's rage and knew that it had been passed down to him from his father. He hoped, after learning about Mekhi's birth, he would be spared of his father and grandfather's evils. But after hearing Money's confession, Hawk knew, right then and there, the baby's future was going to be bleak. Somewhere down the line, he made himself believe that Money was better; cured. As much as he stayed on him about it throughout the years, he thought it was a thing of the past.

"I wish you would have come to me after you found that picture of Jimmy and your mother," Hawk said. "Had you done so, I would have been able to tell you everything...*everything*. It would have been so much easier then."

"You lost me, Unc'," Money grinned.

Hawk folded his arms at his chest and inhaled deeply before releasing the air.

"Your father's dead, son."

Money shifted uneasily in his seat. He struggled to wrap his mind around his uncle's proclamation. He began to rub the nape of his neck as he searched for a reply.

"How do you know that?" Money asked with averted eyes.

"Because I'm the one who sanctioned his slaying," Hawk admitted.

Money's head snapped up. His eyes were wide and puzzled. He searched his uncle's face for a sign, any sign, of untruth. But there was nothing there. Hawk's face was expressionless.

"As you already know, your father was Essex County's most notorious drug lord. What you don't know is that I was his best friend and his business partner. You know me as Uncle D. But the players in the game know me as Hawk," he admitted.

Money's eyes grew wider with shock. *Had he heard him correctly?* His uncle couldn't have been the Hawk who Karma met with two years ago. That was impossible. No one, not even the cops, knew who Hawk was. The Hawk he learned about at the precinct had no record, no face.

"Come on, Uncle D, man. You're pullin' my leg, right?" he asked with hopeful eyes.

"About two years ago, a young lady who lost her mother, came to me and told me she needed help finding her mother's killer," Hawk continued. "I, not knowing the true identity of her or her mother at the time, happily obliged to assisting her in her quest...with one stipulation. She had to do something for me first. Do you remember what that was, Money?"

Money's nose flared in response to his uncle's question. He knew good and well what the one condition was. Karma was to meet a cat by the name of "Pimp" at The Mint on New Year's Eve. She was instructed to get his attention, talk to him for a little while, then lure him back to the Robert Treat Hotel where he'd be killed. Indigo had gone with her that night.

The more Money thought about that New Year's Eve night, the more enraged he became. He and Karma actually fought over her "plans" for that evening. He forbade her to go, but she went anyway. His uncle was the cause behind her suspicious behavior those many moons ago. The excessive late night phone calls from Stuff, the coded text messages, and the secrets she held from him all pointed back to his uncle. Money couldn't believe he was sitting across from the man who permitted his woman to cheat on him with that scumbag from Philadelphia.

"She had to help take out a young man who was trying to make a name for himself over here in Jersey. A little punk who was getting a little ahead of himself. Or as you knew him, Patrick "Pimp" Thomas," Hawk smirked. "And she did." He paused briefly before continuing. "I learned of her true identity from one of my soldiers. He put his job and life on the line to save hers. She returned to my office the following week and spotted a photograph of Jimmy and I on my desk. I asked her if she recognized the man next to me. And she said yes. Satisfied with her answer and knowing her intentions for him, I provided her with the information she needed to locate him."

Money looked away, running his hand over his goatee.

"Are you tellin' me Karma killed my father, man? Is that what you sayin', Unc'?" he hissed.

Hawk said nothing. He just looked at his nephew straight-faced

"Are you tellin' me that *my muthafuckin' woman* killed my pops, man?" A stream of tears began to run down Moncy's face. "The same one that bore my son? And you let her do it? Is that what you tellin' me, man?" he swelled up.

Hawk blinked slowly. He imagined Money would react in this manner. He knew he was guilty of telling the man. After all, he made Karma swear on her life that she would take all that she knew and did to the grave. But plans changed just as much as decisions and people did.

"It had to be done, son," Hawk admitted.

"Don't call me 'son.' I'm not your fuckin' son!" Money blared.

"All right, then," Hawk replied calmly.

Money looked over at his pokerfaced uncle and shook his head. How he could keep a secret like this from him for two years was incomprehensible. What made matters worse was Karma's role in the whole ordeal. She'd lied to him for two years, telling him that she'd given up hope in finding Jimmy; all the while knowing that she rocked him into an eternal slumber. She hadn't gone to KFC that night he and Indigo were playing cards at the house. She'd gone to kill his father. He knew there was something wrong with her when she returned to the house. Her eyes said it all. They were a variation of colors when he looked at them; each color fighting the other for permanent inhabitancy. It was as if her eyes were trying to tell him what she was thinking and how she was feeling about what she'd just done. But he hadn't listened close enough.

Money rose from the booth with his coat in hand and stormed out of the pool hall without saying a word to his uncle. *What else was there to say?* He'd been betrayed by three of the six most important people to him. Imposters. That's all they were. And he wished he could arrest them for impersonating good, honest people.

Karma told him three months ago that he would never find his father because one couldn't find someone who'd already been found. Money didn't understand what she'd meant by it then, but he did now. He hopped in his truck, placed the key in the ignition, and turned it. He had to get away from Jersey...as far away from there as possible. He had no direction, no idea as to where he was going to go. But he did know that if he didn't put that truck in drive and put his foot on that pedal, someone was going to get hurt.

Chapter 22

Dinner was absolutely amazing, Evelyn. Thank you," Lorenzo smiled as he wiped his mouth with a cloth napkin.

"No, *thank you*," she blushed, rising from her seat to clear the table.

She'd invited Lorenzo and Karma over for dinner, cooking salmon cakes, spaghetti with shrimp, and spinach. She thought it would be nice to have the man she'd been dreaming about over for a meal. Evelyn wanted to get to know him better. By no means did she want to disrespect Karma or the memory of her late mother by flirting or throwing herself at her father. But she couldn't help but take interest in the tall, broad-shouldered man with the shiny bald head, peppered goatee, and pearly white teeth sitting at her dining table. He was the finest thing she'd ever seen in the fifty years she'd been alive. She could see the resemblance between him and Karma. They both shared the same bright, beautiful smile.

Evelyn found herself fanning her face and chest throughout the night. Lorenzo made her somewhat uncomfortable, awakening something in her that had been asleep for the last twenty years. Of course, she had her share of men during the

80s and 90s, but none of them stirred up her emotions like Lorenzo had. The man was just so fine...and intelligent, chivalrous, and witty. His feet were big and his hands, strong. The fact that he smelled good didn't help the situation either. She couldn't blame Karma's mother for going against her better judgment and holding on to him. She'd loved that man, a crime so many women committed each and every day.

Evelyn tried her best to keep her composure in his presence. She thought she'd done well. She'd been discreet until Karma gave her a knowing glance from across the table. A mischievous grin grew along her face before she broke into a child-like giggle. Evelyn, flush-faced, averted her eyes and continued to eat her meal. It wasn't long before she was giggling right along with the girl.

"Would you like some dessert, Lorenzo? I made a red velvet cake the other day. I've got some vanilla ice cream in the freezer," she informed him.

Lorenzo looked up at the beautiful, graying woman standing over him and smiled despite of himself. He was a sucker for women with full, succulent lips. And Evelyn had a set on her that could bring any man to his knees.

He cleared his throat, forcing his eyes to meet hers.

"Yes, please."

"All right," Evelyn replied, smiling at him warmly before exiting.

Lorenzo watched her saunter out of the room while Karma watched him. She sat back with raised eyebrows, waiting for her father to acknowledge her. He appeared to be in a trance. The only woman she knew who could put him under a spell like this was her mother. Karma wasn't sure if the attraction between her father and Money's mother was strictly physical or not. She hoped the two wouldn't take things farther than this uncomfortable phase because she surely wouldn't be able to handle them sleeping together. After all, her father was still mourning the death of her mother and she had a child by this woman's son.

"Your slip is showin', Daddy," Karma teased.

"What?" he asked, snapping out of his trance.

Karma cracked a smile.

"Your slip. It's showin'," she reiterated.

"Oh," he laughed nervously. "I'm sorry, baby doll."

"You need to be ashamed of yourself," he taunted.

"Why? What did I do?" Lorenzo quizzed, already knowing the answer.

"You know what you did," Karma countered with serious eyes. "I didn't bring you over here to make her uncomfortable, okay? Behave yourself."

A wide, guilty smile spread across Lorenzo's face. He began to chuckle to himself.

"All I did was tell her how delicious the food was," he shrugged.

"I'm not talkin' about what you said to her. I'm talkin' about how you looked at her when she asked you if you wanted dessert," Karma uttered matter-of-factly.

"How was I lookin' at her?" he grinned with furrowed brows.

"You were lookin' at her like she was askin' you if you wanted some of *her* dessert," she said knowingly.

"Baby Doll--" he began.

"Baby Doll, nothin'. Behave yourself. I mean it, Daddy. She's your grandson's grandmother. Remember that," she stated earnestly.

Lorenzo shifted uncomfortably in his seat as Evelyn returned with a circular tray of cake in one hand and a carton of ice cream in the other.

"Sorry it took me so long. I had to go down to the basement to get the ice cream out of the freezer," she admitted regrettably as she placed the items on the dining table.

"That's all right," father and daughter replied in unison.

Evelyn opened the top to the ice cream and placed it down on the table. Just as she was about to remove the top from the cake tray, she realized she didn't have the utensils she needed to cut, scoop, or serve the cake and ice cream on.

She sucked her teeth in disgust.

"Karma, baby, I forgot the damn...," she paused, looking over at Lorenzo in embarrassment. "Oh, forgive me," she whispered, blushing. "I don't usually--"

"It's quite all right," he smiled.

Evelyn melted. She slowly pulled her eyes away from Lorenzo and set them back on Karma, who rose from the table, shaking her head in disbelief.

"Don't worry. I got it," she huffed as she made her way out of the room into the kitchen.

Karma walked toward the island and settled there for a moment. She closed her eyes and took a deep breath in, then released it. By the way things were playing out between her father and Evelyn; she knew she was probably going to have to drag him out of there tonight. She didn't trust him. He was a ladies' man. His track record was perfect when it came to getting any woman he wanted. He always succeeded and Karma knew better than to let him put his mack down on Evelyn.

The vibrating and ringing of her cell phone broke her out of her thoughts. She pulled the phone from its case, read the name on the miniature screen, and flipped it open. She placed it to her ear and smiled.

"Hello?"

"Karma, it's Hawk. How are you, dear?" he asked sincerely.

"I know who it is," she cooed. "I'm well. How are you? I haven't seen you since Mekhi was born," she continued as she took a seat at the island.

"I know. I do apologize for my excessive absence," he sighed. "I haven't been able to get out and move around as freely as I used to in my younger days."

"Oh, I don't believe that. You're not as old as you think. Really," she replied in a light voice.

"You're too kind, Karma," he beamed. "Too, too kind."

"I just call 'em like I see 'em," she grinned. "Is everything okay? Do you need anything?"

"No, no. I don't need anything," he admitted. "I called because I was wondering if you'd seen or spoken to Money today."

"Uh, the last time I saw him was this morning. He left my house around noon or so to go run some errands. At least, that's what he told me. I've called him a couple of times since then, but his phone is off. Why? Do you think something's happened to him?" she asked warily.

"I can't honestly say, my dear." He paused before continuing. "I met with Money this afternoon, Karma. I told him. Everything."

Karma felt her heart drop into her stomach. She could hear its echo beating in the depths of her ears and bouncing off the walls of her skull. *What did he mean he told Money everything?* They made a pact. He made her swear on her life and on her mother that she'd take what she knew to the grave. And now Money was missing. They didn't know if he was dead or alive, by himself or with company, sane or insane.

"Karma?" Hawk called from the other line. "Are you still there?"

Karma fixed her mouth to speak, but nothing came out.

"I want you to listen to me carefully," he instructed sternly. "Do not tell anyone he is missing. He'll call. I don't know when or who he'll call, but he will call. When he does, act as if you have no knowledge of what is going on. Do you understand me?"

"Y-yes," she stuttered in a whisper.

"I want you to know that what I did was necessary. I didn't want him searching for a man who no longer exists. A man who, had he lived, would have hurt him far worse than that of his stories," Hawk cringed. "I want you to be very careful. Watch your back at all times. He left our meeting raving mad and the mind-set that he's in, he's capable of hurting you and anyone else in his path."

Karma felt the blood from her face drain and settle in her chest. *What had he done?* He put her, Indigo, Stuff, and himself in danger. Money was crazy as hell. And Karma was certain he'd reached his breaking point and snapped. He'd driven somewhere far to think, to scheme. He was going to make a move, one so big that it was going to rock their worlds.

Karma knew he'd fallen into that dark place, way deep down inside of himself. That place where he had no rope or ladder to climb up out of it. She thought about taking the baby and driving down to her father's house in Maryland. Maybe she could hide out there until it was safe to return, until he calmed down some. *What was she going to do?*

"Do you understand me, Karma?" Hawk asked, breaking her train of thought.

"Yes," she replied, her voice quivering.

"Allright. I'll be in touch," he countered before disconnecting his end of the call.

Karma gulped as she pulled the phone away from her ear and snapped it shut. There was going to be a showdown between her and Money. She was sure of it. And he was going to make her explain herself. But he wasn't going to make it easy. He was going to make her pay for her sins.

Chapter 23

Money sat on the edge of the hotel bed, legs wide open, his head hung. His back was facing a naked redbone sleeping on her side behind him. He'd picked her up on a side street off of Atlantic Drive. She was the prettiest out of all the prostitutes walking back and forth on the strip. He pulled up to the utility pole she was leaning against and rolled down his window. He never looked her way as she approached the SUV. He didn't want to. He couldn't deal with the knowing of what he was going to do with her that night. She was dressed in a tanned trench coat that stopped just below her knees and five-inch stilettos on her feet. The wig she wore on her head looked like the ones Diana Ross and The Supremes used to wear in the 60's. Her face wasn't caked with make-up. She had a touch of eyeliner around her bedroom eyes. The crimson-colored lipstick on her pouty lips gave them a fullness that looked like her mouth was fixed in a permanent pucker.

Her name was Candy. She charged ten for oral, twenty for anal, sixty for oral and anal, one-hundred for oral, anal, and vaginal. Money said nothing. He simply opened the door, waited for her to get in, and then drove off to the Regency.

He could tell by the way she screamed during their three-hour rendezvous, he hurt her more than he intended to. But he didn't care. Her pain was no match for his. They'd taken two lines of coke straight to the dome before they began. Candy reassured him that it was best to be high or drunk when tricking for the first. Money never put up a fight. She poured the white powder onto a compact mirror, cut it with one of her business cards, then leaned into her two lines and snorted. Money watched her rub her nose for a brief moment before a smile grew along her face. She looked back at him and gestured for him to take a hit with a raised brow. Money obliged. He took one line up one nostril and the second up the other. His nose burned. He pinched and rubbed, rubbed and pinched until the fire was doused. Then he looked up to see Candy standing before him in all of her naked glory. She kept the heels and the wig on. She watched his manhood grow in his pants and the lust grow in his eyes. She licked her lips and went to work.

In the three hours he and Candy went at it, Money couldn't get Karma off his mind. Every time he thought about what she'd done, he pounded into his Atlantic City trick just a little harder than the last time. He squeezed her neck a little tighter, slapped her behind a little harder, sucked her breasts a little harder; bit her bottom lip a little harder. When he looked down at her, he saw Karma. He wanted her to be Karma. But when he thought about it, there was nothing that he'd done to Candy that had not already been done to Karma. Candy screamed just as Karma had. She fought just as Karma had. And she cried just as Karma had.

He rubbed the back of his neck and listened to her quiet snores. He was finally coming down off of his high. He should have been asleep just as Candy was, but he was too afraid to close his eyes. He'd closed his eyes when he raped Karma. He saw his father when he closed his eyes. The best thing for him to do was to stay awake and figure out what he was going to do next.

Going home was not an option. He was too angry to face anyone, especially Karma. She'd stolen his identity. But he'd stripped her of her dignity. She'd killed his father. But his father killed her mother. They were even now...right? No, they weren't. She was able to know and love her mother for twenty-seven years. He hadn't known his father at all. The longing he had for this familiar stranger who lived inside of him surpassed all of the suns, moons, stars, minutes, seconds, and hours Karma spent with her mother. She'd taken something away from him that he could never get back---his "self."He had no other choice but to do the same to her.

Chapter 24

Evelyn slipped out of Lorenzo's arm and turned over onto her side. It was the thirtieth, one day before Mekhi's first birthday, and the twenty-first day that Money had been gone. She hadn't heard from him since the night she had Karma and Lorenzo over for dinner. He'd called in the wee hours of the morning, telling her that she needn't worry. He was okay and would be home as soon as he cleared his head. She immediately began to bombard him with questions, asking him where he was and what was going on. But he gave her no answers. He said nothing but, "I love you, Mama," before hanging up, leaving her panic-stricken and confused.

She called her brother right away and told him about Money's bizarre call. Hawk reassured her that wherever Money was, he was safe. He told her Money was probably going through something and needed some time to himself. He'd been through a lot during the year and was more than likely reflecting upon it all. He'd reached a point in his life where it was time to do a little soul searching. Every man had to do it sooner or later and Money's time had come. Evelyn insisted that Money sounded suicidal when she spoke to him. But Hawk assured her that he wouldn't do such a thing knowing he had her, Mekhi, Mimi, and Karma to take care of.

Evelyn settled down a bit after digesting her brother's words and let him go to sleep. When she awakened the next morning, called Money on his cell, and got his voice mail. She began to panic again and called Karma, expressing her concern. Karma, expecting Evelyn's call, remained calm and repeated what Hawk told her. She told Evelyn she'd left a number of messages on Money's voice mail, but he hadn't called her back either. Karma stressed it was best they leave him be and trust that he was in one piece.

Even with Hawk and Karma's reassurance, Evelyn knew she wasn't going to rest at night until Money was back home. And she hadn't. Twenty-one days later, she was lying nude beside her grandson's grandfather. She'd spent seventeen of those days crying on his shoulder, kissing his soft, warm lips, and opening her legs to him. She made herself forget about her lost son and his dearly departed wife.

The nights spent with Lorenzo were mind-blowing. They stayed up for hours, laughing and talking about the lives they led. She learned so much about him and vice versa. He was a man who loved and lost hard. His pain was evident in his touch and in his eyes.

Evelyn had no idea what she and Lorenzo were doing. She did know that whatever it was, it was wrong. And if Karma found out, her relationship with the young woman would never be the same. She'd taken Karma under her wing and loved her the only way she knew how as a mother. And even though she had not birthed her, Karma was her daughter nonetheless. Their bond was stronger than an electrical current. But the hold her father had on her mind, body, and soul was far greater than the tie that bound them. She loved Karma dearly, but she was falling in love with her father. And she wasn't sure if she wanted to fall out of it any time soon.

No one should have to spend the rest of their life alone. No one.

Chapter 25

Victor studied his reflection in the mirror. He'd been out of the hospital for two weeks. His recovery had been painful to say the least. But it was nothing like the pain he'd been feeling since Maggie's departure. She walked out of his life the very day he was discharged from University.

They drove home in one of the restaurant's delivery vans. He never noticed the number of suitcases, shoe boxes, and plastic-covered suits in the back of the vehicle. When they pulled up to the house, she put the van in park, got out and walked around to his side. She opened the door and helped him out, retrieved his duffle bag from the space in between the driver and passenger seat and handed it to him. She closed the door behind him and escorted him to the porch of their house. She reached inside her purse for her keys, but she couldn't seem to find them. Something was troubling her. Victor was sure of it. When he reached for her in an attempt to comfort her, she jumped back. It was then that he saw what was bothering her. *Him*. He was the problem.

She refocused her attention back to the missing keys and finally found them at the bottom of her purse. She clutched them for a brief moment before placing them in his hand. Her eyes followed the railroad tracks of stitches leading to his two glossy silver dollars. She grimaced at the sight of him tearing up. Taking a deep breath, she leaned in and kissed him quickly on the lips before turning and walking away from him forever.

He looked like Edward Scissorhands. The doctors said his face, arms, and hands would heal in time. The sutures were going to leave deep indentations in his skin. He was going to be scarred for the rest of his life; not only on the outside, but on the inside as well.

Victor could hear movement and the faint voices of his wife, daughter, and son-in-law downstairs. They were there to get the rest of Maggie's things. He didn't know where she called home now. His current situation was no one's fault but his own. He knew he'd gone too far with talking about his sister and even farther when he punched Maggie in the face for defending her. With actions came consequences and one had to live with both in the end.

******

"Damn, Ma. What'chu got in dis box? A dead body?" Stuff asked as he lifted the large cardboard container up off the floor.

"You got some mout' on you dere, boi," she cringed.

Stuff walked up to her and smiled.

"Better to tell you 'I Love You' wit'," he said before kissing her on the cheek.

Maggie sucked her teeth and blushed as she slapped her son-in-law on the shoulder. He winked back at her before making his way toward the front door and exiting. Maggie proceeded to sort, separate, and place a mountain of clothes into two big, black garbage bags.

Indigo shook her head and grinned. She was blessed to have a mother and husband who genuinely got along. Not many women could say that. Indigo was also grateful that her mother took her advice and left her father. Karma had been a big help in making her transition into the Montclair condominium as smooth as possible. Aunt and niece had reconciled and things were back to normal.

Speaking of her cousin, Indigo looked down at her watch, wondering whereKarma was. She was twenty minutes late. The plan was for her to meet them at the house and help move the rest of Maggie's belongings to the condo. Indigo sighed in frustration. It was too hard for her to be in that house knowing her father was upstairs. He'd been up there since they arrived. And she hoped he would remain where he was once Karma showed up. She doubted another fight would break out between them, but anything was possible when Karma was involved.

"Sorry, I'm late, *Tia*," Karma said, flying into the house. She kissed her aunt on the cheek and proceeded to throw her pocketbook down. She found herself doing that a lot lately; flying in and out of places. *What other choice did she have?* She was afraid for her life and she figured if Money happened to show up unexpectedly, she would already have a ten second head start on him.

"Dat's okay, baby," Maggie replied with a warm smile. "We haven't gotten too far."

Karma scratched the back of her neck as she skimmed over the clutter of clothes, books, and other items scattered around the room. She didn't know where to start. She saw Indigo struggling to wrap a large oil painting of a beach in St. Kitts and decided to help her.

Indigo gave Karma a wary glance as she approached her.

"What?" Karma shrugged. "I got hung up at Party City."

Indigo shook her head in disbelief.

"They had one cashier and she didn't know how to work the register. What the hell was I supposed to do? Mekhi's party is tomorrow."

"It's not that," Indigo confessed in an almost inaudible tone. She looked back at her mother, then reset her eyes on Karma.

"Me going to go to de batroom," Maggie announced, rising from the couch.

"Okay," the girls replied in unison. They watched her leave the room and waited to hear the bathroom door close. When it did, they continued their conversation.

"Then, what?" Karma asked in a whisper.

"I don't want to be here," Indigo shook her head.

Karma let out a quiet sigh.

"I know you don't. But we have to get the rest of her things out of here before she has second thoughts. You don't want her to backslide, do you?"

"No," Indigo sulked.

"Okay, then. Fix your face and get back to work," Karma instructed firmly. "The quicker we go, the quicker we *go*."

The sound of the toilet flushing and footsteps descending the main stairway caught Indigo and Karma's attention. They could hear Maggie making her way back to the living room and Victor's steps harmonizing with his wife's. Indigo and Karma had no idea what to do. So when Maggie re-entered the room and took her place back on the couch, the girls continued to wrap the oil painting. It hadn't been five seconds before Victor emerged in the entryway.

Maggie, Indigo, and Karma's heads rose at the same time. They stared back at the man who'd spent his life trying to make theirs as miserable as his. He was in his navy blue terrycloth robe. His feet were bare, his hair, wild. The stitches in his face and hands were as black as licorice. He shifted his weight from one foot to the other, wringing his hands as if they were sponges. He looked like he wanted to say something, but none of them knew if he even had a voice anymore. Tears began to well in his eyes. Before long they were cascading down his Raggedy Andy-like face. He licked his lips and parted them to make a sound.

"I'm sorry," he whispered breathlessly. "She didn't deserve it."

She. Soleil. Maggie. Indigo. Karma.

Chapter 26

Mekhi sat on his mother's lap at the head of his nanny's dining table, donning a cone-shaped birthday hat on his head and a baffled look on his face. He looked at the Elmo shaped cake before him, then turned his attention to the host of smiling, singing faces gathered in the room. Among them were his grandparents, Hawk and his wife, Maggie, Miguel, Indigo and Stuff, Desiree, Mimi, Captain Pagano, and a number of Money's colleagues from the 5th precinct with their wives and children. Money, unfortunately, was not present.

Mekhi turned his attention back to the cake as the *Happy Birthday* song came to an end. Karma, with the baby in her arms, leaned forward and blew the number one shaped candle out for him. She took his hands into hers thereafter and clapped them. Mekhi, still confused, looked back at his mother and grimaced. Karma and the rest of the family laughed at his classic expression. Mekhi studied his family's smiling faces for a moment before locking eyes with Desiree. Desiree's eyebrows rose and her eyes grew wide, exemplifying her own misunderstanding of what was going on around them. Mekhi, tired of being confused, lunged forward and rammed his hands into the cake. Karma screamed as she rose from her seat, pulling him away from the mutilated Sesame Street character. The family and other guests fell into a fit of laughter. Camera flashes came in rapid succession.

"Dat's what I'm talkin' about!" Stuff cried over the crowd. "Give dat man some cake!"

"Shut up, Stuff!" Karma laughed, carrying Mekhi into the kitchen with Evelyn in tow.

"Lil' nigga's hungry," he muttered under his breath.

Indigo, hearing her husband, nudged him in the arm.

"What?" he asked, knowing the answer. "He is."

Indigo shook her head and laughed in spite of herself.

Karma handed Mekhi over to Evelyn and made her way over to the sink to retrieve a dish rag.

"Bad boy," Evelyn said to the baby before kissing him and setting him down on the island.

"You can say that again," Karma smirked, wetting the dish cloth. She turned the faucet off, rung the rag out a bit, then traveled over to where Evelyn and Mekhi were and began to wipe his hands off.

"Money did the same thing on his first birthday," Evelyn professed while suppressing the urge to cry.

Karma glanced over at her former mother-in-law-to-be before looking back at Mekhi and the mess of icing on his shirt sleeves.

"I thought he would have come back for this," Karma expressed with furrowed brows. It wasn't as if she was lying to the woman. She truly did think Money was going to return for Mekhi's birthday. She didn't care how upset he was with her, his uncle, and whoever else, he was Mekhi's father and he was supposed to be there. He was supposed to put the issues he had with her aside for the baby's sake. But he'd put himself and whatever wave of emotions he was experiencing before their son, yet again.

"I did, too," Evelyn sighed, running her fingers through Mekhi's hair.

"He *should have* come back for this," Karma replied with tears of fury in her eyes.

Evelyn nodded.

"This shit isn't comin' out. I'm gonna have to put another shirt on 'im," Karma confessed frustratingly. She balled up the dish rag and threw it to the side.

"It's all right. I'll do it," Evelyn replied, picking the baby up in her arms. "Go on back out there and try to enjoy the rest of the party," she continued, rubbing Karma's cheek with her thumb.

Karma sighed heavily in response to Evelyn's declaration. She raised her hand to her forehead and began to rub it.

"Go on, now," Evelyn insisted. "You've got a room full of people out there waiting for you."

Karma sighed again and shook her head in discontent.

"Look at me, Karma," Evelyn demanded.

Karma hesitated before obliging.

"You see this gorgeous child right here?" Evelyn asked. "You see him?"

"Mm-Hmm," Karma nodded.

"No one else matters, but him. This is *his* night. You understand me?" Evelyn queried seriously.

"Yes, ma'am," Karma replied, smiling painfully.

"Good. Don't let his father's absence put you in a foul mood," Evelyn urged. "You've been doing well all night."

Karma began to sniffle. Evelyn caught sight of a tear that was threatening to fall from Karma's eye and wiped it away.

"You are not allowed to fall apart. You hear me? Not until this party is over. Hmm?"

Karma nodded.

"Now, pull yourself together," Evelyn pressed before walking out of the room with the baby in arms.

Karma wiped her eyes with her fingertips, took a deep breath in, and released it. Evelyn was right. Mekhi was the only one who mattered. If Money wanted to be an ass and not be a part of their son's day, then that was his loss.

Chapter 27

Karma sat down on the edge of her mother's bed and began to dry her wet hair with a towel. She'd spent thirty minutes in the shower with closed eyes and a heavy heart. The outpour of money, cards, and gifts Mekhi received last night was overwhelming. She was forced to leave half of his presents at his grandmother's house. Her father promised he'd bring the rest home once he finished helping Evelyn clean up, but the last time Karma looked out the window, her car was the only one parked in the driveway.

She was tired---mentally and emotionally drained. She'd spent the first milestone in her son's life without his father and her mother. She set the wet towel down beside her and settled her eyes on a framed black and white photograph of her mother that was sitting on the nightstand next to the bed. It was going to be one of those days. Karma could feel it. She was going to lay her head down tonight and not bother to lift it once the sun came up in the morning. Seven and a half hours until sunrise. Karma often wondered if heaven had sunrises and sunsets. Heaven---a place only people like her mother were worthy of going.

Karma leaned forward and opened the top drawer of the nightstand. She spotted the book she was looking for, removed it, and then closed the drawer. It had been years since she last read the Bible. This one was her mother's, with its black leather front and back covers, gold trimmings, and cedar scent. She had no intentions of reading it tonight. The stories and scriptures weren't of any interest to her, but the letter was. She placed the letter her mother wrote to her in the book after the repast and hadn't touched it since.

Karma slowly opened the Bible and removed the sealed white envelope from the book of Psalms. She held the letter in her hands and studied the beautiful inscription of her name on the front. Karma slowly turned the envelope over, dug her thumbnail into the sealed flap, and ran it along the glued paper. Once she got it open, she gradually pulled the folded sheets of paper out of the envelope and unfolded them. Her eyes began to well with tears the moment she read the first line. She didn't want to read the damn thing. She swore to herself that she would never read it. But she knew her mother wouldn't have taken the time to write it if it wasn't important.

Karma looked to the heavens and sighed before returning her gaze on the letter. It was now or never. She gathered the little courage she had and proceeded to read.

Karma, My Love,

I want you to know that it was not my intention to leave you. My greatest fear as your mother was passing before my time and leaving you behind. I had that nightmare many a night. And I want to apologize to you for making it a reality. Know that I fought to the very end, baby. I know you never understood why I loved Jimmy as much as I did. You probably figured I feared him, if anything, and tried to make myself believe that it was love. I can't blame you for thinking that. Did I fear him? Yes, I did. But I loved him just as much. It wasn't a hard thing to do...loving him. I know you may find that hard to believe, but it wasn't. Because when you come to know a person who never experienced such a thing as love before, you can't help but take pride in knowing that you were " the one" who showed them what it meant to be loved...how it felt...what it looked like. Everyone deserves to be loved, baby. Remember that. And there's always a reason behind the types of decisions people make...wise or otherwise.

Your grandmother once told me that my heart was going to be the death of me. I never understood what she meant by that until the day I laid with your father for the first time after his affair. When I could not deny him of myself, I knew from that moment on, I was guilty of my grandmother's greatest sin—forgiving a man for something he would have never forgiven me for.

My grandmother, Carmen De Leon-Cruz, was a beautiful black woman who grew up on a sugar plantation in what's now considered Old Havana. She was the youngest of ten, the pride and joy of her family. At the age of eighteen, she met a soldier, an Irishman, by the name of Nicholas O'Hara. He'd been stationed in Cuba for some time and had not come across anyone as captivating as her. He had to have her. And he decided from that very moment that he was going to make her his girl. He chased her around that island for months. He chased her until she finally gave in and allowed him to love her. She, in turn, learned to love him back. But their love would eventually die. Because you see, baby, your grandmother was conceived out of their union. And when your great-grandmother told your great-grandfather that she was pregnant, he left her. She was never the same after that. She raised your grandmother by herself.

You see, her family disowned her upon hearing the news of the " bastardo de mulato" she was carrying. She began to live a lifestyle unsuitable for a single woman with a child. She gained a reputation around the island for her promiscuity, often subjecting your grandmother to many of her sexual escapades. She was beaten for the majority of her young life because she looked so much like her father. The beatings stopped eventually, but your grandmother would walk away from them damaged beyond repair. She was sixteen-years-old when her father returned to the island. Her mother received him with open arms and open legs. Your grandmother looked the other way when he came and looked toward the future when he left.

Even though she used to tell me every day of my life that she hated me, I don't believe she meant it. I think she hated the fact that I looked like her mother; just like her mother hated that she looked like her father. We often take the faults of our parents out on our children. And we never learn how to apologize to them for it. So, I want to take this time and tell you how sorry I am for forgiving your father and Jimmy more times than I should have and letting them take advantage of my heart. I'm sorry for forcing you into a position where you may have felt as if you had to be " the one" to mend it. That's too big a responsibility for any child. So, I say to you now, mi amor, Mommy is truly sorry for burdening you with her cross. My heart beats inside of you now. Take better care of it. Remember that God makes no mistakes. He is real. And once you get over being angry with Him, thank Him for allowing you to have a mother at all.

I love you, baby. I am with you ALWAYS.

- Mommy

Karma, her face stained with tears, eyes clouded and heavy, pressed the letter to her aching chest and wept for her mother. How unselfish Soleil was to have apologized for not only her mistakes, but the mistakes of her Cuban-born mothers before her.

The closing of one of the doors down the hall startled her. She placed the letter back in its envelope, put the envelope back in the Bible, and set it on the nightstand. She rose from the bed, wiping her wet face with her hands and made her way into the dark hallway. All of the bedroom doors were closed. She approached the door to her father's room, turned the knob, and opened it. She peeked inside the room and saw that he was not in there. She figured he was still over Evelyn's house. She didn't want to believe that anything was going on between them, but she knew better. It wasn't something that she agreed with and promised herself that she would address it to the both of them when the time was right.

Karma walked to the bathroom across the hall from her father's room and looked inside. It was vacant as well. She closed the door behind her and retied the belt on her bathrobe as she made her way down the hall to the nursery. She placed her hand on the knob, turned it, and quietly walked in. She thought she heard the sound of plastic crackling in one of the corners. So she scaled the wall with her hand in search of the light switch. Once her fingers and the toggle connected, she flipped it up, expecting the room to come to life. But when it didn't, Karma sucked her teeth and cursed under her breath. She turned to walk out of the room to get a new bulb from the linen closet in the hall. But before her feet met the plush carpeting of the threshold, she heard a familiar voice escape from one of the dark corners.

"There's nothing wrong with the light bulb. I have it here in my hand," he said dismally.

"Money?" Karma asked into the room's darkness.

Click.

Money pulled on a string that was attached to a rotating caricature lamp set beside him on a nightstand. He was sitting in the rocking chair he built for her just days before Mekhi's birth. A .380 millimeter gun was resting in his lap. Karma's eyes darted from Money to the gun to him again. She noticed he was sweating profusely and his clothes were filthy. His hair was grown out and matted. His ever so meticulously trimmed goatee was gone. A fully-grown beard danced around his salivating mouth now. He was looking at her through bloodshot eyes. They were piercing into her. He never batted them. He never blinked.

"How did you get in the house?" Karma managed to say.

"I picked the locks," Money admitted. "I don't want to talk about that right now," he said as he began to slowly rock back and forth in the chair. "I want to talk about what you did to my father."

Karma stood frozen in terror. Money was obviously in an unstable state. *What was she supposed to say? Was she supposed to apologize for killing him?* She was at loss for words. She didn't want to say anything that was going to piss him off. He had a gun. She was more than certain he was going to use it. All she had to do was give him a reason, one good reason.

She had to get to Mekhi. She needed to make sure her baby was okay. She looked over at the mahogany crib, wishing she'd gone straight to him instead of trying to turn on the ceiling light upon entrance.

Money followed Karma's eyes, and then reset them on her.

"Don't worry. He's all right," he reassured her.

Karma pulled her eyes away from the crib and locked them with Money's.

"Did he have a good birthday?" Money asked her sincerely.

"Yes. He did," Karma replied, her voice quivering. "You would know that had you come."

Money stopped rocking in the chair. He tilted his head to the side and studied Karma for a moment. As wrong as she'd been for the last two years, she still had the balls to stand across that room and remind him of his indiscretion.

"Well, we can't do anything about that now, can we?" he asked sarcastically. "I mean, if anybody should be feelin' some kinda way right now, it's me. After all, you're the reason why I missed it," he proclaimed, rising from the rocking chair.

"You're the one who kept me away from him. Your lies...kept me away from him." He slowly stepped to the side of the chair and leaned back against the wall behind it. He proceeded to put one foot up on the wall and rested it there. He placed his hands in front of him, one atop the other. The gun remained in his clutch. "I had a lot of time to think while I was away. And one of the things I thought about was what I was going to do to you when I finally saw you. I thought about...fuckin' da shit outta you again. But then I thought I'd enjoy that too much. I thought about... pistol whippin' ya ass. But then I had to ask myself, 'Do I really want to fuck up that beautiful face of hers?' No. So then I just said, 'Fuck it. I'll kill da bitch.' But then I thought against that too. Any and everything you can possibly think of me doing to you, I already thought about."

Karma took a big, rigid gulp. She was trying her hardest to keep her composure, but she could feel herself slowly falling apart. She had no idea what Money had in store for her, but she knew the impact it would have would remain with her forever, if she lived.

"At the end of the day, I could never hurt you, Karma. I love you too much. And when you love somebody as much as I love you, you have to forgive them...no matter how fucked up they are or how fucked up the shit they did," he confessed. "My father, for example, was a fucked up individual who did some fucked up shit. He beat the shit out of women and enjoyed it. He was as fucked up as they came. But what's more fucked up than that is you, of all people, killin' his ass," he exclaimed with raised eyebrows. "I couldn't believe that shit when my uncle told me. It took me some time to really think about what I would have done had I been in your shoes. I came to the realization that I would have done the same goddamn thing. The only thing I would have done different, though, was tell you that I killed him right after I did it."

"No, you wouldn't have, Money," Karma stated knowingly. "Because you couldn't even tell me why you stopped talking to your mother eight months ago," she shrugged. "I had no idea you had any interest in wanting to know your father. You never said anything to me about it. Whenever you spoke about him in the past, it was never positive," she reminded him. "I can't take back what I've done. All I can ask is for you to forgive me. I know, now, that I took away the opportunity for you knowing him and whatever else you wanted to do with him. I'm sorry. Okay? If that's what you've been waiting for...an apology from me, then I'm sorry," she professed wholeheartedly.

"Really?" Money asked with a look of confusion on his face.

"Really," Karma confirmed seriously.

Money raised his hands and grabbed a handful of his hair with them. He moved away from the wall and began to pace back and forth. Karma looked on in uneasiness. Money was mumbling something under his breath. She couldn't quite make out what he was saying. He balled his hands into fists and began to hit himself in the head with them.

"It was the only way to stop it," Money whispered to himself.

"Stop what, Money?" Karma asked apprehensively.

"It was the only way to stop it from growing," he continued.

"To stop what from growing, Money?" Karma asked, walking toward him.

She grabbed him by his arms, putting an end to his pacing. She pulled his hands down from his temples and gently placed her fingertips on his thick neck, resting her thumbs on each cheek. She waited until his wild, penitent eyes met hers.

"Money, baby...please? I need you to tell me what the 'it' is."

Money looked down at Karma and smiled regrettably.

"The monster," he replied with tears brimming in his eyes. "It would have... taken over his body...like it did mine and my father's if I hadn't...killed him."

Karma's mouth fell open. She backed away from Money and crossed over to the baby's crib. He was lying on his stomach. He was still. His face was turned to the side and peaceful. His arms were outstretched above his head; his little hands balled into fists. She didn't see anything unusual. There was no blood, vomit, nothing. So she reached down into the crib, carefully pulled the blanket off of him, and lost her breath when she saw the single bullet wound to his back.

Karma began to tremble uncontrollably. She leaned down into his cradle and tried to pick him up, but her hands were shaking so violently, she couldn't get a decent grip on him. She could hear Money apologizing to her over and over again in the background, but his voice soon faded out. She heard nothing but her heart beating as she pulled Mekhi into her arms and held him close. She palmed the hole in his back and shuddered under the touch of it. Her legs gave way beneath her and she found herself on her knees. A familiar howl escaped from the depths of her soul and filled the room with its resonance. She held her baby to her chest and did what she always did when he was fast asleep in her arms. She rocked him back and forth...back and forth...back and forth.

Chapter 28

ESPN: The Magazine
October 3, 2012

Ever since she shattered the late Florence Griffith-Joyner's 100 and 200-meter records with times of 10.47 and 21.30 in July's Olympic trials, the concern about Alonso-Walker was whether she could come anywhere near those stunning marks in London against the likes of world champions Veronica Campbell-Brown of Jamaica, Allyson Felix of the USA, and Christine Ohuruogo of Great Britain.

She seems a paradox: beautiful but unusually rugged around the edges. "I had a hard life," she says in her velvet contralto. "After you lose two of the most important people in your life unexpectedly, you're never the same afterwards. You never really recover from it."

Alonso-Walker is speaking of her late mother and the father of her four-year-old son. Her mother, Soleil, was a restaurateur as well as a real estate aficionado and humanitarian. Her father, Lorenzo, was a Master Sergeant in the United States Army. "My father was always on assignment somewhere," says

Alonso-Walker. "I spent the majority of my life with my mother. It was just her and I against the world."

Encouraged in all her interests by her mother, Karma grew up to appreciate life and all it had to offer. "Growing up in Newark, you're surrounded by death," she says. Her tone is casual. "There isn't a day that goes by where someone hasn't gotten shot or stabbed. You could only hope and pray that you and your loved ones would be spared."

Alonso-Walker's faith would be tested in 1997 when her mother was diagnosed with ovarian cancer. "I was 17 at the time. I'd set school records in the sprints and I was on my way to California to train with Bob [Kersee] for the MEAC tournaments," says Alonso-Walker. "But after my mother told me she was sick, running wasn't an option anymore."

Alonso-Walker quit the sport of track and field at the prime of her young, promising life and never looked back. Her mother survived her battle with cancer, but even after the storm, Alonso-Walker remained out of the sport's shadows. She graduated from high school and went on to Hampton University, her parents' alma mater. There, she majored in business and restaurant management. "My plans were to become a partner in my family's restaurant business and the co-proprietor of my mother's properties throughout Essex County," she admits.

After graduating college cum laude, Alonso-Walker returned home. Upon arrival, she learned of her parents' decision to separate. "I wasn't surprised. It felt like they'd been separated for most of their marriage anyway," she shrugs. Her golden eyes are glowing. "It was my mother's decision, really.

And I couldn't blame her for making it," she says. "She and my father had two totally different perceptions of how our family was supposed to look and function."

Her parents' separation would last for four years. And in that time, they both found pleasure in the company of others. Alonso-Walker's mother met a mechanic by the name of Jimmy Hayes. In a month's time, he stole her heart. And he would break it fifty-five months later. "He beat her to death. She was almost unrecognizable," says Alonso-Walker. Her golden eyes turn dark. "She and my father were going to get back together. She told Jimmy and he couldn't handle it. So he killed her."

Alonso-Walker would meet her son's father, a Newark police officer, Money Parks, on the night of her mother's discovery. A love affair grew and Alonso-Walker became pregnant with her son soon after. She gave birth to a 9lb, 8 oz.baby boy who she named Mekhi. "He's the joy of my life. He saved my life," she says with a smile. Her eyes are bright again. One can see the pride in her spirit.

Alonso-Walker almost lost her son three years ago at the hands of his father. Parks shot their son in the back a day after his first birthday. "I thought he was dead. I just knew he was," Alonso-Walker says with a cringe. "So I just picked him up and held him. But then he started to gurgle and his head began to move a little," she smiles. Tears brim her eyes. "I ran out of the house and kept running until I got to University Hospital. The doctors and nurses couldn't believe I ran all the way there with just a bathrobe on. No sneakers, no socks...just my bare feet."

Miraculously the bullet curved when it entered his back, missing his spinal cord and other vital organs. He would suffer from a collapsed lung and five broken ribs. Parks was arrested on first-degree murder charges. He pleaded not guilty for reasons of "temporary insanity." He is now serving a ten-year sentence in the psychiatric ward at Massachusetts General Hospital in Boston.

"He had his reasons for trying to kill our son. And those same reasons are what led to his incarceration. That's all I'm going to say about that," she says earnestly. "He's a beautiful man," she says with a genuine smile. "I think about him daily. When I look at our son, I see him. And I'm thankful to have known him...because he thought enough of me to have given me such a special gift."

With a newfound hope and outlook on life, Alonso-Walker stepped back on the track. She called Kersee after an eleven-year absence and told him she wanted to run again. With her son in tow, Alonso-Walker moved to Los Angeles, California and began to train. Each day began and finished with a workout; either a run or a rugged set of leg curls on the hamstring-leg extension machine. This workout strengthened the gluteal and hamstring muscles that blast her out of the blocks. Alonso-Walker asserts that, for her, form assists function.

She broke the late Flo-Jo's 100-meter world record of 10.49 by two seconds and her 200-meter U.S. record of 21.34 by four seconds. Those times are still causing aftershocks. The idea that a golden hair and golden-eyed beauty can run as fast as all but a handful of greyhounds has stirred such interest that the entire Alonso-Walker family has been besieged, and the track star is not one to pass unrecognized. "She's stopped everywhere she goes," says her father, Master Sergeant Lorenzo Walker. "It's a beautiful thing. We always knew how fast she was, but it means so much more now that the whole world knows too."

Alonso-Walker ran five races in three nights. She would adjust her rear block to feel more comfortable than she had in each semi. She would get a terrific start, her early going, smooth and swift. Sensing herself in front, a smile would grow along her face at 70 meters. By 90 meters it would become a glorious grin. By 95 her arms would be up celebrating. At 100 the clock would stop and she would kneel on the track, thank God, and kiss the gold, heart-shaped locket that housed a picture of her late mother. She would rise to her feet, take a flag from a spectator, and carry the stars and stripes for a victory lap that would eventually end in her father and son's arms. Her step-daughter, uncles, aunt, and cousins would hug and kiss her before she disappeared behind the confines of the stadium.

She would later emerge and take her place as number one on the victory stand, walking away with four gold medals and one silver. Tears would fall from her eyes as her country's flag descended from the sky. She would wait for the National Anthem to play and when it did; she would look up to the heavens and smile. She'd granted her mother's undying wish. She ran a good race, her race---the glory race, a race she once dreamed of running so long ago.

"It's a beautiful article, isn't it, son?" Evelyn asked Money as she watched him close the magazine and place it beside the fifty other magazines and newspapers featuring Karma as their cover girl.

"Yeah, it is," he replied with a small, proud grin.

"She still loves you, despite everything that's happened," Evelyn admitted sincerely.

"I know, Ma," Money said in an almost inaudible tone.

"It's going to be a long time before they see fit for you to leave here, baby," the teary-eyed woman expressed. "But I know for certain, God is going to see us through this."

Money simply nodded in agreement.

"I'm not crazy, Ma," Money confessed as he took his mother's aged hand into his own.

"I know you're not crazy, baby," Evelyn cried. "I know that. And Karma knows that."

A deafening silence fell between mother and son.

"I've gotta get her back, Ma," he declared in a whisper. "I've got to."

"And you will, Money. But you have to get better first," Evelyn stated, studying the intensity in her son's eyes.

"I know. I know," he replied sincerely. "And I will," he assured the woman who gave him life. Evelyn, in return, smiled knowingly.

"She's going to be mine again, Ma," Money smirked. "You just wait and see."

WAHIDA CLARK PRESENTS
BEST SELLING TITLES
Trust No Man
Trust No Man II
Thirsty
Cheetah
Karma With A Vengeance
The Ultimate Sacrifice
The Game of Deception
Karma 2: For The Love of Money
Thirsty **2**
Lickin' License
Feenin'
Bonded by Blood
Uncle Yah Yah: 21st Century Man of Wisdom
The Ultimate Sacrifice II
Under Pressure (YA)
The Boy Is Mines! (YA)

COMING SOON!!
A Life For A Life
The Pussy Trap
99 Problems (YA)
Country Boys

ON SALE NOW!

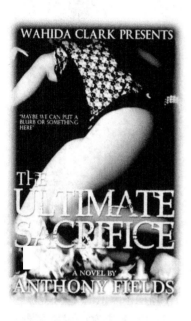

WAHIDA CLARK PRESENTS

"MAYBE WE CAN PUT A BLURB OR SOMETHING HERE"

THE ULTIMATE SACRIFICE

A NOVEL BY
ANTHONY FIELDS

WAHIDA CLARK PRESENTS

KARMA
With a Vengeance

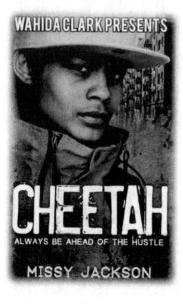

WAHIDA CLARK PRESENTS

CHEETAH
ALWAYS BE AHEAD OF THE HUSTLE

MISSY JACKSON

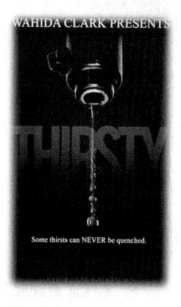

WAHIDA CLARK PRESENTS

THIRSTY

Some thirsts can NEVER be quenched.

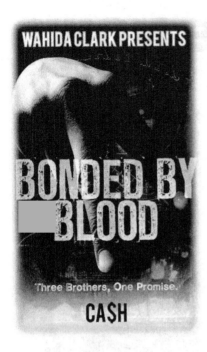

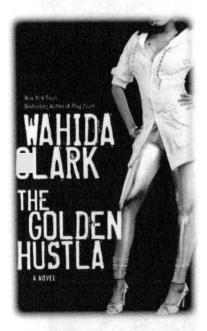

__W__.WCLARKPUBLISHI__G.COM

ON SALE NOW!

WWW.WCLARKPUBLISHING.COM

COMING SOON!

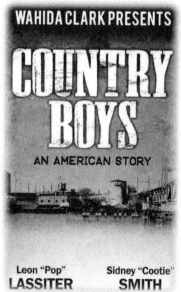

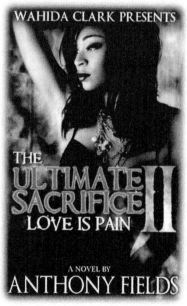